PLAGUE DAEMON

'I MUST KNOW more about this *katharos* whose fate is bound to mine,' Harmis said. 'How may I know it if I ever see it?'

'I wish I could tell you,' Nicodemus replied. 'Alas, it's the kind of daemon which is not easily seen for what it is. Although it is tainted by the mutations of Chaos, as all its kind are, the mutations of a *katharos* are internal rather than external – its true form is masked by illusion. The name means Pure One, but that's an irony, for no daemon can ever be truly pure; what the title signifies is that this kind of evil wears a disguise of guiltlessness, and those who seek to destroy it must first see through its dissimulations.'

More Warhammer from the Black Library

· **THE TALES OF ORFEO** ·

ZARAGOZ by Brian Craig

· **THE VAMPIRE GENEVIEVE NOVELS** ·

DRACHENFELS by Jack Yeovil
BEASTS IN VELVET by Jack Yeovil
GENEVIEVE UNDEAD by Jack Yeovil

· **GOTREK & FELIX** ·

TROLLSLAYER by William King
SKAVENSLAYER by William King
DAEMONSLAYER by William King
DRAGONSLAYER by William King
BEASTSLAYER by William King
VAMPIRESLAYER by William King

· **THE KONRAD TRILOGY** ·

KONRAD by David Ferring
SHADOWBREED by David Ferring
WARBLADE by David Ferring

· **WARHAMMER NOVELS** ·

ZAVANT by Gordon Rennie
HAMMERS OF ULRIC by Dan Abnett,
Nik Vincent & James Wallis
GILEAD'S BLOOD by Dan Abnett & Nik Vincent
THE WINE OF DREAMS by Brian Craig

· **WARHAMMER FANTASY STORIES** ·

REALM OF CHAOS
eds. Marc Gascoigne & Andy Jones
LORDS OF VALOUR
eds. Marc Gascoigne & Christian Dunn

A WARHAMMER NOVEL

The Second Tale of Orfeo

PLAGUE DAEMON

Brian Craig

For Jane Stableford, in recognition of the tolerance which she has shown in coping with her husband's multiple personality.

A BLACK LIBRARY PUBLICATION
First published in 1990 by GW Books.

This edition published in Great Britain
in 2002 by The Black Library,
an imprint of Games Workshop Ltd.,
Willow Road, Lenton, Nottingham, NG7 2WS, UK

10 9 8 7 6 5 4 3 2 1

Cover illustration by Clint Langley

A CIP record for this book
is available from the British Library

ISBN 1 84154 253 9

Set in ITC Giovanni

Printed and bound in Great Britain by
Cox & Wyman Ltd, Cardiff Rd, Reading, Berkshire RG1 8EX, UK

See the Black Library on the internet at
www.blacklibrary.co.uk

Find out more about Games Workshop
and the world of Warhammer at
www.games-workshop.com

PLAGUE DAEMON

Being the Second Tale of Orfeo

PROLOGUE

As SILENTLY AS he could contrive to do it, Orfeo led the two
donkeys away from the sprawling village of tents which
had been raggedly pitched outside the walls of Arjijil.

Most of the fighting men who had arrived with the caravan were standing guard over their masters' wares, and the
solitary sentry who had been set to watch the beasts of burden had fallen asleep, too comfortably coddled by the
blanket which he had set about his body to protect him
from the cool night air. Even so, Orfeo's task was not an
easy one. It was not the first time he had been forced by circumstance to steal an animal, and he knew only too well
how perverse an unwilling beast could become.

Orfeo would far rather have stolen horses than donkeys,
but the caravan had come from Songhai in the south,
crossing the great sea of sand at the leisurely pace dictated
by the harsh terrain. The merchants had forty camels and
a dozen donkeys, but no horses at all. Orfeo and Maro had
not known that when they sneaked out of the fortress –
but had they known, it would not have prevented them

from making their attempt to escape; chance had so far thrown up few enough opportunities.

Camels might well be far more useful to them, in view of their purpose, but Orfeo had never tried to mount a camel, and had heard it rumoured that they were bad-tempered creatures, very difficult to handle for those not expert in their use. The ignominy of being forced to steal a donkey was by no means negligible, but if he should fail to make his getaway because he found out too late that he could not master in an instant the artistry of camel-riding, that would be too much for his pride to bear. In any case, he did not intend to brave the rigours of the Sahra; his intention was to go east along the fertile strip of land which separated the 'twin seas' of brine and sand.

Just as he reached the place where Maro was waiting, with bridles and saddles and such other possessions as they had lately acquired by theft, he heard the hue and cry begin behind him. His heart sank; he had hoped that the watchman might doze until dawn, and give them a full hour's start.

'Quickly, man!' he whispered, when the boy faltered in his work. 'We have no time for fear and fumbling. Put the harness on, and let us swiftly be gone!'

Orfeo had always known that the youth would be a burden to him, and that he stood a far better chance of making his escape alone, but the thought of leaving Maro behind to face the vengeful wrath of Alkadi Nasreen had been too much to bear. The Caliph would be so annoyed by Orfeo's disappearance that he would certainly do what he had threatened and send the boy to Songhai to be gelded as a harem slave.

When he had finished preparing his own animal, Orfeo turned to help Maro, and when everything had been made secure he lifted the boy up into the saddle.

'Hold tight to the rein,' he said, 'kick hard, and pray that your beast will follow mine.'

Then he mounted and immediately set off into the night.

From his high prison in Arjijil Orfeo had measured the land very carefully with his eye, planning the route which he must take. He could only hope now that his mental map was good enough to allow him to outrun the immediate pursuit and be far away from the citadel by the time the news of his escape was carried to Alkadi Nasreen. That Nasreen would send riders after him he had no doubt – not because he was of any use to the Caliph, but because the self-styled Lord of Mahabbah and the Twin Seas was not a man to take insult lightly, and this intemperate refusal of his further hospitality was bound to seem direly impolite.

Orfeo, needless to say, saw things very differently. He was firmly of the opinion that he had more than adequately discharged his obligations as a guest by relating to the Caliph a very full account of the fate of his wayward brother.

He tried to urge the donkey onward at a faster pace, but the animal would not be urged. It was trained to walk and not to trot, having been schooled to a pace which would allow it to keep going for twelve hours a day through the fierce desert heat. To make steady progress in the red lands of the Sahra required dour endurance, not speed.

The pursuers were coming on foot, and because they could run faster than the donkeys would consent to walk, they would certainly catch up if they did not lose the trail in the darkness. But Orfeo dared not abandon the donkeys in order to continue their flight on foot; despite their disguises, he and the boy were too fair of face ever to be taken for natives, and they could not pass for legitimate travellers unless they had animals and packs to sustain the pretence that they were itinerant tinkers. Estalians might be tolerated in Araby if they appeared to have useful skills for hire – mere birds of passage would be sure to attract suspicion and hostility.

Maro cried out to him in alarm, and Orfeo cursed silently, knowing that the cry must be audible to their pursuers. Neverthelesss, he turned to see what was wrong.

By the light of the stars he saw that the other animal had shied, having perhaps trod on a sharp stone or been stung by a scorpion. Poor Maro had been tumbled from its back. The boy was already up on his feet again, but as he tried to catch the donkey's bridle the beast stubbornly pulled it away from him.

Orfeo leapt down and ran back, but as he reached for the trailing rein the first of their pursuers arrived, wielding a broad-bladed knife and calling exultantly to his followers.

Orfeo let the donkey go and drew his sword.

The way the Arab came at him, with the knife raised far above his head, Orfeo could have run him through, but he did not do it. For one thing, he did not want to murder a man who was only trying to protect his own property; for another, he no longer believed that he could make good his escape, and did not want to give Alkadi Nasreen a sufficient reason to have him beheaded.

He used his blade defensively, pricking his assailant on the upper part of his arm and tripping him up. Then he had to dance away in order to gain the space to face two more, one armed with a cudgel, the other with a heavy scimitar.

As they moved apart to come at him from different directions Orfeo saw that they were both clumsy, and knew that he could out-reach either of them by an easy double handspan – but they were two and he was one, and there was no way to change the odds except by killing one.

He tried at first to hurt the hands in which they held their weapons, but failed and switched his attack to their legs. He quickly succeeded in wounding one in a trivial fashion – but then there seemed to be at least a dozen of them crowding all about him, and though he could not speak their language he understood well enough from the manner of their cries that he was instructed to put up his sword.

He had no choice. He stopped and lowered his blade. They gathered about him on every side, and he saw that one of them had already grabbed poor Maro and held the boy tightly.

He dropped the sword on to the sand and one of the Arabs darted forward to snatch it up.

He was seized from behind and roughly held, while a fierce debate began. Orfeo had no doubt that they were trying to decide what to do with him.

'We were prisoners of Alkadi Nasreen,' he said, loudly. 'You might be rewarded, were you to return us to his care.'

When he pronounced the Caliph's name they paused, but it was clear that they could not understand what he was saying. Alas, he did not know the Arabic word for 'reward.'

'If you take us to Arjijil,' he said, 'the Caliph will give you money.'

They recognized the word *money*, even in the Oldworlder tongue – it was a word which tradesmen invariably knew in all languages save for the most arcane. They had the gist of his meaning now, but as they began their debate again he realized that they did not believe him. They were not Nasreen's men, and though they traded willingly enough with the citizens of his little pirate empire they probably did not like him. They must know well enough that Nasreen was an Estalian who had taken the turban for pragmatic reasons, and that the great majority of the victims of his piracy were men of their own kind.

Orfeo's two captors dragged him to a narow gully between two faces of rock, and brought him to an outcrop which had a flat top some three feet above the ground. There they forced him to his knees – but it was not until they tried to stretch his arm out so as to lay his wrist flat across the rock that he realized what they meant to do.

Immediately, he tried with all his might to throw them off.

He sent one of them sprawling in the dust, and his left arm came free. That enabled him to lash out with his fist, but he could not shake loose the other man who held him, and within a few seconds he was securely caught again by four strong men, who struggled steadfastly to keep him still.

When they had him under control, they forced him down again, and levered his defiant arm away from his body, twisting it to make resistance difficult. They forced it on to the table of rock, and then leaned sideways, to make room for a clean strike by the man who held the scimitar.

It was by no means unknown for thieves to lose their hands in the more sternly ruled towns of Orfeo's native Bretonnia – he had seen it done more than once, though never without benefit of a proper trial. He had always thought it a terrible penalty, and because he was a man who loved to play the lute as well as to ply the sword he felt that his whole life and being was stretched out upon that rock, waiting to be split asunder.

He heaved with every last vestige of his strength against the hands which held him, but the Arabs knew him now, and were entirely ready with their resistance. He could not move them, and it was all he could do to stifle an instinctive cry of terrified anguish when he watched the careful swordsman raise his blade, measuring the cut which he intended to make with calm and ruthless precision.

The swordsman could see the expression on his victim's face, and the light of the stars was just bright enough to let Orfeo see the satisfied smile which played upon his tormentor's lips. Then the cruel face became suddenly stony, and the muscles in the swordsman's neck tensed as he began to bring his weapon down.

Orfeo gasped, anticipating the dreadful severance which would change his life forever – and then was utterly astonished when he heard the moving blade intercepted by another, which appeared as if from nowhere to block its path.

The would-be deliverer of summary justice was equally surprised – and somewhat pained, in addition, by the shock which jarred his arms. Whoever had interposed the second blade was clearly a very powerful man.

The caravanners fell back and Orfeo suddenly found himself free. He snatched back his right arm, clutching the wrist with his left hand and hugging it to his chest, delirious with the good fortune of his narrow escape. Then he looked into the face of the man who had come to save him and felt a little of the exultation ebb away. He had seen his rescuer before; he was one of Alkadi Nasreen's bodyguards.

His absence from the citadel had clearly been discovered.

He could not help but wonder whether his hand had been preserved only to make sure that he could go hale and hearty into the untender care of Arjijil's headsman.

He cursed eloquently in his own tongue, and saw that his rescuer understood the motive, if not the literal meaning, of his speech. The bodyguard grinned, the curling wings of his moustache opening up with the smile as if to take flight from his face.

Poor headstrong Orfeo, he said to himself, in the manner which had become his custom. *Oafish as ever in thy dull humanity! What hope can there ever be for one as clumsy as thee in such a world as this?*

He was a long way from the Forest of Loren now – but the world, it seemed, was not one whit more sympathetic to his failures.

'Ah well,' he said, 'it might make a comic tale for lonely tavern nights, if only I can make it a little more exciting. I thank you for my hand, at any rate.'

The Caliph's bodyguard answered with a grunt, and took him by the shoulder, to lead him – unresisting – back to Arjijil.

LATER, ORFEO STOOD at the window of his room, watching the first white rays of the nascent dawn hurl silver light into the waiting sky. The east lay to his left, the west to his right; stretching away before him to the southern horizon was the quiet Sahra, which was briefly tinted by a confusion of pastel shades. When the sun was wholly risen, the harsher yellow light of its full-faced glare would set the sand and rocks ablaze and show the desert in its true vivid colours.

'You should not have tried to run away,' said Alkadi Nasreen, Caliph of Mahabbah and Lord of the Twin Seas. He did not sound angry, but a certain resentment and bitter disappointment were very evident in his modestly chiding tone.

Orfeo refused, for the moment, to turn and face his host. While still staring out of the window he answered: 'I should not have needed to run stealthily away. I had your promise that I would be set free, in return for my tale of the doom of Zaragoz. You swore by the One God, if you recall – and though you were not born to that faith, I did not think that you would hold it in such frank contempt as to violate its oath so casually.'

He felt his shoulder gripped yet again, as Nasreen came to him and forced him to turn around. The Caliph was angry enough now.

'You will not speak to me like that!' he said, his voice sharp and intense.

Orfeo consented to look at him, but tried to remain cool, aloof and unbending. 'Is it not true?' he asked.

'No,' replied the dark man. 'It is not true. I remember exactly what I swore – though you, it seems, do not. I swore that I would not punish you, even if I had cause to be hurt in what you told me; and I swore that you and the boy would receive fair treatment in Arjijil. When you had finished your tale, I declared that I would not sell either of you as a slave. I have kept my word.'

'You said that I need not call you *my lord*,' Orfeo countered, 'because I was to reckon myself a free man. A free man may go where he pleases, I think – even in Arjijil.'

'Even a free man must not steal.'

'How else am I to make my way? Since you have not deigned to see me in these last two weeks I have asked your servants for leave to go. I have asked to be given passage on a ship; I have asked to be allowed to go with a caravan. Perhaps you consider it a fair way to honour your word, to set me free but to refuse me the means to exercise my freedom, but it seems to me an overly nice distinction. No doubt you consider it a fine act of mercy not to sell us for slaves, and expect us to be grateful, but I have ever been a free man, and do not recognize any right you may claim to have seized us in the first place. You swore that Maro and I should have fair treatment in Arjijil, and if this is what counts as fair treatment in the eyes of that God before which you swore, then he is a meaner god by far than the ones by which I swore when I took my oath to tell you the truth!'

Alkadi Nasreen did not flinch at all before the tide of accusation, but met Orfeo's pale eyes frankly with his darker ones. His features, which were as fine as if they had been carved from rich and polished wood, were tautly held.

'You are guests here, not prisoners,' said the Caliph. 'But as guests, you have obligations, just as I have obligations as your host. I have not finished with you yet, and until I have, you should not try to leave my house. You would have gone to your deaths, had the watchmen not caught you, for you do not know this land and its ways.'

Orfeo looked away again, but did not try to turn his back on the other man.

'I had not understood that you have not finished with me yet, *my lord*,' he said, bitterly. 'I have told you everything I can about Zaragoz and what befell me there, as I swore I would.'

'I know that,' answered Alkadi Nasreen, 'And I am more grateful than you seem to think. I believe that you told me the truth, and what you told me has been much on my mind. It is true that I have not come to see you, but that was not because I had forgotten you or ceased to care what happened to you. I have been struggling to understand what you told me about my brother, and I have surprised myself by the intensity of that struggle. The bonds of kinship mean a good deal to the men of Estalia, even when kinsmen learn to hate one another. It is a man's duty to avenge his brother, if his brother be treacherously slain.'

'Treacherously slain! Your brother was seized by dae-mons which he had sought to control for his own ends – there is none to blame for his end but his own ambition, unless you would go to hell to seek amends for his betrayal!'

'No,' said Alkadi Nasreen, grimly. '*That* far I would not go. But I would dearly love to know more about those forces which destroyed him, that I may do what I can to oppose them here on earth.'

Orfeo laughed. Here was a man who desired to take a stand against Chaos itself!

'My lord,' he said, tiredly, 'what is it that you want of me?'

Alkadi Nasreen had released him, but now he reached out again to place a gentle hand on Orfeo's shoulder. 'Orfeo,' he said, 'you are an honest man, and a clever fighter. Join me, here in Arjijil. Take the turban, and become my strong right arm. I do not want you as a ser-vant, but as a friend. I believe that you are the one man I have met in these last ten years who might make such a friend, for though the Arabs make good and loyal servants, they are not my own kind.'

Orfeo was surprised by the offer, but also disconcerted by it, for he had no wish to make a life as a reaver. He pre-ferred a better audience than he could ever expect to find in this barbarian citadel, and he was possessed by a *wan-derlust* which had always forbidden him to make any kind of home.

'I am not Estalian,' said Orfeo, in a tone which was at least half-apologetic, 'and truly I do not know what kind I really am, for I was cast aside by my own kin to be raised by patient elves. And though I have no god of my own I could not take the turban, even in pretence. It is not my way to pay mock homage to any god.'

He knew, as he made this refusal, that he risked injuring the other man's pride. He could not believe that Alkadi Nasreen had ever made such a request before, and knew what generosity and sincere regard there must be in his words.

Nasreen did not show any hurt or disappointment in his face, but there was an undercurrent of regret in the light voice in which he replied.

'I am sorry to hear it,' he said, 'and sorry that you are the kind of man who feels that he cannot be a friend to another.'

'If you would truly be my friend,' said the player. 'Let me go. I am a wanderer by nature, not a pirate, and though I have no mission but my own, I would like to be gone from here.'

'And what is your mission?' asked Alkadi Nasreen. 'I cannot quite understand your hurry.'

Orfeo looked him carefully in the eye. 'I have stories to tell,' he said. 'I have the wisdom of lore and legend to spread throughout the world. If you truly want to strike some kind of blow against the forces which destroyed your brother, you might do far worse than to let me tell my stories to all who care to hear them – for my tales always warn against the corruptions of ambition, greed and wrath, and fight their own small wars for amity and honesty.'

'That is a cunning answer,' acknowledged the Caliph, 'but I hope you will forgive me if I doubt that it is the whole truth. I think there is something more personal in your determination, though I believe you when you say that you are not a spy for Estalia. Still, I will not press you on the point, and will be content to accept what you say. If the wisdom of lore and legend will help me to understand what became of my brother, and to take what little vengeance I can, then I would hear more of it. I want you to tell me more of what you know about this mystery you call Chaos – but I ask that you tell me only tales that are true, not clever fancies invented for the amusement of the lords and ladies of the civilized lands.'

'My lord,' said Orfeo, 'I have had little to do with the agents of Chaos in the course of my life. I think that I would have been unfortunate had I had more. Few of those in whom the powers of Chaos take an interest remain alive to tell the tale. I was given subtle warnings by the elves which raised me; I have heard others from the wiser priests of several gods. But I have only known one man who claimed to have fought a champion of Chaos face to face and won. I believed what he told me, for he seemed to me an honest and unboastful man, but I can only tell you what *he* told *me*.'

'I would like to hear it,' said the Caliph.

'And would you swear to let me go free, as the price for hearing it?' asked Orfeo.

'I do not need to swear,' replied Alkadi Nasreen. 'You are already a free man, as I have said. But I will promise you this: if you tell me this tale, I will give you a fine horse, and a saddle, and thirty Imperial crowns. Only say that you will tell me as carefully as you can the true facts of the case.'

'It is a long story,' said Orfeo, 'and it will keep us up as long as the last one did.'

'Then I will make sure that we have more comfortable chairs,' said the Caliph of Mahabbah and Lord of the Twin Seas, 'and as you seem to feel the pressure of time more keenly than the patient desert-men, we will begin this evening, as soon as the sun goes down. And we will meet every night, as we did before, until the tale is done.'

Orfeo could see that he had very little choice, whether or not the Caliph's promises were to be trusted. Alkadi Nasreen had him, and what Alkadi Nasreen wanted to hear, he must be told.

'So be it,' said Orfeo, with a small bow. 'I accept your conditions, and will do as you ask.'

And before Alkadi Nasreen had gone from the room, Orfeo had begun to compose the tale he would tell. He intended, as always, to be very careful in recalling every last detail of what had been said to him by the man whose tale it was, and in improving discreetly upon those incidents which seemed to need improvement.

CHAPTER ONE

YOU WILL HAVE heard, my lord, of a region to the east of the
Tilean city-states, divided from them by the Apuccini
Mountains, which is sometimes known as the land of the
Border Princes. It has the Black Mountains to the north,
the mountains of the World's Edge to the east, and the
Black Gulf to the south, so that it forms a wide rectangle
which is virtually cut off from what we would term the civ-
ilized world.

This land is reckoned by its own people to be civilized
enough, and it is not unlike Estalia or Tilea in that the men
of every little princedom think themselves better than their
neighbours, and are ever-ready to consider that they have
been deprived of some portion of that share of wealth and
privilege which would be theirs if justice prevailed
throughout the world.

Nowhere is the land of the Border Princes very fertile;
much of it is wilderness, and even in the valleys where its
life-giving rivers run the soil is often poor. Its woodlands,
such as they are, consist in the main of short and thorny

trees which usually form a thick and impenetrable undergrowth. The eastern princedoms are perennially plagued by unruly goblins, and in many of the hilly regions there are bands of creatures called mutants, which some people believe – wrongly, I am certain – to be half-castes birthed by human women who have been impregnated by daemons. The presence of such quarrelsome and nasty creatures makes order very difficult to maintain, and it must often be dearly bought by the ruthlessness of princes and their men-at-arms.

Men of Estalia or the Empire will confidently assure you that there are no cities in the region and that even the grandest of the so-called princes are merely upstart brigands. Those whose notion of a city is formed by knowledge of Magritta or Altdorf are justified in saying that no such place exists in the Border Princes, but there are walled towns in the region much greater in size than Arjijil, which the people – who know no better – think of as great cities. Such places are sometimes little more than huge fortresses, to which the entire population of a region might retire in time of invasion. Each one has its own prince, and each one has its own tiny empire – for even such small cities as these must rely on the produce of a legion of farmers.

I say that these petty empires are tiny, and indeed they are, for you will understand well enough that the size of an empire depends upon its communications. The mighty Empire which was restored by Magnus the Pious is nowadays held together by the amity of its electors, but the true bonds of that amity are the good hard roads which carry its carts and coaches, and the broad and placid rivers which carry its boats and barges.

In the Border Princes the roads are poor, and its rivers are often forced to race through ravines or tumble over cataracts. For this reason, there is no common cause between the scattered cities, and the territories over which each prince can exercise his dominion are far from wide.

Despite their tininess, these little empires are as hungry as empires everywhere for expansion. This has less to do with the greed and vaulting ambition of princes than is commonly supposed, and more to do with the tendency of populations to increase. Men and women lead more comfortable lives when they are protected by fortifications, and the population of walled towns always grows unless it is cut back by famine, war or plague. If such an increasing population is to be fed, then the ruler of the city must extend his dominion to encompass more farmland.

In the Border Princes, where there is so much wasteland, such expansion is not easy, and the hold the cities have over their outermost lands is often weak – tested as much by the ruggedness of the terrain which separates them from the seat of power as by the resentment of the farmers against the taxation of distant landlords.

It is all too often the case that these outlying farming communities are constantly threatened by marauders and bandits who live in the neighbouring wilderness, and the men-at-arms who are stationed there must be brave defenders as well as careful oppressors. Such situations breed dour and mistrustful men, but the best among those men are always hard as iron – the stuff of which heroes can easily be made.

This tale concerns the affairs of one such petty empire, and one such iron-hard man.

THE CITY OF which I speak is named Khypris. It was built long ago at the centre of a square of unusually fertile land cut out by a right-angled bend in one of the wider rivers of the region, which is called by its people the Tana Dante. The Tana Dante forms the northern and western boundaries of the fertile square, while the eastern boundary is made by bare and broken mountain crags and the southern by a very dry and stony desert, both of which are virtually impassable to foreign armies.

Thus isolated, the core of Khypris has usually been considered very safe from invasion, and the people of the city

are among the more prosperous denizens of the Border
Princes. The inevitable result of this prosperity, however, is
that the rulers of Khypris must ever be eager to extend their
control from this heartland to the less fertile lands beyond
the river, annexing to the little nation two territories which
the Khyprians call the northlands and the westlands.

Each of these two regions consists of interrupted wilderness, desolate moorland containing isolated vales of
various sizes, whose people can sometimes grow grain but
are more often restricted to the cultivation of turnips, beets
and cabbages. Such vales produce surpluses which are very
small, and would hardly be considered worth the effort of
subjugation and taxation were they outside the boundaries
of richer nations, but as the hunger of Khypris increases, so
does the market value of the food these distant coverts produce.

The further reaches of the northlands and westlands are
more desolate still, merging by degrees with the foothills of
the Black Mountains. Here there are vast tracts of land
which are very liberally decked with thorny trees and
bushes. No crops can be grown there, but there is a kind of
cattle called aurochs which can find adequate grazing. The
aurochs have very shaggy coats and very horny mouths, and
are thus enabled to be quite careless of the thorns. These
beasts are gathered into herds by nomadic tribesmen, sup-
plying them with all that they need in order to live: meat to
eat, leather and coarse wool for tents and clothing.

These tribes are numerous, each one having its own
name and traditions, but the differences between them
mean little to the farmer-folk, who refer to all the hillmen
as the Zani, and think of them as a single barbarian race.
In fact the hillmen are very rarely inclined to band
together in a common cause, and the only thing that will
make them do it is the threat of famine, which sometimes
causes them to bring their herds down from the higher
hills to graze in the fertile vales. In order to do this, they
must combine their warbands into a greater horde, for
that is the only strategy which will suffice to defeat the

trained and disciplined forces the prince of Khypris can put into the field.

In exactly the same way that the slow increase of the population of Khypris forces the prince to extend his dominion as far as possible into the northlands and westlands, the gradual increase in the numbers of the Zani requires a steady growth in the size of the herds which they keep. These expanding herds thin out the thorn-scrub year by year, until the tribes are forced to look to the fertile lowlands as a source of richer grazing for their animals.

When such a time comes, the chiefs of the Zani tribes make overtures to one another, and look for a warlord who will lead them into the lowlands, driving the defending armies assembled by the prince of Khypris back to the heartland beyond the Tana Dante. In the meantime, their united herds will lay waste all the croplands in their path. The confusions which such invasions cause are inevitably exploited by bandits of all kinds, who take full advantage of their opportunity to plunder and pillage.

The man who told me this story assured me that before his own adventure began, the historians of Khypris had preserved the memory of several such invasions by the Zani, and knew that they followed a consistent pattern. The northlands and the westlands could not be properly defended, but the Zani horde invariably found it difficult to bring their warriors and herds across the Tana Dante, and even if they succeeded in doing so, were so depleted that they had not the resources to storm the city walls. Khypris itself had never fallen. For this reason, the strategy followed by the Khyprians was always the same: the prince's men-at-arms would retreat, forming up into a considerable army on the inner bank of the great river. Those northlanders and westlanders who had horses and carts would flee, trying to cross the bridges into the heartland before the Zani arrived to destroy them.

THE MAN OF whom my story tells was named Harmis Detz. He was a Khyprian through and through, though I judged that his remote ancestors must have been immigrant adventurers from the banks of the Reik in Sudenland, for he still had the look of such folk about him. He was not tall, but he was powerfully built, with heavy chest and shoulders and knotty muscles about his thighs. He moved with a sinuous ease. His face had been severely ravaged by childhood disease and was pockmarked, but he was not unhandsome by the standards of his kind. He had brown hair but his eyes were grey and intense; his stare was difficult to meet.

When I knew the man, he was something over sixty years old – a good age for one of his kind – but when the events of this tale took place he was only thirty-three. He had been born in the walled city, the eldest son of a servant in Prince Faramond's stables. He had a younger brother, whose name was Lavarock.

When they came of age, Harmis and Lavarock both decided to train as men-at-arms, so that they could wear the colours of their master in what seemed to them the grandest and noblest way, as fighting men. Their heads had been filled, as the heads of all children are, with tales of bold knights – for the myths and legends of the Templars and Knights Panther travel faster and further than the knights themselves ever could – and the arts of war seemed far more glorious than the care of horses.

The two brothers mastered the skills of war well enough, and soon began to spend half of every year in the northlands, helping to keep the peace and defend the unsteady borders of the nation. There they learned the realities of politics and war, and came to understand that no man would call them friend. To the villagers and farmers the claret-and-gold which were the colours of Faramond's family were symbols of oppression, despite that it was the sworn duty of all who wore such colours to risk their lives in protecting the vales against the continual nuisance of Zani warbands and bandits. The only gratitude the prince's men ever received was grudging, and the business of fighting soon lost the gloss of glamour which

Harmis's and Lavarock's childish ideals had bestowed upon it.

When he killed his first Zan raider, Harmis Detz was exultant; when he killed his tenth he felt nothing but sour relief. When he first bested a hillman after a ten-minute duel with swords he was already too wise to be intoxicated with the romance of it, and was resentful of the danger it had placed him in. He knew by then how infinitely preferable it was to strike a man cleverly from behind with a thrown knife, or to put a strangling-cord stealthily about his throat.

Harmis and Lavarock belonged to a company called the Border Guard, though it was a common joke among them that no one could say exactly where the border was. They knew, though, that the men who were guarding it were strung out across a line more than two hundred miles long, in very small groups. Their job was to pursue small bands of raiders – which they could not catch on four occasions in five – and to send urgent warning to Prince Faramond and his commanders of any major incursion from the hills. There had been no such incursion during the fifteen years in which Harmis had worn Faramond's livery, nor in the thirty years before his service began.

Harmis, at this time of his life, had never been married, and had accumulated very little wealth. First among his possessions was his horse, a mare named Sable. Like the helmet for his head, the armoured coat and the wooden shield which he carried into open conflict, Sable had been given to him by the prince's armourers, but custom dictated that she could not be taken from him until he died. Should he live long enough to retire into less violent service, and she long enough to retire with him, he would be allowed to keep her. Second among his possessions was his sword, also given to him by the prince's armourers, but on similar terms – the army would not reclaim it, unless he died with it in his hand.

He would also have received a knife, on the same terms, if it were not that he possessed an heirloom of his family, hard-won and faithfully handed down by another Detz who had fought for his prince. This heirloom consisted of a fine matched pair of knives, weighted for throwing; Harmis carried them in a harness which crossed the scabbards behind his back, so that he could draw one by reaching back over either of his shoulders.

Lavarock, being the younger brother, had no such inheritance, and so had only a small token given to him by his mother in addition to what he had acquired on entering the profession of arms. Lavarock, unlike his austere brother, had once taken a wife in Khypris, but she had died in childbirth while he was far away in the north; she had left him a son named Medard, who was already being schooled to follow in his father's and uncle's footsteps.

ON THE NIGHT when the events of the story began to unfold, Harmis Detz was standing guard on a tower built from logs, which stood on the outskirts of a village named Vimera. His station was twenty feet above the ground, and was supposed to give him a commanding view of the surrounding slopes. The Zani had never come that way in force, for the territory was not conducive to the gathering of the herds, but small warbands would occasionally ride through the gullies to raid Vimera and its neighbouring villages.

Though spring was already making way for summer, the night was cool and misty, and while Harmis stood aloft the fog intensified by slow degrees, so that he first lost sight of the northerly slopes, and was then cut off from sight of the house in the middle of Vimera where his fellow guardsmen were billeted.

In the end, he was completely isolated from the world at large by dense walls of grey mist, which were damp and clammy and seemingly full of vague shadows. Since he could see nothing, he wondered whether the officer in charge of his unit would send a man to tell him to come down, but he did not expect it; duty was duty, and a watchman could not expect to be relieved of it merely because circumstances prevented him from discharging it efficiently. He concentrated on keeping warm, and on listening for ominous sounds – though the fog seemed thick enough to muffle sound as well as to obscure sight.

Sable was tethered at the foot of the tower, beside the ladder. She seemed restless, but that signified nothing, for there was no grass there for her to crop.

When he heard a movement down below he was startled by the realization that the man had virtually set foot on the ladder before his presence was detectable, but Harmis relaxed quickly when he saw that it was only Lavarock, come to bring him a cup of warm mead.

'I might as well be in my bed for all the good I can do here,' said Harmis, as Lavarock joined him on the tower and handed him the cup.

'Aye,' said Lavarock. 'The Zani may be stupid barbarians, but they're not such fools as to go abroad on a night like this. Even as far above the ground as this the fog is well-nigh dense enough to be drunk. Should I stay to keep you company?'

'For a few minutes,' said Harmis. 'But there's no need for two of us to suffer for long. You might as well be warm in your bed, and free to enjoy the sound and dreamless sleep of the virtuous.'

'I'd prefer the chance to be gently wicked,' said the younger man, 'and would gladly pay the penalty of a little sleeplessness. But these farmer-folk are very careful of their daughters, and I swear there's not an honest whore in the district!'

'The nearest brothel's a whole day's ride away in Aldium,' Harmis told him, pretending that Lavarock might be too innocent to know already. 'Though they say that the great magician who lives by the Black Tarn has a girl apprentice now, who'd surely take a tumble for an ounce of gold or a cupful of blood.'

The Black Tarn was a nearby place of mystery where the magician Astyanax lived, pursuing his arcane researches. The Border Princes were as poor in magic as in grain, but

Astyanax had the reputation of being a very learned man,
who could have gone to the Empire if he wished, where
he would surely have been welcomed with open arms by
the masters of the Colleges where the Arts Magical were
said to reach their highest achievement. Harmis had seen
Astyanax once or twice on previous tours of duty, but had
not yet clapped eyes on the new girl apprentice of whom
he had heard rumours.

'Oh aye,' said Lavarock. 'Had I an ounce of gold to spend,
I've much better ways to use it, and I'd not lend one of her
kind a drop of blood, let alone a cupful.'

'They say that a little knowledge of the Arts makes girls
more skilful,' Harmis observed, 'but you must be very sure
to please them well enough, or they'll certainly curse you
with warts.'

'You've tried it, I suppose?' said Lavarock, ironically.

'Many a time,' Harmis assured him, not expecting for a
moment to be believed. 'And warts are the one disfigure-
ment that I've never suffered from.'

'If only you'd lasted a few minutes more,' said Lavarock,
'she might have smoothed away those pockmarks which
spoil your looks entirely.'

Had the remark come from anyone else, Harmis would
have considered it an insult, but Lavarock had a licence to
make such jokes.

'Oh no,' said Harmis. 'I like the girls who don't mind a
scar or two about the face, for they're never the kind who
want to marry me and turn me into a farmer.'

'I don't mind the marrying kind, for myself,' answered
Lavarock, with a hint of melancholy. 'And nor would you,
save that you hate to take those knives off, even when
you're at the trough.'

'The voice of jealousy,' said Harmis, dismissively. 'Had
you beaten me to our mother's breach you'd proudly own
the knives yourself, and I'd be well content with that
amulet you wear about your neck.'

Lavarock lifted a finger to touch the place beneath his
jerkin where his mother's gift rested. Despite that Harmis

called it an amulet, it was only a mirror, and it had no virtue at all except to show them their rugged faces, and to remind them both whence they had come.

'I'm well enough content,' said the younger brother, soberly. 'You throw the knives far better than I, and while you have them to defend us both, I'm better defended than I could ever be if I had to hurl them myself.'

'Depend on it,' said Harmis, and gave him back the empty cup. He had twice saved Lavarock's life with the knives. Once he had used them to strike down a cunning brigand who had his own dagger ready-raised; then he had killed a yellow-eyed hillman in a head-dress of aurochs-horns – which marked him as a petty warlord – who had closed coarse hands about his brother's throat.

The fog had thickened even more by now, and when Lavarock went carefully down the ladder it seemed that he was lowering himself into a veritable ocean of confusion.

Harmis resumed his futile watch. Mere minutes passed before his eye was caught by something darting hither and yon about the tower, visible only as a fluttering shadow in the gloom. He held out his lantern, but could not see the thing at all, and had to guess that it was a bat. There were usually songbirds nesting in the tower, but this year they had not come – one of his companions had called it a bad omen, but like most soldiers he was a man forever on the lookout for gloomy auguries.

Harmis brought the lantern back and hung it up again, but the fluttering continued. The bat, if bat it was, seemed intent on circling the tower.

Perhaps, thought Harmis, it is lost in the fog and desperate to find a landmark. But he knew that bats were almost blind on the clearest of nights, and could not get lost.

There was a strange odour in the air, as though the fog were somehow tainted. He thought again about the wizard who had a house by the Black Tarn, no more than seven miles away. Like most men of his stripe, Harmis had little to do with spellcasters, and was content to avoid them when he could. He had never gone to a witch-woman or a hedge-wizard in order to bargain for a love-potion or a protective amulet, and had never asked to have his future told. In Harmis's uneducated opinion, formed mainly by whispered tales of wonder and malicious rumour, all wizards were necromancers at heart, and even the best of them were at least half-mad.

He had to jerk himself awake suddenly, and surprised himself in so doing, because he had thought the night too chilly to allow him to fall easily sleep. The mead, he supposed, must have warmed him better than he knew – and though there could surely be no safer night for sleeping at his post, it was still a silly thing to do.

But the scent on the air seemed somehow to have taken the chill out of the fog; its drifting vapours were not unpleasant now, and the scent they carried made him feel slightly dreamy. His armoured coat, which he was forced to wear when he was on sentry duty, felt unusually heavy.

With difficulty, he pulled himself together, forcing himself to think in order to resist the temptation of sleep. He dismissed wizardry from his mind and thought instead of where his own small company would next be taken, and where he would most desire to go, in terms of efficient kitchen-service and bed-service. Vimera, alas, was as short of competent cooks as it was of willing girls.

Aldium, he decided in the end, would be the best of the likely postings. It was a more sizeable village – whose people reckoned it a town – some miles to the south of Vimera. It was conveniently distant from the border, and civilized by the standards of the region. But if his luck was bad, they would be sent further west to Malko, a place much like Vimera, of which he had no fond memories at all – though he had not been billeted there for three years and more. He tried to remember whether there was a pretty girl in Malko, or in any of the other godforsaken hamlets even further to the west.

He did not sleep; to that extent at least his determination succeeded. But when he heard the first shouts of alarm from behind him, he realized that he had not conserved attention enough to do his work well. In all probability, he would not have seen or heard the raiders had his wits been at their sharpest, but he would never be sure that he could not have caught some faint but telling sound had he been fully alert.

He came down the ladder very quickly, and untethered Sable. The cries of alarm had given way to screams, eerily distorted by the clinging mist, and he could not tell how many voices were joined in the cacophony. One thing was clear: Vimera was under attack.

Once mounted, he urged the mare immediately back towards the billet, without bothering to get his second foot into the stirrup; but before she had taken half a dozen steps there were other horses about him, which seemed to have come at a gallop from those northern hills he had been appointed to watch. They were riderless, but not wild – for he could hear the crack of whips as they were driven along. It made no sense to him, for the Zani always rode their horses, while the goblins did not keep them, and were quick to kill and eat any that they captured.

He drew his sword, and cut at a shadow which suddenly loomed up in the mist. The caster of the shadow obviously had not realized that he had come so close to an enemy, and there was as much surprise as injury in the cry of pain which followed the blow – but the cry made Harmis's blood run cold, for it seemed to him that it came from no human throat.

These are not Zani! he thought, in anguish. We are beset by goblins!

They were clustering all about him, and yet he could not see them in the fog – and one of them cut at him just as he had cut at the other, with a blade whose tip seemed to emerge by magic from the cloak of mist. Sable saved him by shying away, but suddenly she stumbled as she was shoved sideways from the narrow path by another horse. Harmis, having been so casually careless in the matter of placing his foot in the second stirrup, was unceremoniously tumbled from her back.

Though the fall bruised him, he came quickly enough to his feet. His sword was still firmly gripped in his hand – but one more riderless horse came galloping out of the fog, and though the hard-driven beast could not have seen him, so fast did it come, Harmis was ridden down and hurled to the ground.

A flying hoof caught him on the side of the head and knocked him silly. He lay on the ground for what seemed like a long time, trying to get up again, but he was far too dizzy. In the end he took a deep and dreadfully sweet breath of the curiously-fragrant mist, and felt his senses leaving him.

His head fell back on to uncaring stone and he knew no more.

CHAPTER TWO

WHEN HARMIS WOKE, Sable was beside him, waiting there patiently, as though she were standing guard to protect him from attack.

The day was bright and cloudless, every last vestige of the fog having disappeared as if by magic. There were no attackers in sight, but when he climbed out of the gully into which he had fallen he saw immediately that they had made their dreadful mark upon the village.

He ran towards the houses, and then along the curved street where most of the cottages were gathered, heading for the big house where his brother and the rest of his companions had been lodged.

He could see there had been a massacre of sorts, yet the evidence of it which met his eyes seemed oddly less than horrible. There were no huge lakes of spilled blood; the dead men who lay in the street were not so grisly a sight as might have been imagined. They had come from their houses bearing axes and pitchforks and had been struck down, as often as not with a single blow. Those who had

died harder had fallen back within the doorways they had
tried to defend. The marauding goblins – if goblins they
had been – had slain them with alacrity, but apparently
had not paused to loot and pillage.

Outside the guardhouse there were signs of a more considerable fight, but by no means a pitched battle. Had
Harmis been able to give warning while the attackers were
still approaching, even with a single shout, the soldiers
would have been out of their beds and ready by the time
they had to defend their makeshift fort. As it was, the
enemy had been at the doors and the windows while the
defenders were still struggling to throw away their blankets.

There was only one corpse lying outside the barrack-
house; Harmis immediately recognized it as a mutant. It
was taller than most men, but thinner, with a flattened jaw
and jutting teeth. Its arms seemed unnaturally long, and
its hands were claw-like. It was lightly armoured with
wood and leather, but whatever weapon it had carried had
been recovered by the survivors of the fight.

Inside, things were much worse.

Harmis stood in the doorway and patiently counted the
dead men. He knew before he stepped across the threshold
that no one had escaped. Here there was blood aplenty,
and many of the bodies had been considerably hacked
about – the mutants must have worked themselves up into
a kind of frenzy, as their kind often did when about the
business of killing.

It was not immediately obvious which of the dead men
was Lavarock.

There were three more mutants – orcs lying dead among
the humans – by no means a poor total, in view of the sud-
denness of the attack. Harmis checked their bodies
carefully, to make quite sure that none was still alive; only
then did he look about for his brother's corpse.

He found Lavarock in the far corner of the dormitory.
His brother's body was bent double about the shaft of a
spear which had been hurled at him with force enough to

go completely through his abdomen. Harmis could see the scar on the wooden wall where the weapon had nearly pinned and held him like a dreadful trophy – but Lavarock's weight had been too great to allow that to happen; he had fallen in crumpled agony, and had died soon afterwards, choking on his own blood.

Harmis stared down at the body, accusing himself with angry bitterness of failing in his duty, failing in his affection, failing in everything. He was momentarily resentful of whatever godly mercy it was which had allowed him to survive, feeling that he fully deserved to have been killed, because he had let the death-dealers pass beneath him while his only concern had been to keep himself awake.

Had he been able to change places with his brother at that moment, he would have done so; he would have given up his own life to save the one which he had unwittingly left undefended. After all, it was the duty of an elder brother to protect a younger – and Lavarock had a son, while Harmis had no one at all to mourn him. His parents had died, one after the other, less than a year ago.

Lavarock had taken off his jerkin when he went to bed. The loose undershirt which he wore beneath it was unbuttoned. The little round mirror he wore – their dead mother's gift to him – was lying uselessly on the floor. Harmis gently lifted his brother's head, so that he could remove the ornament. After taking off his armoured coat, which he intended to pack away in the bag behind Sable's saddle, he placed the mirror's cord around his own neck, and opened his shirt to hide it within. It felt cold against his skin, and the uncomfortable notion struck him that he had willingly taken the chill of death into himself, where he would nurse it carefully as a silent cry for vengeance, token of a debt to be redeemed in mutant blood.

Then he went to the other bodies, one by one, scrupulously searching for signs of life.

There were none.

Outside again, he breathed deeply of the cleaner air. He looked back at the village, wondering if he should search the houses for survivors. But he could not expect to find survivors there; anyone who had escaped would have run away into the misty night, as fast as they could go. They would not come back while there was any chance that the mutants were still around.

Harmis wondered why the marauders were not still there, enjoying the fruits of their victory. Such a raid was by no means unprecedented, but the incident had certain strange features. The mutants had horses with them, which they must have captured in an earlier raid – but they had not paused to enjoy the spoils of that earlier attack either. It seemed that they must have some further purpose still in mind, and that these raids were part of a concerted campaign – but such creatures, though cunning enough, were rarely given to complicated planning, and would far rather kill and eat captured horses than drive them along as the Zani drove their aurochs.

Why had they gone so quickly? Where had they gone?

These thoughts reminded him that there was a duty which remained to be done. He had failed to give warning to his brother and his brothers-in-arms, but there was still warning to be given. If the marauders had some further objective in view – presumably another village – then he must do what he could to make sure that their attack was not as unexpected and as easy as the one which they had visited on Vimera.

And there was another duty too, which he had not performed because he was Faramond's man-at-arms and sworn to defend the empire, but because his brother had been cruelly and treacherously slain: a private duty to seek and obtain revenge.

With these duties before him, Harmis could not linger long in Vimera. He had to be on his way, to find the killers, and – if he could – to frustrate whatever plan they had to commit further mayhem in Khypris. There was no time to bury Lavarock or any of the others, nor could he lay them on a cart and drive it to Aldium. He had more urgent and more dangerous work to do.

He carefully gathered together everything he needed,
and secured the resultant bundle to Sable's saddle. Then he
climbed up on her back, making very certain that both feet
were securely set in their stirrups. He set forth without
delay, riding southwards along the crude road which connected Vimera with the inner part of what the Khyprians
were proud to call their empire. While he rode he looked
carefully for the trail the mutants must have left, in their
hurry to be on their way. He had no difficulty in discovering the place where the band had left the road – and after
a moment's hesitation, he followed them.

THE TRAIL CURVED to the west, away from the flatter farmlands and into a region of steep slopes and ravines which
– had they not been bare of all but coarse grass and purple
heather – might have been reckoned to belong to the Zani
rather than the northland marches.

The mutants and their captive horses seemed to be following the course of a fast-running rill, heading upstream.
Harmis could not at first guess any reason for it, but it
struck him suddenly, in a way which made him feel stupid
for not having guessed it before, that the stream must be
one of the outlets of the Black Tarn.

The tarn was set high in the hills, having formed in a
broad hollow where rainwater was trapped in a natural
reservoir cut into the grey granite which was the bedrock of
the region. Harmis had occasionally ridden along a ridge
from where the southern edge of the tarn could be seen,
but he had never been close to the wizard's lair on the
northern shore.

He wondered whether Astyanax might have sent the
raiders to murder the soldiers in Vimera, but he dismissed
the idea almost immediately. Though wizards and
mutants might be considered similar in that both were
somewhat beyond the pale of ordinary human society, he
had never heard that Astyanax was an evil man, or one
who would stoop to the use of such instruments. But still
he was puzzled by the evident fact that the raiders were

headed for the wizard's house, for they were not a large band – probably no more than a dozen strong, to judge by the marks of their passage – and they would be very reckless indeed were they to attack a wizard's stronghold. The house of Astyanax was certain to have magical defences of some sort as well as sturdy walls, and mutants were not known for their courage in the face of wizardry, though they were always cocksure of their prowess with ordinary weapons.

Once he was certain that he knew where the subhumans were going, Harmis left the route they had followed. He did not want to be below them, and knew that they would certainly take the trouble to check their rear occasionally when they had left such carnage in their wake.

With this in mind, he carefully guided Sable up a long and difficult slope which would allow him to make his way to the tarn by a much higher route. He knew that he would have to keep in mind the peril of being silhouetted against the bright sky, but he was confident that he could do it. He had been billeted in Vimera half a dozen times in the last seven years, and knew the territory reasonably well. He considered himself a skilful man in the soldierly arts, as any man with his fifteen years of experience was entitled to do.

As it happened, he came upon the mutants sooner than he expected, for they had dawdled on the way and then had stopped. The horses which they led – increased in number by several they had found in Vimera, including the bay which had belonged to Lavarock – were roped together as a string. The horses were drinking at the stream while the mutants were sprawled upon the bank nearby, laughing and jeering at one another after the fashion of their kind. Sometimes, Harmis knew, such jocularity could disappear in an instant as the banter slipped over the edge of mortal insult, but the mood of this company seemed good enough.

Harmis did not like that, for it showed how much they had enjoyed the work which they had recently done.

He managed to find a narrow canyon in which to hide Sable safely away; then he crept to a place where he could watch his enemies without undue danger of being seen. There was no way to get close to the group, for its members had stopped in a place where there was no substantial cover for ninety yards, but he was content to wait for a while. He counted their number as eleven, and knew that it would be very foolhardy to tackle them alone, even if he waited for the small hours of the night, when the greater part of their number would be fast asleep. He might easily murder a couple of sentries with the aid of his strangling-cord – and he knew from experience that unhuman throats were as easy to close as human ones – but once the rest had been alerted to his nearness and his murderous intentions he would be very lucky indeed if he were able to carry forward a successful war of attrition.

Given half a chance, though, he was determined to try. Though his companions had always reckoned him – with some justice – a cold and uncommunicative man, the loss of his brother pained and shamed him. He knew that he could not be sure that his brother's murderer was dead unless he saw all eleven of these monstrous creatures slain, and to achieve that end he was prepared to set aside the caution which had preserved his life through fifteen years as a fighter.

He thought at first that the raiders had stopped to rest their horses and make a meal, but when he saw that they had made no preparations for eating he realized that he had been stupid again. The monsters had been in a hurry when they left Vimera; if they were not in a hurry now it must be because they had reached their immediate destination. So this must be a point of rendezvous – but who were they to meet, and why?

Was it possible, he asked himself, that they were not headed for the Black Tarn after all? But he dismissed the idea; it was far more likely that they *did* intend to attack the wizard's house, but needed help in order to do it. They must be waiting now for reinforcements.

Again, it was brought home to him how very unusual the behaviour of these beings was. It was almost as if they had been conscripted into some dread army, contrary to everything he knew about their habits and their inclinations. Something strange and sinister was happening in the northlands – something worse, perhaps, than the invasion of the Zani for which the Border Guard had patiently watched for three generations and more.

Harmis wondered whether he ought to go back to Sable and ride on ahead, to warn Astyanax of the lurking danger. He hesitated, not only because he was not sure that it was the right thing to do, but also because of his innate dislike of spellcasters. He told himself sternly that there was no need for any particular anxiety, because the wizard was well-known in the region as a good man, and surely depended on the farms and villages of the district for his mundane supplies of bread and meat. Nevertheless, he waited where he was.

After all, he said, silently, he is a wizard, and should not need warnings to be carried to him by ordinary men.

HE DID NOT have to wait for long. Mere minutes had passed when he sighted a rider coming up the gully with several others on foot behind him. They too were following the course of the stream. Because the leader was mounted he knew that they could not be goblins from the moment he caught sight of them, but when they came close enough for him to judge what they might be instead, he drew in his breath very sharply. They were most certainly not what he had expected – or, indeed, anything he could have expected. He had not seen their like before, nor ever known that such as they existed.

The rider, to judge by the staff he carried, was some kind of sorcerer; but *what* kind, Harmis did not know. The staff itself seemed to be compounded from twisted bones – whether human or animal there was no way to tell – and its knobbed crown was decorated with strips of dried and shrivelled flesh. The man who bore it was tall, and carried himself like a man of strength and power, but the skin of his well-muscled arms, left bare by the sleeveless tunic which he wore, was marked with many sores and scars and leprous patches. His face was even more remarkable, and Harmis could think of no other way to describe it than to imagine that the skin had at some time been scraped off, kneaded like dough with something dark and foul, then spread upon the underlying flesh to set again as hideously as the artist could contrive.

And yet, the eyes which were set in that awful face seemed bright and keen – keen enough to make Harmis crouch down where he was, more afraid by far of being seen than he had been when he had only the common-place ugliness of the mutants to intimidate him.

The retinue which this monstrous wizard had brought with him was equally frightful. They numbered only four, but they were creatures such as Harmis had never seen, even in his nightmares. Perhaps they were men of a kind, just as the sorcerer was apparently a man, but they seemed to Harmis to have far less of the human in them than the mutants did – and what the remainder was, he did not dare to guess, for even in that first moment of astonishment it was obvious to him that they must have parents far more horrible than he could imagine.

Harmis had heard tales of daemons and beastmen, as everyone has, but he had never known how much trust a man should put in such horrific nightmares. Now he saw that the tales had truth in them. These must surely be beastmen or daemons – for how else could their human attributes be mingled so intimately with aspects of loathsome beasts?

One of the creatures was somewhat snakelike in its features, with coarse scaly skin which seemed to be in the process of being sloughed off and replenished from beneath. Its skull was horned and hairless. Its tongue, which seemed too large to be contained by its mouth, was serpentine in form, and it appeared to have a smaller mouth of its own.

The second creature had similarly ravaged skin, some-what ruddier in hue. It had horns more twisted than the first, the ends of which bore strange rubbery suckers.

The third was hairier than its companions, though the brown skin beneath its hair seemed very moist with sweat or exuded mucus. It was more corpulent than the others, and its appearance was made more wretched by the fact that its discoloured eyes were weeping thick tears.

The fourth, astonishingly, was the worst of them. Although Harmis struggled to think of something to com-pare it to, it defied immediate analogy. It was as if its face had somehow been turned inside-out, so that it wore its warped skull on the outside, instead of masking it decently with flesh. Like the others, its head bore twisted horns, and its body was covered in scars and sores.

The horse on which the repulsive sorcerer rode was ordi-nary enough, but it was of uncommon bulk, and its piebald coat was mottled by the marks of some strange infection.

The sight of these newcomers was so appalling to Harmis that he could not help but wonder at the fact that even mutants could bear to be with such creatures or con-sent to be their servants – and when he looked at the company awaiting these new arrivals he saw that the mutants were indeed rather uneasy.

Harmis had spent his life fighting Zani warriors, who liked to prove their manhood by descending into the low-lands in groups a dozen strong, with their shaggy coats and their horned helmets – but at that moment he would have been delighted to see a Zani warband come swarming down the canyon, shooting their deadly arrows and whirling their axes about their heads. He had earlier toyed with the notion that the mutants might be agents of the Zani, come to smooth the way for an invasion, but now he made mute apology. The Zani would never seek allies like these; this affair was a wizards' war of some kind – and very much more dangerous than he had thought when he had set out to track the marauders who had fallen on Vimera.

But it was not *only* a wizards' war, he reminded himself, for the mutants must have slaughtered the guardsmen in Vimera to prevent their taking a part in it. He remembered, suddenly, the batlike thing that had fluttered about the watch-tower, and the peculiar scent which had been in the air. He knew then that he *had* been narcotised while the mutants came into Vimera, and knew also that the fog had been thickened by enchantment.

He felt sick to his stomach, not only because he knew better now what kind of hand had casually reached out to crush his companions-in-arms, but also because he felt that the task of properly avenging his brother's murder must now be reckoned impossible. A wizard as powerful as Astyanax might be able to make a worthy stand against a company like this, but not a mere man like Harmis Detz.

On further thought, however, he realized that even a wizard might need eager hands to bear weapons on his behalf, if he were to be faced by a sorcerer who could match and nullify his magical power and a company of warrior beastmen. So far as he knew, Astyanax had only two apprentices with him, one of them a girl. Perhaps, he thought, there might yet be something he could do, to aid the good magician against the bad.

When the combined forces of the mutants and the sorcerer's monstrous minions moved off again, heading for the Black Tarn, Harmis Detz moved too. The mutants did not take their captured horses, but left them safely roped, and Harmis likewise continued on foot. He took great care to remain hidden from those he was following, but he took equal care to ensure that they did not pass out of his sight.

Duty still drove him on – and for the moment, his desire for revenge was fierce enough to subdue his horror and his fear.

CHAPTER THREE

THE WIZARD'S HOUSE was built on a rocky promontory, so that the waters of the tarn were on three sides of it. It was by no means a palatial edifice; its foundation was a rounded rock of no great size, so that the house too was rounded, and twice as high as it was broad. The causeway connecting it to the shore looked to Harmis as though it had been deliberately narrowed at one point, so that only two men afoot or one on horseback could comfortably pass through the bottleneck. The causeway was not very long – only thirty yards or so – but it was obvious that the house would be difficult to invade by that route.

The tarn was very still and unnaturally dark. There was little enough wind, and the rocky ridges around the lake shielded its waters, but still there was an odd absence of waves. Though the sky was clear and the sun shone the water was not blue, even in the unshadowed centre; the tarn fully deserved the name which had been given to it, for its surface was indeed almost black. Harmis could not tell whether this was because of the colour of the rocks which trapped and held the water, or whether it was some mysterious property of the water itself.

There was no evident way to approach the house clandestinely, for it had narrow windows on every side, and there was not so much as a bush or a bramble-patch anywhere along the shore. Nevertheless, the mutants and their monstrous masters paused well below the level of the tarn, and the sorcerer dismounted. Then he and his companions made their way cautiously forward, walking along the edge of the lake in single file, as though they crouched behind some protective barrier.

Harmis, still watching them from above and behind, realized that the magician with the contorted face must be shielding them in some way to prevent their being observed from the house, but that he had not troubled to shield them from the view of watchers in a place where no watchers should be.

Harmis regretted now that he had not ridden on ahead of the party to give warning of their coming, though he was still very uneasy about the prospect of taking a hand in the battle which would shortly commence. Reason suggested that if the attackers were creeping so carefully they must expect to derive a considerable advantage from surprise; he could only conclude that a conflict of wizards might benefit as much as any other from forewarning and time to prepare.

Was it still possible, he wondered, to give such a warning?

There was no way now to race ahead of the monstrous company below him – not, at any rate, without exposing himself to their attention and whatever violence they might be able to aim at him. He realized, though, that he had other resources, and he took out the mirror he had taken from Lavarock's body, pausing to polish it briefly on the sleeve of his tunic.

Without removing the cord from around his neck he angled the face of the mirror to catch the sun and deflect a narrow ray across the dark water, aiming at the highest of the windows which faced him. The distance was so great, and the window itself was so deeply shadowed, that there was no way to know whether anyone was in the room, or whether the flash of reflected light could be seen if anyone was.

He tilted the mirror from side to side so as to send an intermittent signal which would be more readily glimpsed, but after a few minutes he stopped and put it away. He clicked his tongue in frustration, because he could not be certain that anything would be achieved if anyone within the house had caught sight of the winking light, if the sorcerer's spell of concealment was sufficiently effective.

Feeling utterly helpless, he watched the mutants and their dreadful companions make their way painstakingly to the end of the causeway.

He saw the attackers distribute themselves as though for a rush, and wondered briefly whether the sorcerer intended to blast the door from where he stood. In fact, though, the dire magician stood back, and it was one of his unhuman companions who stepped forward, bearing a heavy halberd, ready to make a solitary charge. The three remaining monstrosities spread out, two with longbows at the ready, the third with a massive spear.

The halberdier was the one with the scaly skin and snakelike tongue; he was the most powerfully muscled of the beastmen, though he was not as huge in the midriff as the one with slimy fur. When he charged the door, Harmis was astonished by his speed, and it seemed as though he might cover the thirty yards in a matter of three seconds despite being weighed down by ragged armour.

But the snake-tongued monster had covered no more than half the distance when something reached out of the water and caught his ankle, bringing him down at the narrowest part of the causeway. It was a long, black tentacle, smooth and leech-like.

Harmis had heard of creatures called lashworms which could thrust out a saw-edged tongue in whip-like fashion to sting a victim, but if this was a relative of such creatures it was far cleverer than they, for the tentacle was clearly attempting to coil itself as tightly as it could about the body of the man which it had tripped.

The halberdier tried at first to pull himself free, as though he could not believe that such a thing might hold him against his will. But though he heaved with all his weight, the black thing merely stretched, absorbing the strength of the pull. Then the scaly titan slashed at the prisoning cord with his weapon, trying to cut through it. The tentacle was severed, and the part which was still anchored underwater was snatched back beneath the surface, gouting purple ichor – but the disconnected part still writhed and wrestled at the snakeman's feet, as if trying to knot itself about his calves. And when the one tentacle was severed, three more rose sinuously from the depths to wrap themselves around the prisoner's other leg, his waist and his arm.

Harmis saw the sorcerer signalling angrily to the reluctant mutants, urging them to run forward with their swords to cut and slash, but they moved forward very reluctantly, with one eye on their own feet – and as they rose from their crouched positions to run to the aid of their misshapen ally, an arrow flew from a window high above the door to take one full in the chest.

If the advantage of surprise had not been lost as soon as Harmis sent his signal, it was certainly lost now, and whatever resistance the inhabitants of the house could make had been mustered to the cause of its defence.

One of the hideous bowmen immediately sent an arrow through the window from which fire had come, while the spearman tried with threatening gestures of his weapon to urge the mutant troops on to more enthusiastic action. The mutants, realizing that they were within easy bowshot of four or five different windows, became keen to reach the cover offered by the walls of the house, and ran forward to help the beleaguered halberdier.

The snakeman was quickly freed by the chopping of their swords, but the mutants were instantly made targets themselves, and as the severed ends of the tentacles squirmed about them they became panicked and began to get in one another's way. One, accidentally cut by a companion's blade, howled in anguish and in pain. Another was tumbled into the water – Harmis could not be sure whether he had been seized by another of the groping tentacles, or tripped up by a severed end, or simply bundled over by one of his own kind.

Harmis looked back at the sorcerer and saw him moving his arms, as though willing his servants to succeed, or at least to press on more ardently. He knew nothing of magical combat save for what rumour had told him, but he had always been sure that tales of magicians hurling lightning-bolts at one another were over-imaginative. The wise fighting man, as he knew from his own training and experience, tried to exhaust his opponent while sparing himself, and Harmis judged that some such tactics were being used here. The hideous magician was determined to draw his enemy's fire before unleashing his own – his mutant pawns were little more than cannon-fodder in his eyes, and even his monstrous servants were being urged forward to take a heavy burden of punishment upon themselves, so that their master's task might be light enough to bear when he finally consented to unleash his own power.

Another arrow soared from the house – not from the same window as before – and struck one of the misbegotten bowmen full in the chest. But he did not fall; instead he ripped the arrow from his own flesh with a grimace which made his gargoyle of a face uglier still; with a defiant flourish and a contemptuous cry of rage, he hurled it away. The other bowman had returned fire instantly and accurately, but whether his arrow might have struck home inside the house there was no way to tell.

The snakeman had reached the door by now, and two of the mutants were still with him – though three more were now blocking the causeway while they struggled with all their might to throw off the serpentine coils of the liberated

tentacles. More of the black things were already rising from
the dark water to join in the attempt to anchor them. Those
of their companions who were as yet unencumbered were
bustling about behind them, trying as best they could to
cut them free, but the causeway was not wide enough to
make the task easy.

Harmis knew only too well that he would be out of his
depth in such a fight as this, but he nevertheless began to
move closer. He wished that the slope behind the fighters
was steeper, so that he might think of starting a landslide,
but the bare and weathered rock held no such promise and
he had no bow with which to fire at them from a distance.
The best he could hope for was to come to a position from
which he could throw one or both of his knives – and that
a situation might somehow develop which would allow
him to do so without being instantly slain in reprisal.

The halberdier was hacking at the door now, his blows
seemingly driven by superhuman strength. It was clear that
his weapon had a very sturdy blade – he was wielding it
almost as though it were a battle-axe, though no merely
human arm could possibly have used it thus. The door was
splintering already, and now there were four mutants waiting with him, though one more had been dragged into the
turbid water while two others had won free and two more
had been entangled in their turn.

As the door caved in, an arrow sped out, obviously fired
from very close range. It hit the snakeman squarely in his
throat, and though he had his own scaly armour there the
point cut through it. The arrow must have grazed past his
spine, for it cut clean through his neck to jut out behind.

The shot would have killed a man on the instant, but
this monster did not fall dead. Instead he staggered back,
clutching at the bloody wound with his hand. As he staggered, his other hand – which still held the halberd –
jerked convulsively, causing the blade of the weapon to
describe a deadly arc which struck the head of one unwary
mutant from his shoulders and made the others screech
with dire alarm.

For a moment or two the snakeman tottered, but then – incredibly – he recovered his balance. Harmis was almost sure that in spite of the arrow through his neck he would somehow have recovered sufficiently to continue his attack, but while all eyes were briefly on him there was a strange explosion within the fabric of the broken-down door, which turned all of its splinters into flying wooden daggers.

The splinters showered the attackers clustering about the wounded snakeman – though he must have taken the main force of the blast himself, because eight or ten more makeshift arrows were suddenly standing out from his torso and belly. The force of their collective impact, which caught him while his balance was still precarious, swept him backwards and sideways so that he plunged into the tar-black water with a mighty splash, and sank with unnatural rapidity.

One more mutant was struck dead by the flying splinters, and two others howled with anguish as smaller slivers of wood drove into their bodies. One of them had received a thin sliver in the right eye, to judge by his reaction, and Harmis saw that he had lost all further interest in carrying the fight into the vestibule of Astyanax's house. But one of his companions, whose blood was well and truly up, leapt boldly into the breach – and the fact that he had done it seemed to all those looking on to be a significant turning of the tide of conflict.

All of a sudden, the whole company was charging, careless of the danger which still waited on the causeway – but Harmis saw that the black tentacles had been too badly cut about to offer much more resistance, and it was obvious that the first enemy to hurl himself through the door would by no means be the last.

Again the bowman within the house fired through the doorway, and again his target was one of the unnatural things – this time the hairy and tearful one which was the largest of the four – but even though the arrow hit it in the chest the monster was not stopped in its charge.

Harmis came closer, moved to hurry in spite of his anxieties. His heart was hammering harder than it ever had before, and could not have raised more fever in his blood had he been in the thick of it. Now that he saw how badly the battle was going for the defenders of the house he was frightened and alarmed, but he did not turn and run from the fight because he still felt that it was his fight as well as theirs – that the conflict had first been joined when the mutants attacked Vimera, and that he had never been out of it.

Ahead of him, the sorcerer was still gesticulating wildly, urging his vile companions on with little cries of delight. Harmis reached the last possible hiding-place, no more than a dozen yards behind the foul-fleshed creature, but there he stopped and dropped out of sight. Reason and panic were curiously allied within him, urging him to wait and husband his resources.

When he looked up again, there were only two figures left standing on the causeway. One was the creature whose face was a twisted skull; the other was the semi-blinded mutant, who was trying to defend himself one-handed from a single groping tentacle while clutching his wounded eye with the other hand. The others had all gone inside, and what magic tricks they might still have to face Harmis could not tell.

He did not have to wait long for one of them to return, for barely three minutes had passed when the creature with the most curiously twisted horns ran out, his loathsomely ruddy skin catching the bright sunlight vividly. He was waving wildly at his ugly companion and the wizard on the shore. Even as he came, though, he was caught in the back by a fearsome bolt of force which almost split him in two, and as he was bowled over by it he cannoned into the bone-faced creature and knocked him down.

The skull-faced monstrosity tried immediately to rise but his arm was seized by one of the black tentacles, and then by another. It seemed that they combined what force they could still muster in order to make one last assault upon him, grappling with him in a seemingly desperate attempt to hold him down. Like the snakeman earlier, the creature with the inside-out face had not sufficient presence of mind to cut and slash in deft fashion – instead he wasted his strength in heaving and hauling and trying futilely to break the bonds which held him.

But if this was a victory of sorts for the defenders, the sorcerer was not in the least dismayed. He ceased his excited gesticulation, standing erect and holding himself rigid. He raised his bony wand and pointed with it, and Harmis knew that the moment of crisis had arrived. This was to be the final blow.

Harmis saw two mutants staggering from the blasted doorway, intent on making their escape from whatever fury they had found to face them in the house; their one-eyed companion turned also to face the spellcaster. All three of them put up their hands in useless protest when they saw that they were not to be given time enough to reach the shore; clearly they did not relish the prospect of being caught in this kind of crossfire.

One of the mutants actually dived into the dark water of the tarn rather than face the bolt of wrath which was coming – the others tried as best they could to move around the rock on which the house was standing, to obtain whatever shelter the curving walls could provide.

Harmis saw that someone else was in the doorway – but after the briefest of glances the figure retreated inwards again, unwilling or unable to face what was coming.

Harmis imagined that he could feel the radiation of power from the sorcerer as the beam of destruction was gathered into his skeletal staff, ready for dispatch. Harmis had ceased to calculate consequences by now; he had only the dimmest awareness of the fact that while the sorcerer was working his spell he might be vulnerable, and that was not the reason why he acted when he did. It was blind determination which drove him – something more akin to madness than to intelligence.

But whatever it was which impelled him, Harmis nevertheless stood up, and snatched the knife from the scabbard at his right shoulder. He took three paces forward, and hurled it with all his might at the sorcerer's broad back.

It was a blow which would certainly have killed an ordinary man, yet it was almost as if the sorcerer did not feel it at all. He did not fall, nor was his body convulsed by the shock. Neither did he turn; it was as though he was so utterly wound up within the spell he was casting that no earthly force was capable of interrupting him.

Harmis saw no obvious physical manifestation of that spell's culmination; no jet of flame sprang from the wand's knobbed head, no bolt of lightning flashed through the air. Yet the air seemed to hum and throb with a strange, barely audible sound.

For two seconds, that was all. Time itself seemed to have been suspended.

Then there was such a shock within the stone walls of the house that they crumbled and split, and a terrible noise of cracking wood and falling debris could be heard within.

The surviving mutants shrivelled within their skins and died; the creature which had defied nature by wearing its twisted skull outside the flesh of its face ceased immediately to struggle, and was dragged into the water by the black guardians of the causeway.

Harmis, without thinking, threw his second knife.

Like the first, the second dagger hit the sorcerer hard and true. There was no way, Harmis had supposed, that any living creature could survive such a double blow, and he was glad to see that now the spell was discharged the sorcerer fell, releasing his wand and collapsing in a heap.

Harmis took one step forward, but then he paused, for the sorcerer was not yet still.

The grotesque spellcaster tried to stand up, pushing down with his hands on the rock, as though he could not believe that he had not the strength to lift his raddled but muscular body. Try as he might, though, he could not do it.

When he had accepted that he was unable to raise himself, the sorcerer turned in agonized fashion to see who had struck him down. Harmis, nauseated by a thrill of pure terror, felt that he would only have to catch sight of the bright, keen eyes which were set in that sick and mutilated face to be struck dead in his turn.

He did not want those frightful eyes to look into his own, but when he tried to turn away, he found himself as helpless to run as the sorcerer had been to rise to his feet. He was compelled to wait for the awful wizard to look at him, and though no more than a second could have elapsed before the gruesome head turned, it seemed like a long time.

He caught the merest glimpse of a look of hatred which must surely have hurt or blinded him, but then the magician's vile and dreadful face was caught by a rictus of pain which made it somehow less terrible. Then, and only then, was Harmis sure that he had actually achieved the death of his enemy. His terror was abruptly tranformed into the wildest exultation as he realized that he had killed a mighty man of magic – that he had become a hero fit for the stuff of legend.

It did not matter that he had struck from behind like a hired assassin; it did not matter that his enemy had been distracted, channelling all his power into a bolt to be hurled at an enemy who was his equal. All that mattered was that he, Harmis Detz, had destroyed a great evil – and had reaped such incredible vengeance for the slaughter in Vimera that his brother Lavarock must be screaming his triumphant thanks in the cold night of the afterworld.

But the sorcerer's eyes, clouded as they were with pain and death, had not entirely lost their power to hurt. While the thrill was still in him, Harmis felt as though a cruel hand had clutched his throat, and he was brought to his knees within an instant, choking and vomiting.

That wretched nausea was not the worst of it, for he felt something else which he could not quite describe. It was as though a cold dark tide was gathering inside him – a dire sickness of the soul which would surely leave an expanding void at the core of his being, an emptiness which could never be filled again. He was invaded by the sorcerer's sight in a way he had not thought possible, laid open to expose abyssal depths within his being whose existence he had never known. And though he knew full well that he was not being killed – that his heart would not stop and that use and command of his senses would return to him – he was aware of being altered, and made into something other than he was.

He understood – because it was part of the sorcerer's intention that he must understand – that a curse had been put upon him by those eyes. Though he was untouched by the leprous and claw-like hands, he was *marked*. He had been deliberately tainted by a gaze which had the power to make him more vulnerable to foul disease, and might serve him worse than that, by making him an object of attention for the daemons that served the Master of Uncleanness to whom this sorcerer had sold his soul.

Harmis suffered an instant's painful nightmare, lest he too should be hideously distorted in his physical appearance, and made into a thing which ought never to have been created or enabled to live, but that nightmare did not last.

As he fell unconscious, his last thought was that it was not, after all, such a pleasant sensation to be a mighty monster-slayer.

CHAPTER FOUR

HARMIS WOKE TO the touch of cold water on his face. When he opened his eyes the cloth which carried the water was taken away momentarily, then applied to his chest, which had been bared.

He gasped, not simply with the shock of it, but because the water stung him in a strange way. He could almost have believed that liquor was being poured on to lacerated skin, yet he was whole and it was only water: the dark water of the Black Tarn.

The girl who was dabbing at him with the cloth had black hair and dark eyes. She wore a man's hose rather than a skirt and her hair was cut short, but she could not be mistaken for a boy at this close range. She was below medium height and rather stocky, but might have had a little growth left in her, for she seemed no more than sixteen years of age.

Her face was round, and not overly pretty – but after seeing such faces as he had been forced to watch all morning her ordinariness was very reassuring, and her plainness seemed more welcoming than any hectic beauty could have been.

Harmis sat up, and tried to stand, but she would not let him. 'I must bathe you in the tarn's dark water,' she said. 'It has a certain power to soothe, and after this day's work we will need every protection we can find.'

Soothe! The word struck him hollowly, for the touch of the water still sent a shudder through him, as though the laving were reaching mordantly into his inner being.

'Are they all dead?' he whispered, reaching up to touch his forehead. The sun was past its zenith now, but a few hours of daylight yet remained and it was warmer by far than it had been in the chilly mists of the night before.

It was not the girl who answered but another, whose shadow fell across him when the speaker moved to stand beside him. 'All dead,' was the reply. 'Thanks to you and the good gods. We owe you our lives.'

Harmis looked up at the speaker. It was a young man in his twenties, whose general appearance suggested that he came from much the same Tilean stock as the girl; his hair was very dark, his eyes brown. He was dressed in similarly plain style, and might have passed for a serving-man but for the way he carried himself. He was handsome, but his features were tensed with pain, for he had been thrice wounded. He had an ugly sword cut just beneath the line of his jaw, his right arm was bound as if broken, and he was limping.

'You seem to have done your part in saving yourselves,' said Harmis, gruffly. 'Were you the bowman who fired from the windows?'

'I was,' said the wounded man.

'Then you're as fine a shot as I have seen, and it's a dreadful pity that your arm was hurt.'

'Aye,' said the other. 'I was caught by fallen beams when the house was blasted, and I'll not fire another shot for a goodly time. But I'm alive, and I'm twice in your debt for that. My name is Nicodemus, and this is Averil – we are apprentices to Astyanax of Violtis.'

The girl finished mopping the skin which she had bared.

'Now,' she said, 'you must drink a little of the tarnwine.'

Harmis shook his head, for he did not like the uncomfortable feel of the water on his skin, and felt sure that it would poison him.

But she said: 'It is necessary. You must trust us, for you do not know what peril still remains, despite that the Lazarite is dead.'

She had a cup in her hand, half-filled with the unnaturally dark water. When he would not take it from her, she put it to his lips.

'She is right,' said Nicodemus. 'That sorcerer whom you slew did not leave you unmarked. Though you may not know it yet, you are in need of healing. While your soul struggles to resist the curse which was put upon you, your flesh will thirst most avidly for the tarnwine. If you do not drink, you will suffer for it.'

Harmis stared uneasily at the young man for a few moments, then drank – at first just a sip, but then a deep draught. He expected it to roast his throat with fire, but the actual sensation was very different. The liquid sent a weird thrill through his body, which was partly unpleasant and partly calming.

He drained the cup.

As the plain girl turned away to take the cloth and cup back into the house, he struggled to his feet. He saw as he watched her go that the house had not fallen completely into ruins, though its topmost storey had caved in and he knew there must be a great deal of rubble and wreckage inside.

'What is your name?' asked Nicodemus.

'Harmis Detz,' he replied. '*Twice* in your debt, did you say?'

'Astyanax saw your signal from the hill, and it alerted us to danger soon enough to make preparation. And had you not struck at the Lazarite when you did, he would certainly have completed his work of slaughter, for Astyanax had not an ounce of strength left in him. Even as it is, we must count ourselves fortunate, for the evil which was in *these* men is such as can live after them, had we not magic to ward it off. The waters of the tarn have a special virtue, which Astyanax has laboured long and hard to impart to them, and he has made other preparations against this day, whose coming he and Ritandyr have feared for some years.'

Harmis was glad that Lavarock's mirror had played a part in the vengeance which had been won against his murderers, but he was very confused. 'What is a Lazarite and who is Ritandyr?' he asked.

'A Lazarite is a magician whose magic is donated by a particularly loathsome god, who must pay a price for his reward in flesh tormented by disease and morbidity. Ritandyr was apprentice here before me; he went to Khypris years ago to give warning to Prince Faramond of the peril to come, then went into the westlands to keep a vigil in Alynda, for Astyanax could not be sure which way the enemy would come.'

Harmis touched his brow, still moist with the water which the girl – Averil – had called tarnwine. He took two steps towards the body of the sorcerer, intending to retrieve his knives, but Nicodemus was quick to stop him. 'Not yet,' he said. 'Astyanax must say that it is safe before anyone dares to touch him. As I have said, his evil did not end with his life, and your knives may carry his taint more dangerously than you do yourself.'

Harmis shuddered at the thought of such a taint, though he did not really know what was implied by it. Ever afraid of magic and its works, he could not relish the thought of being hurt by the servant of a 'particularly loathsome god.'

'The mutants killed my brother,' Harmis muttered. 'They massacred the border guard in Vimera... and struck down many of the villagers in their homes. I thought they were just bandits, and did not realize soon enough they had magic for their aid, or I might have been too cowardly to come after them.'

'You are a brave man,' said Nicodemus – but Harmis knew that it was not the whole truth. There had been a small measure of courage in what he did, but a greater measure by far of simple foolhardiness.

'Come into the house,' said Nicodemus, gently. 'Astyanax cannot come out, for he took the full force of the daemon-lover's malice, and two great beams lie across his fallen body. His back is broken, and both his legs. He has not the power and I have not the skill to do more than ease his passing. He will be dead before nightfall, and you must see him before then.'

Harmis was half-inclined to say that he was too sick in the head, having been rendered unconscious twice within eighteen hours, but Nicodemus seemed very anxious for him to come, so he followed the younger man across the causeway, unmolested by any guardian of the way. They came through the blasted doorway into the wreckage of the tower.

As he had imagined, the extent of the destruction was considerable, though some few of the beams which held the floorboards of the second storey had not cracked – and that had provided shelter enough for Averil, and nearly enough for Nicodemus too.

The magician, on the other hand, had stood facing the doorway, making what use he could of his power to repel the invaders and withstand the spell of destruction. In saving the lives of his apprentices he had sacrificed himself. He lay face upwards, with one colossal beam across his belly and another across his legs. It was obvious that his body was very badly broken, yet his pale grey eyes were open, and his ancient face was not contorted by pain.

'This is Harmis Detz,' said Nicodemus. 'He struck the Lazarite down with throwing-knives – his double blow was timed to perfection.'

The wizard looked up, blinking against the dust which still swirled about in the warm and lazy air. 'I would take you by the hand, if I could,' he said, 'but I can barely raise my arm, and my fingers could not bear the clasp. I am Astyanax of Violtis.'

'Harmis Detz,' said Harmis, 'of the Border Guard.'

'Do you have a courser?' asked the wizard.

'Aye,' said Harmis. A courser was a running horse, such as might be used to carry urgent messages. Sable was fast enough.

'Good. When I am done with, you must go with my apprentices to Aldium, and find a man named Rolf Humbold. He is forewarned that this day would come, and has the means to send a message to Khypris. You must instruct him to have the bridges broken, without an instant's delay.'

Harmis started, for he understood only too well the import of those words. 'Have the Zani crossed the border?' he asked.

'They have,' replied Astyanax. 'I am certain of it, not by virtue of any spell of divination, but because this attack says that it is so. The herds must be on the move, somewhere to the west. The news would probably have reached Vimera today, but for the Lazarite's minions.'

'Even so,' said Harmis, anxiously, 'it will be six days and more before they reach the Tana Dante, for aurochs cannot gallop like horses and the terrain is dificult. The captains in the river-towns will know when the bridges must be broken – if they are broken too soon, thousands of our own people who might have fled to the heartland would be left at the mercy of the Zani.'

'They must do it sooner than that,' said Astyanax, almost as faintly. 'Alas, they must – else Khypris itself will certainly fall.'

Harmis looked down at him, and said: 'The Zani have never taken Khypris. They never could, were they unwise enough to try.'

'The Zani are not all that Khypris has to fear,' said the wizard. 'They believe, as all men do, that they are masters of their own destiny, and have brought their herds across the border for their own reasons – but this time, the hill-men are also the instruments of another invader, which seeks to spread its own seeds of destruction amid the panic they will cause. The other enemy is more dangerous by far.'

Harmis said nothing, but he was very uneasy, and Astyanax must have seen it.

'You are a soldier, are you not?' asked the wizard, his voice suddenly sharper. 'You are a man who knows the meaning of duty.'

'Aye,' said Harmis, resentfully. 'But I am not so sure where my duty lies, in this confusion.'

Astyanax studied him carefully, and Harmis shivered at the thought that the magician was looking into his very soul. But the wizard only said: 'Did Averil bathe you in the tarnwine, and did you drink a little of it?'

'Aye,' said Harmis.

'And did it feel like cool water upon your skin? Did the draught which you downed slake your thirst, and nothing else?'

'No,' said Harmis, very uneasily. 'Do you tell me now that you have tried to poison me?'

'Not I,' said Astyanax, with a sigh. 'But there is a kind of poison in you, more deadly than you know. I do not know what kindly god impelled you here, or whether the whim was truly your own, but you are now part of this unfolding pattern of destiny, and it is I who must tell you where your duty lies. You must join forces with my apprentices whose lives you have saved. You will need the tarnwine to undo the curse which the Lazarite put upon you as he died, and they may need your lucky daggers – and your good throwing arm – to defeat an enemy more powerful than the one which is already slain. Duty demands this of you – and more than duty, for the thread of your destiny has been securely trapped by this dire affair.'

This speech seemed to exhaust the magician, who sank back and closed his eyes for a moment.

Harmis did not know what to say, and in the end it was the watching Nicodemus who spoke. 'Our own horses are dead,' he said, soberly.

'There are a dozen horses tethered by the stream,' said Harmis, unthinkingly. 'The mutants brought them, in expectation of a feast.'

'Do not touch the horse on which the sorcerer rode!' said Astyanax, in a faint but urgent whisper. 'Wash the others in water from the tarn, to be safe.' The magician seemed to be gathering the last vestiges of his strength, and the strain was evident in the way he spoke.

'Aye,' said Nicodemus. 'I will do that.'

'Go do it now,' said Astyanax, 'and leave our rescuer with me, that I may try to put his mind at rest. Find Averil, and tell her to douse the body of the daemon-kin in the virtuous tarnwine, and then to put wet cloths about her hands to draw the daggers from his diseased back. She must bring them to me, for in snuffing out an evil life they have gained in power, and that power may be turned to virtue's cause, if we are clever enough.'

Nicodemus nodded, and promptly turned away. Harmis stayed, looking down uneasily at the stricken man.

'Kneel beside me,' said Astyanax, 'so that I need not speak loudly.' When Harmis knelt, the wizard somehow found the strength he had said he did not have, and contrived to move his arm a little, so that he could rest his fragile fingers on the soldier's arm.

'I am sorry, my son,' he said, in a low tone. 'What threatens Khypris now is worse by far than ambitious herdsmen hungry for the loot of the northlands. The evil man you slew was a magician as powerful as myself, but still he was the lesser of two evil creatures which have turned their malevolent eyes upon this little nation. The greater of the two will not declare its nature with a retinue of beastmen, for it is one of the *katharoi*. It is a daemon of sorts, but it was human once, before it pledged its soul to the god of plague and pestilence in return for power over the fates of those it had cause to hate.

'I wish that I could arm you more fully to face the *katharos*, but it has taken me many years and greater effort than you can know to prepare the water of the tarn for the work it must do. You must trust the tarnwine's virtue, no matter what pain it causes you – but I think that your thirst will make sure of that. Nicodemus is not without skill in magic, nor is Averil – but they are children in the art of war, and I must ask you to protect them if you can from the rigours of the journey which they must take in order to combine forces with Ritandyr. Your strength and courage have already proved themselves, and now that you have been inwardly marked by the Lazarite, fate will surely draw you together with the *katharos*. If you can face the daemon boldly, inspired by courage and by duty, you may have the strength to slay it; otherwise, I fear that you would surely fall victim to its malice.'

Harmis wanted to shake his head in ardent refusal, to say that this was far too deep a matter for the likes of him, but he could not. He could see the nearness of death written across the face of the old magician, and could not turn away from a dying man who was begging him for help.

'I know nothing of daemons and sorcerers,' he said, helplessly.

'Those daggers which you carry have a sorcery of their own now,' said Astyanax, struggling to speak more rapidly as he realized how near his end might be. 'They will be dangerous to use, but they may have power enough even to slay the *katharos*. Still, you will need a name – a true name, to guide the power of your thrust. That name is Ystareth. I beg you not to speak it aloud to anyone until the time comes. I wish that we had met in a better way, Harmis Detz, for then I could have shown you clearly where your duty lies – but I can say only this: if it is your heart's desire to avenge your brother's death, and save the nation which your master rules from cruel devastation, then do as I ask. Bear the burden of the tarnwine's healing bravely, and stay with my servants until this evil day has run its course.'

The last words of this speech were followed by an exclamation which sounded ominously like a dying breath, but in fact it marked the arrival of the girl, who was carrying Harmis's twin knives, with the hilts wrapped in dampened cloths. The blades were quite clean, and Harmis could only assume that she had washed them in the mysterious water.

Averil reached out as though to place one of the knives in her master's broken hand, but he shook his head.

'The points!' he whispered, impatiently. 'Touch the points to my eyes!'

She seemed almost as surprised as Harmis was, but she was clearly no stranger to odd requests. Astyanax closed his eyes, and she reached down, with a knife in each hand, to rest the sharp tip of each blade, very gently, upon an eyelid. Harmis could not resist a shudder as he thought how utterly simple it must be to blind a man who would accept such a touch. But the girl took the blades away after a few seconds had passed, and the wizard opened his eyes again.

'Oh yes,' he said. 'There is power there – power which might be turned to the best of ends. Sheath the knives, my son, and never draw them idly, for they carry a curse upon them now which must be gently nursed. You will be safe, at least as long as the tarnwine lasts, and when fate draws you to the *katharos*, as it surely will, you might become the very stuff of legend.'

But am I not already the stuff of legend, thought Harmis, furiously? I have slain a sorcerer – must I take up arms against the gods themselves?

Averil moved behind him to sheathe the knives for him. Harmis felt a painful knot of anxiety in his throat, which he could not swallow. The wizard was desperate to say something more, before the breath finally departed from his body.

'He who is touched by Chaos,' whispered Astyanax, 'may harm Chaos... but must always beware, lest he become the instrument of Chaos instead of its destroyer.'

Then, after a pause, he tried to begin again, saying: 'Averil...?'

'What is it?' she asked, quickly. But whatever instruction had been in his mind was stillborn. Though the old man opened his mouth, no words came out. His grey eyes still seemed to be looking up at his young apprentice, but there was no mind now behind the stare.

Harmis took Lavarock's mirror from his shirt, and put it close to Astyanax's lips. There was no hint of condensation upon it. The wizard was dead.

When Harmis stood up again, he said: 'I could not begin to understand the meaning of his words. What is this daemon called a *katharos*? Why does he say that I have been touched or tainted? Why must the bridges be broken now? And what is the meaning of that *true name* he told me?'

He stopped when an expression of utter horror crossed her face, and she put a hasty finger to his lips to instruct him to be silent.

'There is a danger in speaking true names,' she said, 'for names have power which might be wasted in repetition, and might be heard in other worlds by things whose attention is better not caught.'

Had he heard such words from Lavarock or any other of his former comrades Harmis would have laughed, but what he had seen today forbade his laughter, and he merely shrugged resentfully. This, he reminded himself, was the girl he had named a trollop just the night before, on the assumption that any girl indentured to a wizard could be little better than a whore. This was the girl whose price he had computed by guesswork to be an ounce of gold or a cupful of blood. It had seemed amusing at the time; it did not seem funny now.

'What is this *katharos*?' he asked again, in a low tone.

'A kind of daemon,' she said. 'A champion of a vile god, able for a brief while to walk the earth, venting its spite upon those among whom it was once unluckily born. It can do more to destroy this nation than the war-horde of the hillmen. But I am only an apprentice; there are many secrets which I do not know, and many others which I am sworn not to reveal – I beg you not to question me too closely.'

Harmis felt himself lost in a welter of confusion and frustration. 'I do not like this message we have been told to carry,' he said dourly, feeling that some assertion of his manhood was necessary. 'I have spent my life in the marches of the north and the west, and though I do not like the people any more than they have liked me, I would far rather give them a chance to quit their land and seek refuge across the Tana Dante than commend them to the mercy of the wild hillmen.'

'The message may not be so very important,' she told him. 'Humbold will know what to do – and it is possible that the news will have reached him before we do. But we must pass through Aldium anyway, on our way to find Ritandyr. You must stay with us, because we need you – and though you do not yet understand why, you need us as much as we need you.'

'I'm Faramond's man-at-arms,' he said, uneasily. 'I cannot ride away upon some whim, to guard two enchanter's apprentices in search of a third. As soon as I reach Aldium, I'll be given to a band of fighting men and sent against the forerunners of the Zani.'

'You have a higher duty than that,' she said, confidently. 'Humbold will see to it that you receive a proper commission when Nicodemus explains what has happened here.'

She turned away, to avoid his complaining stare. Harmis looked down again at the body of the virtuous wizard, who seemed peacefully asleep beneath the burden of the fallen ceiling.

When he followed the girl outside, Harmis saw that Nicodemus had fetched five horses, including Sable. Lavarock's bay was not among them. The apprentice was busy loading packs on two of the animals, and he told Averil to go back into the house in search of anything else which might be of use. Harmis saw that the pack-animals were already burdened by an odd assortment of flasks and bottles; he assumed that they contained magical water taken from the tarn. He wondered whether it was fit to drink to slake an ordinary thirst, or whether it must be saved for more solemn things than that.

While the others were busy he went to look at the corpse of the viler wizard, whom he had so cleverly – or so luckily – destroyed.

He was astonished to find that there was nothing left within the sodden rags of the Lazarite's clothing but a whitened skeleton. It was as though the tormented flesh had been dissolved from its supporting bone by the water which had been poured over the corpse. There were viscous puddles lying all around, though a good deal of the liquid had seeped into cracks in the rock, and he wondered whether that seepage had carried away the foul solution of the sorcerer's unhumanity.

This, he thought, is what becomes of those who treat with daemons. Harmis had always thought of daemons as rather comical things, like giant bats with leering faces or flying toads with dripping fangs, but he had now had a hard lesson in the true ways of evil magic. He knew now the limitations of an imagination fed on common-or-garden scarifying tales. This creature had been rotting while he lived. He had been a walking pillar of corruption – and the things that were his servants, which must surely have been beastmen, had been born of an uglier nightmare than unkind sleep had ever brought to Harmis Detz.

I am a hero, Harmis reminded himself. I have stood against foul magic, and defeated it.

Then he spoke to himself more honestly, and said: I stabbed foul magic in the back, while all its power was distracted. I am the deftest of coward-assassins, not the bravest of the brave.

But then, in a less censorious vein, he thought: but this is the Border Princes, not Sigmar's glorious Empire, and I am a common soldier, not a wielder of the fearsome warhammer. When it happens that a man sees evil and corruption from the rear, should he hesitate through niceness to stab it in the back, and insist instead on looking into its deadly face?

'Harmis,' called Nicodemus. 'We are ready to go, and must not tarry here, for there is much work still to do.'

'Oh aye,' said Harmis, as he came to mount his patient mare. 'We have the empire to save, and Faramond's great gratitude to win. No doubt we'll all be nobles of the realm when our work is done – if only we can cross the Tana Dante before the bridges are down and the fire of scorching fields is at our backs.'

They set off, riding along the shore of the dark lake at a pace which gradually quickened. Nicodemus – despite the pain which his injuries must have caused him – led the way in a very determined fashion.

Harmis knew, in his heart, that his life could never return to the dull routines which had previously shaped it. He did not fully understand what mark had been put upon him by the sorcerer's curse, but he understood that he *had* been marked, and changed.

From now on he must be content to be ruled by a duty and a fate more ominous and difficult than any which had ever ruled him before.

CHAPTER FIVE

THEY CAME TO Aldium in the fading twilight, having ridden without pause. All five of their horses were very tired, and Nicodemus – weakened by his injuries – was desperately pale. Left to himself, Harmis would not have come so quickly over such awkward terrain, but he had allowed himself to be hurried by the urgency which the magician's two apprentices obviously felt.

Aldium seemed at first sight to be undisturbed: children were still playing on the commons around the town, and groups of labourers were making their slow way in from the fields after taking full advantage of the bright day. It was clear that no raiders had ventured this far into the northlands, and that no news had yet arrived from Vimera. And yet, there was an undercurrent of unease, which Harmis felt as soon as they rode into the streets.

The streets stank of rotting garbage and excrement, whose odour had been brought to fullest fruition by the heat of the day. The pockmarked faces of the children who ran to watch the strangers ride by were more fearful than

usual. Because of his livery, and the direction from which
he rode, they took Harmis for a courier, and something in
the wind had already told them to expect bad news. The
fact that he had a wounded man with him would be a
ready cause for further anxiety.

The whispers began before they had dismounted.

Are the Zani coming?

The Zani are coming! The Zani! The Zani!

Most of the people refused to meet Harmis's eye as he
looked about; they had no particular love for the men-at-
arms whose task it was to secure their lands for Khypris,
and their anxiety made them more careful than usual.
Only the children called out to him. Averil and Nicodemus
drew more inquisitive stares, though no one seemed to
know who they were.

Nicodemus was uncertain which way to go, so Harmis
took the lead and brought them to one of the larger
shrines to which the town played host. It was a shrine of
Morr, set close by the graveyard, and was only a little
smaller than the shrine of Shallya at which the majority of
the townspeople worshipped. It played host to the dead
and the bereaved, of whom there was always an adequate
supply. The third deity of some importance in Aldium was
called Arya, though she was better known to the world at
large as Rhya; her worship was mysterious and clandestine,
and had to do with assuring the fertility of the fields.

Harmis had come to the shrine because of Lavarock and
what had happened in Vimera, but also because he reckoned the priests of Morr the wisest men in the town. Those
who keep company with the dying and offer comfort to
the bereaved hear a greater measure of honesty than ordinary men, and few secrets are hidden from them. There
was not a family in the town the priests of Morr did not
know, for children flooded from the wombs of Aldium's
women like raindrops from a heavy sky, and many died of
the infant pox and other fevers.

As Harmis dismounted in the street, one of the priests
came out of the building where Morr's company was

lodged. Having taken one appraising look at the newcomers he beckoned to a group of youths standing nearby. While Harmis helped Nicodemus down, the priest ordered the boys to see that the horses were properly stabled behind the shrine. Harmis asked Averil whether she had any money, and when she nodded he told her what to give them. Nicodemus seemed anxious about their supplies, but Harmis knew that while their belongings were under Morr's protection none but the most brave and foolhardy thief would dare to touch them.

When they were inside, another black-robed priest came forward, and said: 'You would do better to take that man to Shallya's shrine, for he is not dying.'

'It was not for his sake that I came,' said Harmis, 'but to bear bad news. Mutant marauders fell upon Vimera under cover of last night's mists, and slew at least two dozen. How many fled I could not tell, but they will need you, and I beg you to send out to them as soon as you can, for there will be none among them who has not lost kin and friends. I must offer my own prayer to your god, for I lost a brother.'

While the priest was still acknowledging this information with anxious nods, Nicodemus broke in: 'Do you know a man named Rolf Humbold? If so, I beg you to tell me where he is to be found, or to send for him.'

The priest frowned, and replied: 'We are the priests of Morr, not messengers.'

'Forgive him,' said Harmis, quickly. 'He too has suffered loss. He was apprentice to the enchanter Astyanax, who was brutally killed today by monsters whose like I have never seen before. The wizard believed that the Zani have crossed the border in the east, though I have only hearsay to rely on in making my warning.'

The priest could not help but start at such news, and lost a little of his funereal dignity as real fear showed in his face.

'Astyanax!' he said, as though it was very difficult to believe. 'Astyanax killed! By whom, in the god's name?'

'Best ask Nicodemus by whom, and why it was done,' said Harmis grimly. 'I know only that they were of a very foul kind, and that if their like should come to Aldium, the people must flee before them.'

The import of these words made three of the priests who had heard them come quickly together, and when the Superior had asserted his authority two of them went scurrying away.

'We will send a boy to find Rolf Humbold,' said the remaining priest. 'The priestesses of Shallya must be informed of this also. Tell me, my son, what happened to your master?'

The way in which he pronounced the words 'my son' put Harmis very much in mind of the dying magician.

'Beastmen,' said Nicodemus, who was sitting down in a chair, and breathing very heavily, as though all the strength had gone out of him. 'They were led by a Lazarite sorcerer, and had mutants with them too. All are dead, thanks to the house's magical defences and this brave soldier, but the threat to Khypris is by no means ended.'

As the young man said this he sagged forward, and Averil had to catch him up to prevent his falling to the floor. The Superior turned away, to fetch a cup of wine, which he gave to Averil because Nicodemus could not hold it himself.

'What does all this mean?' asked the priest of Morr.

'I cannot tell,' said Harmis, to whom the words had been addressed. 'I know nothing of Lazarites and beastmen, save that I hope I never see either kind again as long as I may live. But Astyanax told me that some kind of daemon is loose in the land, which may cause destruction greater than the Zani horde if we cannot stop it by magic.'

'I am sorry to hear that Astyanax is dead,' said the priest. 'If the northlands have lost the wisest and best of their guardians to evil magic, every one of us is under threat.'

Harmis lowered his head, to signify that there was nothing more to be said. He was content, for the time being, to move into the heart of the shrine in order to make his own plea to the god of death for the soul of his fallen brother.

Now that Lavarock was dead, he had no kin in all the world save for Lavarock's son in Khypris, whom he had not seen for nearly three years, when the boy had been ten years old.

He offered up a further prayer as well, though Morr had never been his own god. He prayed that the path upon which he was now to be led by duty and fate would not be so very hard, and that he would reach its end safely. Morr was a god of death and dreams, but he was not – so far as Harmis knew – a god who was so hungry for the deaths of men that he would be annoyed by a plea for death to be delayed. In any case, he thought, there would be deaths aplenty in Khypris now that the Zani had come – and perhaps in greater profusion still, if the *katharos* had its way. In all that flood of dying, what could the life of a single soldier count?

WHEN ROLF HUMBOLD arrived at the shrine of Morr one of the priests tried to keep him outside, protesting that the shrine was not to be employed for the conduct of worldly affairs – but Nicodemus was still suffering the after-effects of his long ride, and the Superior indicated that the prince's man must be allowed to enter.

Humbold was a short, barrel-chested man with sandy hair and a ruddy complexion. His clothing displayed Faramond's claret-and-gold far more gaudily than a soldier's livery, and his slender sword was sheathed in an ornate scabbard. His cap was very pretty and his boots were polished, but he was no mere fop – Harmis was certain that the man had won his high standing in Faramond's service by means of intelligence as well as breeding. When it was confirmed that he would be allowed to pass, Humbold bustled unceremoniously past the priest who had tried to stop him, muttering beneath his breath in an impatient way which did not please the Superior – or, for that matter, Harmis.

It was to Harmis that this master of couriers came directly, saying: 'What is this ill news from Vimera, which

must be sent to Khypris without delay? Is it true that the
Zani have come?'

The rumours, it seemed, had already taken wing.

'This man,' said Harmis, pointing to Nicodemus, 'has a
message for you from Astyanax of Violtis.'

Humbold had not recognized Nicodemus before, but
when he realized who the wounded man was he became
instantly very agitated. 'Nicodemus!' he cried. 'What has
happened?'

Harmis felt perversely relieved that he would not have to
speak the awful words of the magician's message, though
it made not the slightest difference. The message was given
and received, and to Harmis's great surprise Humbold did
not stay to receive details of the battle at the tarn, or even
to hear whether Astyanax was dead or alive. The words of
the message were enough in themselves to send him scurrying forth after a scrivener, who could write a letter to be
attached to the leg of a carrier-bird.

The Superior seemed equally surprised by the man's
alacrity, and was very deeply concerned by the message
which he was forced to overhear. He drew Harmis to one
side, and said, in a low tone: 'I do not know why Astyanax
has asked that this be done.'

'Nor I,' said Harmis. 'But the birds will carry this word to
Prince Faramond much faster than a man could ride on
the fastest courser in the land. If he does what he is bid, the
northlanders will be trapped on this side of the river.
When the Zani warriors come with their herds, there will
be slaughter on a frightful scale. Is it not true that the
bridges have only been broken before at the end of a long
campaign, when as many people as the heartland could
contain had crossed the Tana Dante to be safe?'

'It is true,' answered the priest, frowning with concern
and biting his lip.

'Then this is your hour,' said Harmis, bitterly, 'for there
will be such work for the priests of Morr to do that–'

'Be silent,' said the priest, in justified annoyance. 'You
are in the god's house, and must not mock him with your

anger. Morr knows what work there is for his priests to do.'

'I am sorry,' said Harmis, sincerely. 'Brother, I know it is not your way to intervene in the common run of men's affairs, or to use what magic you have to any other ends but the care of the dead and dying, but I beg you to tell me what the likes of you and I might usefully do, now that this message has gone forth.'

'What can we do?' asked the priest. 'You can only join the others of your kind, to make what defence you can against the Zani, while I... I have a darker mission, and for once the ends of the dead and dying may justify more public action than is common.'

'You know something of what is happening,' Harmis charged him. 'You understand far better than I what news we have brought – and you know, too, that the hand of fear has already touched the people of Aldium. I beg you to explain what is going on.'

The priest hesitated for a moment, but then he said: 'You are right, my friend. There is a new fear in the town. I had thought that Aldium was saturated with fear already, for life here is never easy, but there is always room in human life for extra fears. I do not know how the people know it, but they have tasted it on the wind. There is dark magic abroad, which comes ultimately from the far east, beyond the mountains of the World's Edge. Something is spilling into the world, and spreading tentacles of evil through all the nations of men. I fear that this may be one of many ugly wars which the Border Princedoms will have to fight, if they are not to be given entirely to the daemons and their kin.

'You may think that the gods which are already in Aldium are dark enough, but they are gentle and generous in their fashion. Morr is the lord of death, but his priests are comforters; the followers of Arya spill blood upon the fields, but she is the fecundity which sustains their lives, and it is a petty price to pay for her benevolence. There are darker gods by far than these. There are gods of wrath and horror, whose dominion is growing in the world of men.'

'I have heard of them,' said Harmis. 'But I have never been afraid of them, for I cannot see what would lead men to their worship, save for madness.'

'Madness is more a penalty of that worship than its cause,' said the priest, sadly. 'The cause is terror, for when men see evil in the world, and fear that it will claim them, their courage often fails, and they try to placate the force of evil instead of standing against them. You know how many of the children of this region die, and you bear the scars yourself of the disease which kills so many. The priests of Morr are bound by honour to lessen the pain of bereavement, but ours is not the easiest counsel to heed.

'You are a man-at-arms, schooled to a tolerance of unkind death even when it strikes down your own kin, but these farmer-folk are not; the temptation is sometimes strong in them to pray in secret to evil gods, saying: *take another's child in place of mine.* That is how evil takes root in the minds of men – and there is a god of pestilence and plague which hears such prayers. If he has sent his favourites against Khypris, we face a time of trial in which terror may come to reign supreme.'

Harmis remembered the twisted creatures which had gone to murder Astyanax, and had no difficulty at all in understanding how horrific the reign of such monsters might be. And yet, he thought, if it were possible to form great armies of such things as that, would not the world of men have been overwhelmed long before? If ten thousand of those beastmen could be marched into the northlands, surely there would be no hope at all. These daemon-kin must be rare enough, and mortal enough in their fashion, to be forced to formulate their schemes more subtly.

'There is a god of pestilence and plague,' murmured Harmis, echoing what the priest of Morr had said. He had a notion now of why the message had been sent forth to Faramond to break the bridges. It was not the warbands of the Zani which threatened Khypris itself – they were only herdsmen, driving crowds of people as they drove the aurochs. It was some unnatural plague which Astyanax had sought to keep at bay – something best fought by magic. But the guardian who had planned to make magic against that menace was dead, and only his apprentices remained to carry forward that cause... only his apprentices, and Harmis Detz.

'The sorcerer who destroyed Astyanax was himself destroyed,' said Harmis to the priest, 'but as you have heard, there is a daemon abroad in the land. Astyanax told me its name, and said that I must be its slayer or its instrument.'

The priest made no reply to that, being seemingly lost in thought.

'I do not understand it,' Harmis persisted. 'You are the spellcaster, not I. I need your guidance. He told me a true name, which I am commanded to use against this mysterious *katharos*, as a kind of power – but I do not know what I am supposed to do. Would it not be better if a man like you had the name and whatever power it contains?'

'What magic I have is dedicated to the work of Morr,' replied the priest. 'It is his and not mine. If Astyanax has claimed you, he must have an adequate reason. If you would know more, you must ask Nicodemus or seek out Ritandyr.'

Harmis could only shake his head. He looked at Nicodemus, to see what possibility there might be of obtaining reassurance from him, but there was none. He was left alone when the Superior went to confer with others of his company, who seemed very anxious. A priestess of Shallya was with them, having returned with the man sent to carry the news to her own shrine.

When the Superior spoke to Harmis again, it was to say: 'The priestesses of Shallya wish to hold a special ceremony, to implore her to show what mercy she can to the women and children of Aldium. They have asked us to attend, as a mark of respect, and to help ensure that all the townsfolk are there. The shrine is far too small, but there is a small hill on common land, which is often used for festivals. Will you help us to carry the sacred portal to the place?'

Harmis nodded, and said: 'Yes, I will gladly do that.'

THE NIGHT WHICH fell upon Aldium was very dark, a light haze occluding all but the brightest stars; only the fainter of the two moons was in the sky. There was no sign, though, of the thick mist which had hidden the mutants while they came to Vimera, and it was not cold.

As the great procession wound out of the town and on to the commons Harmis felt unusually conspicuous. Having been appointed by the priests of Morr to carry the lintel-stone – part of the portal they would erect on the site of the ceremony – he was preceded among Morr's men only by the Superior, while four novices carried the two uprights on which the lintel would be set. The lintel was shorter than the supporting blocks, but it was heavy enough to be a taxing burden for one man, and Harmis felt awkwardly pressed down by the weight upon his shoulder.

Beside the Superior walked the High Priestess of Shallya, her white robe contrasting sharply with his black one. Her followers were far less awkwardly burdened, being obliged to carry only a pair of wicker cages, in which white doves were contained.

There was a fire on the hillock where the rite was to take place, which burned red and bright, but not many lanterns, for these townsfolk were inclined to be frugal with their oil. Harmis helped the priests of Morr to erect the symbolic portal in front of the fire, and was very glad indeed to be free from his burden; he hoped that another volunteer might be found to carry it back again.

He looked around, wondering where he should stand, given that he was an outsider here. In the end, he followed the priests of Morr, and sat beside one of the novices. A little later, he was joined by Averil and Nicodemus, who clearly considered that they were now his companions, their fates bound to his.

Harmis looked round at the townspeople, astonished by the size of the crowd. The women and children, as might be expected, were to the fore, while their menfolk held back. Though everyone here was prepared to pay homage to Shallya, the first – but unadmitted – allegiance of the men would be to Arya; and some, perhaps, offered secret prayers to other gods.

The High Priestess wasted little time before beginning the ceremony. She stood to the right of Morr's portal, intoning the words of her rite in an arcane language which could not have been understood by the assembly even had they been able to hear it clearly. As things were, the priestess's voice was not sufficiently strident to carry far, and the crackling of the wood which was hungrily consumed by the angry fire drowned the words. But the words were not of much importance; silhouetted as she was by the leaping flames her gestures were clear enough as they moved through a sequence of familiar signs.

The shadows which the priestess and the portal cast moved eerily as the flames flickered, and Harmis fancied that the shadow of the priestess – whose sleeves were loose and waved like fluttering wings as she moved her arms – had some resemblance to a raven, which was a symbol of the god of death. Was Shallya really here at all, he wondered, or did the shadows speak more honestly than the muttered words and the mechanical passes? What mercy could these people really expect, if their villages and fields were to be pillaged by the Zani and their escape to the heartland cut off?

The women who were regular attenders at Shallya's shrine murmured their responses at the appropriate moments of the rite, their collective voice much louder than the celebrant's. Harmis fancied that he could hear a deep anxiety in the voice of the town, and knew that an undercurrent of whispers must be surging back and forth among the throng. Before the rite was done, everyone would know what message had been given to Rolf Humbold, and what wild rumours had been invented in order to interpret its meaning. He knew only too well that he was not the only one there who could find little hope and consolation in the sight of the gesticulating priestess.

The eyes of the smaller children, glowing redly in the firelight, seemed rapt and excited. For them, this was an occasion, a distraction from the dull routine of their lives. The people further back had a different manner, and though Harmis knew well enough how much of it was due to their distance from the fire, he knew that it spoke honestly enough of a darkness in their hearts. They were very much afraid, already possessed by the daemonic powers of terror and despair. He was suddenly certain that this ceremony was not serving its intended purpose. He could understand the determination of the priests of Shallya to hold it, and thus to make demonstration of their defiant hope, but he knew that the townspeople already felt themselves to be beyond Shallya's help.

The priest of Morr had already told him what secret thoughts these people had, and now he understood how the people were wont to respond to the stink of evil in the wind. The women here – the mothers – might be paying proper homage to Shallya, but the men muttering in the rear might be speaking in their hearts to other gods, saying: *Come if you will, for we cannot keep you back, but spare me! Spare me!*

The high priestess was slowing down, approaching the end of her invocation.

When he had been a child, and his own mother had told him that magic was being worked in rites such as this, Harmis had been awed – but his opinions had hardened long before he was fully grown to manhood. Oh, there was magic, to be sure – he had never doubted *that* – but he had ceased to believe that any such magic would work for him, or if it did, would prove adequate to defend him against the awful burden of misfortune which was the worldly lot of men of his low station.

He could believe himself cursed far more easily than he could imagine himself blessed. For that reason, he felt an urge to abandon Nicodemus and Averil, and go his own way, but he was not sure that he dared do it, after all that had been said.

To make matters worse, he felt a strange thirst in his belly – a thirst not for any ordinary water, but for the mysteriously virtuous wine of the Black Tarn. He had not liked its taste, but he craved it now.

When the rite ended he expected the crowd to break up and return at a run to their homes, eager to make their practical preparations for the evil time to come – but he was wrong. The people showed no inclination to be off, and seemed quite fascinated by the fire. The children did not want to go home; they wanted to play. And though the ration of comfort which Shallya had contrived to give them was meagre enough, the parents were able to take a little comfort from the mere fact of being a crowd, instead of men alone.

Some had brought mead or fiercer liquor, and stone bottles were being passed around. Small groups of children began games, involving rhymes and dances – their own private rites of comfort-seeking. The priests of Morr seemed in no more hurry to be gone than anyone else, nor did they move to dismantle the portal which they had brought to signify their presence. Thus freed from anticipated responsibility Harmis went to where Nicodemus sat, and asked Averil how he was.

'Ritandyr,' said the wounded man, seemingly on the verge of delirium. 'We must find Ritandyr.'

'Tomorrow,' said Averil, gently. 'Sleep now, and tomorrow you might be fit to ride.'

She took from her cloak a corked phial, and Harmis did not have to ask what it contained. She let a little of it fall on the tongue of her fellow apprentice, and did not seem surprised when Harmis reached out to demand some for himself.

The feel of it trickling down his throat was still alarming, but something deep inside him – perhaps his endangered soul – was grateful for the taste of it.

Harmis said nothing, and would have turned to go away when he had returned the empty phial, but Averil stopped him, and mutely begged him to stay with her. There was grief in her shadowed eyes, and the infection of fear which had spread through the whole company had her in its grip. Harmis sat beside her, and put his arm around her shoulders. Despite her plainness, the gesture made him think of an ounce of gold or a cupful of blood, but he put all carnal notions out of his mind. He could not harbour such thoughts at an unfortunate time like this.

'Fear not,' he said, as much to himself as to the girl. 'We are not dead yet, and if there is indeed a curse upon the nation or ourselves, we must meet its fury as bravely as we can.'

CHAPTER SIX

HARMIS AWOKE, UNCOMFORTABLY, to the silvery light of dawn. His arms and legs ached, but he had slept deeply – all the better because sleep had come to him naturally for once. He sat up, brushing some of the dirt from his grey-green sleeves.

The priests of Morr were gone and so was their portal, but not all the villagers had returned to their homes. Many of the labourers were well used to sleeping in the open at this time of year; the hovels in which they lived offered no greater comfort and had to be shared with all manner of vermin. Nicodemus slept nearby, turning and murmuring in the grip of an unpleasant dream.

Averil had apparently kept watch over them both; she was sitting up, huddled within her dark cloak. The fire had died in the night, but thin plumes of smoke still rose from its ashes.

Harmis stood up and looked around. He was surprised by the number of people who lay about in couples, the state of their clothing suggesting that they had not gone immediately to sleep. But anxiety was, after all, a kind of excitement, and the people of Aldium had last night valued company above privacy. Most of the children had gone to their homes, but there were more than a hundred still here, some now beginning to awaken in the grey morning light.

The wind was blowing from the north – from the Black Mountains – and Harmis breathed deeply in to see if he could detect the taint of evil magic or the smell of the Zani's aurochs. There was nothing; the breeze seemed fresh and cool.

He felt thirsty, but not for any ordinary water. The appetite which only the tarnwine could satisfy was again exerting its demands. He suppressed a sharp pang of fear, telling himself that the apprentices knew of his condition, and that Astyanax had implied that it would not last forever. But he could not altogether quiet his anxiety; although he was a fighting man, for whom bravery in the face of physical danger had become mere habit, the knowledge that he was accursed sickened his thoughts as much as the curse itself sickened his soul.

'What will they do now?' asked Averil, turning her head so that her gaze played over the ragged crowd.

'I don't know,' said Harmis. 'Some will pack up and run; some will wait until the Zani come – or until the soldiers come to fire the fields, to prevent the aurochs grazing here. In the end, most will take to the roads, intending to cross the Tana Dante to the heartland.'

'What hope is there for them, if the bridges are broken?'

Harmis shrugged. 'Who can tell? Who knows when the bridges will be broken? Prince Faramond will receive your master's message, no doubt, and his commanders and petty noblemen will be quite content to see it obeyed. But when the order comes back from Khypris to the captains in the river towns I'm not so sure they'll obey with any great alacrity. If the Zani war-horde is close by, that will be one thing – but if the Zani are still far away, the captains may calculate their duty in a different way.'

'We must go to Ritandyr immediately,' she said, with conviction. 'He is our best hope now.'

'*You* must go to Ritandyr,' he said. 'I am obliged to find Faramond's commander in Aldium, and must place myself under his orders.' He said it uneasily, because he knew that he needed to stay with the apprentices, not simply because they had the tarnwine but also because they were the ones who seemed to understand how the curse with which the Lazarite had stricken him could be cancelled out. And yet, he could not set aside by himself the call of his other duty, which he owed to Faramond's militia. If the Zani had come, then those who had previously fought the Zani – as he had in a dozen bloody skirmishes – would swiftly be sent to face them again.

He was surprised by the sharpness of her reply. 'You must not do that!' she said. 'You have the knives which killed the Lazarite. You must do *our* work now, whether the commander wishes it or not.'

Harmis scowled and shrugged, unwilling to be instructed so firmly by a slip of a girl, who thought herself better than him because she had been servant to a great wizard while he was a very ordinary man-at-arms. 'I am a loyal servant of the prince,' he said, trying to sound proud.

'Then we must see Humbold again – he will tell the commander what you must do.'

'Humbold may well be gone by now,' Harmis said. 'What reason would he have to stay, when he has sent such a message to Khypris? He will ride until his mount can run no more, then take another and another.' He paused, and added: 'But he will not need to reach the Tana Dante before the bridges are broken; for a man like him they will send a ferry-boat, and I suppose that soldiers will hold back the crowd to make sure he crosses safely. He stands high in Faramond's service.'

While he said it, it occurred to him that there was reason enough why he should not want to linger in Aldium himself. He was one of the messengers who had brought the bad news, and he knew only too well that if murderous ire

were to be aroused in the town the people might seize
whoever was nearest to hand to take the blame.

With this in mind, he said: 'Wake Nicodemus. We must
go to Morr's shrine, where our horses are held. Then you
must go, with all possible speed, while I go to the commander.' Even while he said it he felt the pangs of his
strange thirst again, and knew that if his orders called him
away from the apprentices, he might find it very difficult to
go.

'You are very stubborn!' she complained. 'Astyanax
trusted you, because of what you did, and we need you. We
have the black water of the tarn to keep us safe, and those
weapons which you carry are too dangerous to bear if you
do not have it also. The priests of Morr will speak to the
commander for us if Humbold has gone – if it is really
your sense of duty which preys upon your will.'

He set his mouth tightly at the accusation, but he was
doubtful enough of himself to wonder whether she was
right. Was it only fear which impelled him futilely to wish
for the company of his own kind during the impending
time of crisis? He knew only too well that it had been fear,
rather than religious faith, which had brought the towns-
men out in force to pay lip-service to Shallya. Was he any
better than they?

'The Prince has augurs and haruspices in Khypris,' said
Harmis, dully, 'and war-magicians too. Why is the nation's
need so strange that only you and I and that wounded
man at your feet will serve it?'

'Some few of the Prince's magicians have virtue,' she
answered, as she tried to rouse Nicodemus with apologetic
prods, 'but far the greater number of those conjurors who
delight to flatter rich men and princes are mere charlatans.
True wizards seek solitude, time to learn and to exact the
disciplines of mind and body which prepare for the exercise of power. Ritandyr was pupil to Astyanax for many
long years, and now that Astyanax is gone, he is the only
man in Khypris who might attempt the kind of spell which
would save us. This is not the Empire, where there are great

Colleges of powerful magicians to help defend the world against the playfulness of wicked gods and their horrid daemons.'

Nicodemus groaned, seemingly reluctant to be brought back from the sanctuary of his dreams – but when he saw Averil, and remembered where he was and what his mission was, he tried to sit up. His face was as white as chalk, and he touched the fingers of his left hand first to the cut below his jaw and then to the wrist of the arm which was paining him.

'We need to find a bone-setter also,' said Harmis, 'for that binding is uncertain and must be better done.' He helped Nicodemus to his feet, and remained close to him while Averil led the way back to the shrine of Morr.

All the way to the shrine Harmis nursed his tarnwine thirst – but when Averil brought more of the elixir from the packs which had been stored at the shrine, he tried to conceal how fierce was his need for it, in the cause of preserving his battered pride.

Harmis then took leave to beg the Superior for further assistance, and found him more helpful than he had dared to expect. They were given food, and one of the older priests consented to reset Nicodemus's arm-bone, making a better job of it than most hireling physicians could have done. Surprisingly, the Superior was also persuaded by Averil's urging to send for the commander of Aldium's contingent of the Border Guard – and more surprisingly still, that officer came to hear what he had to say.

When the priest had spoken to him in private, the commander came to Harmis and ordered him to go with Averil and Nicodemus, and to guard them with his life until they should have no further need of him. He plainly did not know why he had been asked to give the order, but it was equally plain that he did not consider Harmis so valuable a man as to justify quarrelling with a priest of Morr.

The commander also said – much to Harmis's surprise – that he would find a scrivener, and send a written order as soon as possible, so that no one would interfere with

Harmis or his companions. When he had said all this, he hurried off – for he, like everyone else in Aldium, was fearful of a dreadful time to come, and needed to make what preparations he could.

As the commander had promised, they had not long to wait for the written order which Harmis was to carry. He received it with a certain sense of awe, and made Nicodemus read it to him carefully. Afterwards, he looked very carefully at the array of symbols awkwardly scrawled in black ink; though he could hardly tell the characters from the blots, the complex pattern seemed to him as replete with magic as any device which the apprentices carried.

Never in all his life had Harmis been given a piece of paper. Paper was even rarer in the Border Princes than parchment, for want of factories where discarded linen might be collected and pulped; all the paper which made its way to Khypris had originated in Tilea. Harmis folded his prize very carefully, fearful of its fragility. In all likelihood, no one to whom he showed it would be able to read it, but the mere fact that he possessed a written order would compel belief in his story.

When he received the paper, some of the confusion Harmis had felt was dispelled. Though he could not read, the writing told him very clearly where his duty lay; it bound his fate inextricably with the fate of Astyanax's apprentices, and there could be no more questioning of that decision. Whether they had power of command over him, or he over them, remained unspecified, but their mission was now his mission also.

And so, as soon as Nicodemus declared himself ready to ride, they mounted up and set forth along the road to the south.

THE ROAD WAS busy. The exodus from Aldium was a mere trickle as yet, but it had begun. All the traders who were temporary residents of the town had loaded their carts, without much regard for filling them in a businesslike way, and many of those labourers who were hired by the day or by the week to work the land had decided to take themselves and their families to places which might prove safer.

Not even the oldest of the region's inhabitants could remember the last time the Zani had come in force, but there had been several incursions since Faramond's ancestors – who were descended, it was said, from Tilean soldiers of fortune – had first raised the claret-and-gold in Khypris. The combination of political stability and the repetition of the event had allowed an automatic response to be firmly engraved in the wisdom which was handed down from father to son, and the people were in no doubt as to what they had to do.

Alas, if Astyanax's message was heeded, their flight would be in vain.

Harmis told himself that there might yet be some sense in the exodus. Even if it transpired that these people could not cross the Tana Dante, there were places easier to defend than Aldium: remote places where the Zani would not deign to pause, and larger towns like Mentreda which the enemy might avoid for fear of taking heavy losses. The people of a siege-bound Mentreda surrounded by ruined fields and hungry herds would soon be starving; but two men in three might be expected to survive a siege, whereas it might easily be the case that less than one in five would survive a massacre.

The progress which Harmis and his companions made was more modest than it had been during their hectic ride of the day before – by necessity, for the horses could not stand punishment of that sort very long or very often. For this reason they were sometimes overtaken by horsemen on the Prince's business, who could switch horses at every way-station.

Harmis was surprised to see Rolf Humbold ride past them at noon, acknowledging their presence with a courtly wave as he swept by. He had four men-at-arms in attendance. Clearly he had not been quite so anxious to depart as Harmis had expected him to be – but as Harmis had

observed, his kind did not need to fear the breaking of the
Tana Dante's bridges; there would always be boats and
oarsmen for such as he.

At this more gentle pace it was possible for Harmis to
ride alongside Nicodemus and question him, and he took
advantage of the opportunity.

'Where exactly are we going?' he asked.

'Ritandyr went into the westlands,' said Nicodemus, 'to a
place named Alynda. I don't know exactly where his house
is, but if we ask for him we'll find him – ordinary
people are always anxious to gossip about the whereabouts of wizards.'

'I've never been stationed so far south,' said Harmis, wor-
riedly. 'And we may not find it easy to get there, if the Zani
have already brought their herds down from the hill country. If your friend has wind of what is happening, will he
not try to get to Khypris before the bridges are down?'

Nicodemus shook his head. 'I don't think so. He'll guess
that if the Zani are coming then Chaos has also come to the
Khyprian lands, and that the day has come for which he
and Astyanax laboured long to prepare. Astyanax assured
me that he will wait where he is, until a message reaches
him. But I'm not magician enough to communicate with
him at such a distance, and I can't tell whether he knows
that Astyanax is dead. I'm only certain that I must add my
own strength to his greater power, so that our resources
may be combined in the attempt to frustrate the *katharos*.'

'And will your combined powers be enough?' asked
Harmis.

Nicodemus laughed, humourlessly. 'Who can tell?' he
answered. 'I'd be more confident if I were whole and well;
I'm no more master of the arts and the elements in my present state than I'm master of the bow. I fear you mustn't
look to me for anything more than petty tricks until I've
recovered from the battle at the tarn – and Averil, I fear, is
a mere beginner. Her one assured talent is making light to
keep the dark at bay, though if anyone were to attack us, I
think she could hurt them.'

'If anyone attacks us,' said Harmis, stonily, 'I can hurt them myself.'

'I know it too,' answered Nicodemus. 'And you've seen that your courage and skills are very useful, even when magic is involved. The most powerful magician may be slain by strength and cleverness, when his own attention is given to other work. In any case, good luck has given you a magical weapon more powerful than I could have forged with the utmost exercise of my skill. You're a wizard-killer now, and your daggers are tempered for the taking of dae-monic life. But Harmis, I implore you to remember what was said to you. Use your sword first – for in becoming doubly dangerous to your enemies, your knives have become hazardous even to their handler.'

Harmis remembered well enough what had been said to him, and he was not inclined to forget or disregard it.

'I must know more about this *katharos* whose fate is bound to mine,' he said. 'How may I know it if I ever see it?'

'I wish I could tell you,' Nicodemus replied. 'Alas, it's the kind of daemon which is not easily seen for what it is. Although it is tainted by the mutations of Chaos, as all its kind are, the mutations of a *katharos* are internal rather than external – its true form is masked by illusion. The name means Pure One, but that's an irony, for no daemon can ever be truly pure; what the title signifies is that this kind of evil wears a disguise of guiltlessness, and those who seek to destroy it must first see through its dissimula-tions.'

'That's no help to me at all,' protested Harmis. 'Should I expect to see it in the robes of a priest, or the finery of a nobleman, or the livery of a militiaman like myself?'

'I wish I knew,' said Nicodemus, quietly. 'I hope that I'll be able to detect the taint of Chaos, even if it wears a mask, but while I'm hurt and exhausted... I do not know. I've no more experience in this matter than you have, and can tell you only what Astyanax told me. His belief was that this daemon was once a human being, whose soul

was willingly bartered to the god of plague in exchange
for the power to hurt. No doubt there's more than one
motive which makes men champions of Chaos, but one
of the most common is the lust for revenge – of which, I
think, you understand a little yourself. Astyanax guessed –
and it was a matter of guesswork, not of divination – that
this daemon, having gained power and favour in the service of the god it came to love, is returning to the realm
which was its birthplace when it was a human being, to
pay out some grudge its former self had against Khypris...
which is to say, against Prince Faramond.'

Harmis considered this information carefully. There
were many, he knew, who were bitter against the prince he
served, for many different reasons. Men descended from
Empire stock often thought it unjust that they should be
ruled by the descendants of Tileans; the northland and
westland farmers resented the fact that they served the city
folk; members of other branches of Faramond's own family were always prone to imagine that the crown might and
ought to have been diverted in their direction at some crit-
ical moment of misremembered history. Then again, it was
in the nature of princes that they should make frequent
exhibition of their sternness and cruelty, lest they lose their
position. Faramond was no more cruel than most, nor was
he any less cruel. But everyone surely knew that this was
the way of the world; only a madman would sell his soul
to a god of suffering, ambitious to become a loathsome
daemon, in order to strike back at a prince who simply
behaved as all princes must.

And yet, Harmis knew well enough what a rage had possessed him when Lavarock was killed – and was it not the
consequence of that wrathful duty that his inmost soul
had been marked by an evil curse, and the knives which
were his most personal possession tempered by the taint
of murderous magic?

This train of thought would have taken him further, but
Sable's nostrils flared at that moment, and she whinnied
anxiously.

Harmis sniffed at the air, and felt a prick of anxiety as he smelled smoke. He turned round to look back at Aldium before realizing that the wind from the north had died away, and that this smoke was drifting from the fields to the east of the road. But it was not the beginning of the scorching of the fields, by which the northlanders might try to deprive the aurochs herds of sustenance. It was only a fire built by tinkers in a field.

Then he saw another column of smoke, much blacker, rising in the south ahead of them, and heard some commotion carried by warning cries back along the road. At first he paused uncertainly, seeing that those travellers who had reached the ridge of a shallow hill in front of them were halting there, startled by some unexpected sight. Then, feeling that uncertainty was worse than unpleasant revelation, he urged Sable into a trot, and rode ahead of his companions.

Several minutes passed before he was able to bring Sable to the top of the hill, and before he had quite crested the rise he heard the distant clash of iron upon iron which told him that men were fighting with blades. When he finally reached the point where he could see what was happening, where three dozen people now stood looking fearfully down, he saw that Rolf Humbold's party had been attacked by a troop of riders more than a dozen strong. The riders were not Zani, but northlanders – probably bully-boys owned by some petty landholder whose allegiance to Faramond was weak at the best of times.

The men-at-arms had been putting up a fight of sorts, but Harmis could see almost instantly that they were not being asked to fight for their lives; the bandits sought only to drive them off. Knowing that, Humbold's defenders had put up token resistance, and crossed swords for show, but they were now consenting to be driven back. Later, perhaps, they might give one another a bloody nick or two and agree to double the odds which they would claim to have faced, thus making the account of their escape seem

little short of miraculous. In the meantime, they left Rolf
Humbold to the men who wanted him.

Harmis watched, with a dreadful tightness in his throat,
while the northlanders took the retribution wrath had led
them to. They tied a rope around Humbold's neck, then
threw the end over a thick bough which extended from an
ancient twisted tree by the roadside. They used the power
of a horse to haul him up, until his feet were snatched
from the ground.

Humbold kicked and thrashed desperately against the
strangling pressure, his fingers scrabbling at the confining
knot while his face went unnaturally dark. It did not seem
to be an easy death; at any rate, he continued to kick
against his fate for a long time, while the brigands who
had taken him rode around and about, jeering and spitting.

'Can we not help him?' asked Averil, who had come up
beside Harmis.

Her only answer was a bitter laugh – but it was not until
the kicking grew less violent that Harmis realized what an
imbecile he was to wait on the skyline, marked out in silhouette for the convenience of those who might next turn
their attention to him.

He wheeled Sable around, and caught the rein of Averil's
horse. 'Ride!' he said, in a tone which he kept low in spite
of its urgency. 'Ride down the hill, then west – and keep
going, until we've put five miles between those men and
our own tender necks.'

She looked him full in the face, and he saw the alarm in
her eyes. Then she looked at the crowd gathered about
them, to see if any would leap forward to hold them there,
so that they too might be sacrificed to the fear and anger of
the northlands. But the men in the crowd were a different
breed, dourer of temper and duller of wit than the murderers, and so they were able to ride away down the hill, and
then to go west across the fields and into the wilderness.

There was no sign of pursuit, and because he was anxious about Sable Harmis ceased to urge her on when they

had gone only two miles – but he kept looking back after that, and did not begin to feel safe again until late in the afternoon, when they stopped at a stream to water the horses and to rest.

'Why did they do that?' demanded Averil, letting loose a little of the anger which had simmered inside her since she had seen Humbold hanged. Anger made her rounded face much ruddier, but not one whit less plain.

Harmis did not need to answer, for Nicodemus turned on her with his face contorted with pain, and said: 'You know why. He betrayed their trust. The world itself has betrayed their trust, for Chaos is come and they know not how or why it is that their fate must be written in suffering and blood. We're alone, and can look for help to no one but ourselves. Don't expect it!'

She recoiled before his bitterness, and Harmis was astonished. When Nicodemus turned away to nurse his aching leg with his one good arm, Harmis plucked at her sleeve and led her away.

'Don't be hurt,' he told her, awkwardly. 'It's *his* hurt which speaks for him.' But she seemed hardly to have heard him, and her eyes were wide with horror. He knew that she was remembering Rolf Humbold's face as he had fought so desperately and so hopelessly against that strangling rope. Whatever defensive magic she possessed would not be proof against such a death, if they could ever get the rope around her neck.

'If we are attacked, my lady,' he said – and he did not use the title ironically, though she was certainly not of gentle birth – 'remember that however bloodthirsty the men may be, their horses are fearful beasts at heart. Frighten their animals, if you can, and you'll stand a better chance by far of escape.'

As an item of advice it was humble enough, but it was all that he had to offer.

'Will we be attacked?' she asked him. She had been attacked only the day before, but she had been in the house by the tarn then, with its sleek black guardians and

the master magician Astyanax to defend her. Now, she felt
exposed and virtually friendless, for she could not yet trust
Harmis Detz to be her faithful ally.

'Yes,' he said, frankly. 'We must expect to be attacked. Not
by those men, I think, for they have sated their spite for
now – but the journey to Alynda is a long one, and if the
nation's enemies are already within its borders we're very
likely to cross the path of their scouts and raiders. I pray
that we'll not face such ugly foes as those who came with
the Lazarite sorcerer, but if we're to avoid the warbands
who will come ahead of the hillmen's herds we'll be very
lucky indeed, and we dare not reckon on such luck as that.'

'No,' she said, having recovered much of her composure
while he spoke. 'We dare not reckon on such luck as that.
And we must not forget that the daemon might also try to
find us, to make us pay for what we did to its servants at
the tarn.'

It was a thought which did not help Harmis to increase
his peace of mind.

Oh well, he said to himself, I suppose I may still hope
that I am an inconsiderable thing, altogether unworthy of
the attention of dark gods and their daemons, despite that
my knives have spilled the foulest blood that ever spoiled
this nation's thirsty soil.

As a consolation, it was meagre, but it was all that he had
to cling to for the time being.

CHAPTER SEVEN

AS THE SUN set that day, while they still headed south-west towards the westlands and Alynda, Harmis saw the first evidence that the hillmen had indeed brought their herds down to the lowlands. The northern skyline, which should have offered a chain of clear-cut ridges and peaks on such a bright and cloudless day, was blurred by a dull haze which the dying sunlight turned fiery red; it was the dust kicked up by tens of thousands of aurochs driven with some haste across infertile ground, crowding the narrower valleys and pulverizing the sandy soil.

When he pointed this out to his companions, Nicodemus said: 'They're a long way off, and the beasts will surely stop to graze when they reach farmland.'

'The Zani will be as hungry for plunder as their lean beasts are for good grazing,' Harmis told him. 'The hillmen don't fight as a disciplined army, and won't gather together into a horde until they're faced by one. There will be small groups of raiders riding out before the herds, such as I have faced before. I know them well, and they're hard men to best. We must try to stay ahead of them until we reach Alynda.'

'We could ride through the night,' suggested Averil.

'No,' said Harmis, 'that we cannot. We can't get more horses if these break down, and we've used them sternly enough as things are. To ride over rough land at night, with only the paler moon in the sky, is to invite disaster.'

'I can make light for us,' she said. 'I have that much magic.'

'Light which would show us to the Zani scouts,' said Harmis, sourly, 'and bring their bowmen swarming all around.'

'Harmis is right,' said Nicodemus. 'Strength must be conserved – ours as well as the horses'. There will be work for us to do, when we have found Ritandyr, and I'm so battered and bruised that I couldn't even make a light. We must stop when the twilight fades.'

They found a stream within the hour, and stopped there; it was a desolate spot, but in Harmis's view that was all to the good. In coming so far from the road they had reached a sparsely populated region where there were few farms. Here they were not very likely to meet Khyprians – and hence, perhaps, unlikely to be seen by the Zani.

Averil inspected Nicodemus's wounds carefully. She then insisted on checking Harmis's head, where he had been kicked by the horse which rode him down when the mutants attacked Vimera, but she found no trace of any infection. She gave them both dark water to drink, and the way that Nicodemus seized the jug and supped from it suggested to Harmis that the apprentice's thirst for it was as determined as his own.

If I am slave to this poor wine, he thought, and so is he, then what will happen when our supply is exhausted? But there seemed no immediate danger of that, for the multitudinous jugs and bottles still rattled in the horses' packs.

Harmis found Nicodemus a place to sleep where there was sufficient grass to spare his bones, and the young man took prompt advantage of it, while his companions were still drinking tea made from ordinary water and from herbs which Astyanax had kept. Harmis had lit a tiny candle rather than put Averil's light-making skills to the test, and she made no objection, having taken to heart her fellow apprentice's warnings about conserving such power as she had.

'It's not an invigorating potion,' Harmis observed of the tea, whose taste he did not much like. It was an oblique reference to the effect which the dark water had on him.

'It has no magic in it,' agreed Averil, 'but it has its virtues nevertheless. Astyanax was ever anxious to tell us there is much that can be achieved without magic, using only the natural properties which plants and the elements have. Great magicians, he said, must have knowledge and skill as well as power in order to make a seed germinate in the hand... but water and light will have the same effect upon the same seed in the soil, and need no education at all.'

Harmis laughed. His thoughts suddenly turned again to the ounce of gold and the cupful of blood, but he did not try to turn the conversation to amatory matters. He was curiously intimidated by her, though not by her meagre magic or occasional haughtiness. He told himself that she was too plain to be worth any effort on his part, but the real truth was that she seemed so odd and intense and self-absorbed that he did not like to try her out.

He went to sleep as soon as he could, though he slept lightly and fitfully, as befitted his anxious situation.

NEXT MORNING THEY started out with no delay, and were glad to see that it promised to be another bright day. They passed four remote farms, and Harmis called to the labourers in the fields to warn them that the Zani were bringing their herds south – but to some at least the news was no surprise, and he realized that preparations were being made in every case to abandon the land, though it was far too early in the year to take up much of the planted crop. The green fields were being left to take care

of themselves – but if this earth was to be scorched, the
burning would have to be done by other hands.

It was about noon when they saw the first Zani warriors
in the distance – a group of eight, galloping southwards.
Though Harmis quickly sought what cover he could there
was no doubt that the hillmen had seen them, and he
urged his companions to make what haste they could in
turning to the opposite direction.

'They may be scouts and not adventurers,' he called to
Nicodemus, 'and if so, they'll not chase us for long. Even
if they are out for blood, they may turn aside to one of the
farms.'

But when he looked back from the next ridge, he saw
that the riders had not turned back, nor turned aside – and
he judged from the dust they were throwing up that they
were still pushing their horses hard. He cursed, but knew
well enough that if there was a hunt on he had no alternative but to be hunted.

For the next hour he tried hard to figure out a way to
dodge the Zani. He led his party over stony ground, took
care to put what woodlands there were between himself
and the hillmen, and tried in every way he could to throw
them off the track – but when he checked again, as carefully as he could, he saw that the followers had merely
fanned out to hunt for his tracks, and that they were evidently disinclined to be shaken off.

By the time another hour had passed he had abandoned
the hope that the Zani were merely playing a game of
which they would grow tired. Indeed, the suspicion was
growing in him that their pursuers had some particular
motive for hunting them – and Nicodemus too was afraid
that this might be the case.

'The Zani have their magicians too,' he said to Harmis, in
a dry voice, when they slowed down for a moment in
crossing a ravine. 'Like most nomad folk they keep seers
and shamanistic healers, not all of whom are charlatans
and incompetents. The daemon may be using them without their even knowing it – and it may be at the daemon's

command that these men have been sent forth to seek us out.'

Harmis knew a little about the magicians the Zani were supposed to keep, though it was all from hearsay. They were diviners rather than men of power, much given to seeking omens in dreams. Rumour had it that they were clever enough, except when vaulting optimism led them astray. How much he had to fear from them, he did not know.

'Tell me, sir magician,' he replied, ironically, 'how we might shake them off. What spells can you cast to send them another way?'

Nicodemus shook his head. 'If I could only draw my bow,' he said, 'we might pick them off from ambush... but I can't make us invisible, or hide our trail.'

And so they kept going, using the tricks of soldiery which Harmis had been taught to stay ahead of the pursuit, and – as much as was possible – out of sight. Mercifully, the Zani eventually ceased to force their horses on at a run; like those they pursued, they had no chance of finding others. By the time the afternoon was well-advanced the pursuit had slowed to a walk, and seemed set to become a crawl by nightfall.

Later, though, they came to a wood which was far more dense than anything through which they had passed before. It was typical Khyprian woodland, rich in low-crowned thorny trees and thick bushes, but there were some cedars and other high-crowned trees, and the profusion of greenery was adequate to hide a legion, let alone a party of three with five mounts. Harmis knew that there were bound to be foresters in the wood: foragers and charcoal-burners, who would have every reason and motive to fight if the Zani came among them.

It did not take Harmis long to catch the smell of smoke within the wood, and he immediately guided the tired horses towards it. Being cautious, though, he did not take his entire party forward all at once, but went on ahead to see whose fire it was.

His heart fell when he caught his first glimpse of the fire, for the smoke came neither from a charcoal-burner's pyre nor a cutter's cabin. It was an open campfire built between three painted wagons, made by gypsies. That was unfortunate, for gypsies were generally thieves and brigands who had no conspicuous loyalty to any monarch and no sense of belonging to any nation. Gypsies, more than any other people in Khypris, regarded those who wore Faramond's livery as enemies, and those who carried arms on the prince's behalf as objects of hatred. Alone, he dared not approach them.

The gypsies would, of course, be no friends to the Zani either – but they could not have heard word that the Zani horde was coming, and until they had seen the warriors for themselves they would not trust the word of one of Faramond's men.

Harmis judged that if the gypsies became aware of the nearness of his own party, their first thoughts would be of plunder. Five horses and two sizeable packs, defended by one man-at-arms, one injured man and a girl, would surely offer a temptation they could not resist.

Harmis wormed his way to the edge of the camp and tried to count the gypsies as they moved about the camp. There were three families, one to each wagon. All of them were dark of hair and skin. The men wore moustaches – which made them seem kin to the Zani, whose warriors had the same habit. They sported brightly-coloured scarves upon their heads, tunics of green, and silver earrings. The women, though, wore pleated skirts patterned in blue and green – very different from the trews of aurochs-hide which Zani women invariably wore. They wore an abundance of jewellery made from cheap metals and coloured stones.

Harmis judged, when he had completed his count, that there were only five men who were young and strong – but they had an old man too, and three boys of tender years, as well as three wives, two girl-children and a barely-nubile young woman. Harmis could not relish the prospect of a fight with such a company; nor could he believe that he could easily make friends with them.

He made his way back to Nicodemus and Averil, and explained the situation.

'We could go on,' he said, 'and hope to find better allies. But it may be that our best hope is that the Zani will run into the gypsies just as we have done. Perhaps they'll turn back or turn aside in consequence, but it would be better for us were they to attack, so that both groups of our potential enemies would be weakened in fighting one another. It would be useful to know what happens.'

'We can't go much further,' Nicodemus answered. 'Let's make ourselves as safe as we can near here, and stand watch all night against all our enemies.'

Harmis led them carefully around the gypsy camp, so that the brigands were between themselves and the pursuing Zani. Then he found a sheltered spot surrounded by thick bushes, with a taller tree nearby from which a watch could be kept. They lit no fire or lantern, but used what was left of the evening in making an adequate meal. Then Harmis told Averil and Nicodemus to take turns in staying awake, and to use what magic they had to warn them of any approach by enemies. For his own part, he set out to return to the gypsy camp, and placed himself where he could see what went on there.

By the time he got there the gypsies had finished their meal, but he was glad to see that they had no intention of putting out their fire and retiring. Indeed, they seemed intent on making a noise, for two of them brought out their fiddles and began to play, while all the children and the nubile girl were set to dancing. This was not solely for their own enjoyment, but to practise their performances, for playing and dancing were reckoned as a way of earning coin by such folk – perhaps the only honest way they had.

It was inevitable that such innocent recklessness should attract the Zani, and Harmis felt a certain temptation to make himself known and give a warning – the travellers evidently thought themselves utterly safe. But he restrained himself, for it was clearly in his interest that the gypsies should offer a very tempting target to the Zani warband. He found a tree he could safely climb, and took himself up into its branches.

When the twilight faded, the gypsies lit lanterns which they posted on hooks at three sides of their wagons, and continued to make merry. Though he knew that they were ruthless folk, Harmis could not help but feel a bond of human kinship with them, and when one of the men went to see to the horses and did not return he felt an awkward lump in his throat. Once again he had to suppress an impulse to call out and warn the others of their imminent peril.

He stayed silent, and caught his breath as the Zani attacked with swift efficiency.

One of the fiddlers was felled by an arrow, and the obvious intention of the attackers was that the other able-bodied fighters should be similarly shot – but when the first shot was launched, the gypsy men made up for their earlier incaution with a very quick response, for they moved like lightning to take what cover there was and reach for their weapons. Half a dozen arrows sang in the air as they flashed into the camp, but only two hit home, one hitting the old man in the thigh while another struck an infant in the neck.

The Zani should have stayed where they were, and fired more arrows from the darkness, but they had already made a more precipitate plan of attack, and they leapt into the space between the wagons from two opposed sides, brandishing their blades. Had the gypsy men kept their own weapons closer to hand it might have been an even fight, but they had not, and they had to come to hand-to-hand conflict with whatever was near to be picked up and wielded. Even so, one of the Zani went down in a cascade of burning oil as a lantern was flung at him, and another was hit by a dagger thrust into his thigh by one of the boy-children.

The confusion was far too great to allow Harmis to track every blow, but he saw the remaining gypsy men bloodily cut down – not smoothly, but quickly enough and very brutally. The few blows they traded for their mortal hurts were bruising ones, but they had no swords with which to cut deep.

One of the startled women wasted time in fruitless screaming, but the two other wives were quick enough to enter the fight with cooking-knives, and all the children were driven furious by desperation. The Zani cut about themselves with great abandon, but they had come a little too soon to the slaughter, careless of ungrown enemies, and made themselves more trouble than they need have done. Harmis saw the screaming woman nearly beheaded – but that was a silly blow, for she was the only one who posed no threat at all to the attackers, and he was pleased to see that the man who struck her was stabbed in the belly by a child, then hit higher up by an axe which the oldest girl-child swung with amazing ardour.

There was more screaming as one of the children was thrust into the fire – though the Zani badly burned by lamp-oil had not screamed at all, and had killed two enemies by slashing wildly in his frenzy. As the firewood was scattered it became more difficult to see, and more difficult still when another lantern was upturned and doused – but as the action slowed Harmis was all-too-easily able to perceive what havoc had been wreaked in the course of the battle.

When the Zani ceased their slaughter all nine of the males were slain, including the three boy-children. Both of the small girl-children were dead, and two of the wives. One wife and the oldest girl had been disarmed and were held, but both of them seemed badly hurt, for they had not allowed themselves to be disarmed without a desperate fight.

The Zani looked much debilitated now, though not a single one of them was dead. The burned man was suffering greatly, and the one stabbed in the belly and wounded by the axe was flat on his back and writhing – Harmis judged that he could not last the night. Three others had been wounded by stabs, and one of them was bleeding very freely from the thigh. This left only three unscathed, and even they had probably taken a bruise or two in the course of the melee.

Harmis was almost tempted to attack on the instant, feeling sure that he could fell all three of the uncut Zani with his two knives and one good thrust of his sword, but he knew better than to assume that wounded men had no fight in them, and he could not trust the two injured women to rouse themselves again to give effective help to an unexpected rescuer. He knew that it would be better to wait, and make what use he could of stealth.

He was determined now to carry the fight to the Zani, even though it might mean using his knives in defiance of the warning which Astyanax had issued. He had no partic- ular love for gypsies, but the blood of these people was on his own hands as well as the hands of the Zani, for he had not warned them, and he owed it to them to take what vengeance he could. In addition, there was no guarantee that the depleted warband would give up their pursuit, and he would never have a better chance to finish the hunt for good and all.

Alas, his decision to wait meant that he must watch the next phase of the drama, for the Zani were anxious to take what recompense they could for their painful injuries. They had already begun the sickening business of search- ing the dead for any items of value before carrying the bodies away to be discarded in the bushes.

Harmis chose not to watch too closely what happened after that, but he could not help but hear the cruel laugh- ter of the Zani, and though he did not know their language he understood the quality of their cursing and their crow- ing. Nor could he help the stench of the discarded dead reaching his sensitive nose.

I will kill them all, he promised, though he did not know to whom the words ought properly to be addressed.

I swear by all the gods who care that these Zani scum will receive angry justice for what they have done tonight.

Then he cursed himelf for too much tenderness, reminding himelf that he was a man-at-arms, and that bloodshed was his trade. Tactics, not rage or squeamishness, must dictate what he did, and how, and why.

When the Zani had finished all that they had to do, and had brought their horses into the camp, they finally settled down to sleep. They did not go into the wagons to lie upon the makeshift beds which were there, for hillmen always preferred to lay their blankets on the ground, even in winter; nor did they extinguish the last of the lanterns.

They posted a sentry, but Harmis judged by their attitude in taking the decision and drawing lots for the watch that it was a token gesture. They were less pleased with their work than they had looked to be, now that they had counted their hurts. Their minds were entirely on themselves, and not on the possibility of being attacked. They had too little imagination, it seemed, to be afraid of the quarry they had pursued all day.

Harmis knew better than to expect a Zani sentry to go conveniently to sleep, but he knew that when the night was at its darkest he would have every chance to reach the man unobserved, and kill him silently.

He became more confident still when the man who had been stabbed in the belly and cut by the axe became delirious because his own spilled juices were burning his entrails, and began a helpless low moaning. The noise would no doubt ensure that the other Zani slept less soundly than they might, but it would cover his approach.

He did not dare go to sleep, but he made himself as comfortable as he could on his branch, and relaxed as much as he was able until the right moment came for him to stir himself.

CHAPTER EIGHT

HARMIS LET HIMSELF down gently, holding tightly to his branch until he felt his feet touch the ground. Only when he had found a sound foothold did he transfer his weight to his feet; then he breathed out very carefully as the strain on his arms relaxed. His clothing rustled slightly, but the sound could not be audible to the sentry.

Now he was down on the ground he had lost his good view of the camp, the low-burning lantern having been eclipsed by the bulk of one of the wagons. He checked his memory methodically, so as to be certain that he knew where each of his enemies was; then he flexed his muscles and tested his joints, lest he had become unduly stiff while he crouched in the branches.

When he was satisfied that he was ready to fight he made an effort to concentrate his mind, to wipe it clean of irrelevant thoughts as well as unnecessary emotions, clearing a way for the reflexes which had been drummed into him by his training and long practice in the craft of soldiery.

He did not pause to draw his sword before moving off, but took out instead the length of strong cord which he kept for the business of strangling.

As he wound it about his palms the memory of past occasions when he had used it came very vividly to mind, as it was bound to do. He had killed three men this way: all Zani youths, come to the lands which were claimed by Khypris in order to put to the proof their power as warriors. They had all been very young men, their moustaches hardly grown and trained, all with so much more courage than wisdom that they would not have deigned to do the same thing themselves. Harmis knew that he had lived to be thirty-three only because his own education in the craftsmanship of murder had taught him not to be so particular.

He slid forward, choosing a route which would not make too much of a stir in the cluttered undergrowth, and moved around the wagons so that he could come at the sentry from the side.

With catlike stealth he stalked his victim, refusing to be hurried by impatience – though he could not stop his heart hammering in his chest.

At last he was close enough to pounce. He moved his hands swiftly over the Zani's head and pulled the cord tight with a single smooth action. Although the man made a slight gurgling noise in his throat he could do no more to warn his companions.

Had the sentry's sword been in his hand he could have stabbed backwards with it, but his hands were empty and he fell prey to an instinctive response which made him clutch at the cord in a futile attempt to pull it away.

Harmis could not help but remember poor Rolf Humbold, scrabbling at the rope which had hanged him. The Zani's struggles did not last as long as that, for Harmis had powerful muscles in his forearms, whose strength made the cord cut deep into the flesh. He did not let go at once when his victim's struggles ceased, but maintained the pressure for a full two minutes more. Then and only then did he lower the body to the ground, as gently and soundlessly as he could.

Only five Zani were now in a condition to fight him, and three of those were carrying light wounds.

He knew that three strides would take him to a place beside the nearest of the sleepers. Still he did not draw his sword; instead he made a quick exploration of the body of the man he had killed. He was pleased to find that the Zan had two knives tucked into his belt – not his own, but ones he had taken from the gypsy boys. Harmis tested the first blade and found it very sharply pointed; the second was duller but good enough for the purpose he had in mind.

The first Zani lay flat on his back, sleeping peacefully – seemingly quite untroubled by nightmares, the low moans of his companion or the stench of spilled blood. The man's hands were clasped loosely to his collar-bones, the crossed wrists protecting his throat and one forearm masking his heart; he was clearly a man of careful habits.

Harmis knew better than to risk an ordinary disembowelling thrust through the belly and up into the cavity of the chest, that being a more useful thrust against a man erect. Instead, he raised the sharper of his stolen blades high into the air and plunged it vertically down into the sleeping man's left eyeball, with sufficient force to carry it through the thin bone behind the socket and into the forebrain. He did not try to pull the blade out again, but left it where it was.

The dead man expelled his last breath in a low, hoarse whistle, but it sounded very like a snore, and if any of the others heard it, they were not alerted to the presence of danger.

Harmis moved to the next sleeper, who lay on his side with his head pillowed on a garment taken from one of the wagons. This man too had his arms up about his shoulders, but the side of his neck was exposed and vulnerable to a stab which, if cleverly directed, would sever the artery there and instantly fill the throat with sufficient blood to prevent a cry of pain.

The barbarian warrior was only a boy, no more than fifteen or sixteen years of age, but he had come on a man's mission and must take a man's risks.

Harmis plunged the duller knife down, striking again with careful force and all the precision of which he was capable.

Alas, the blow failed in its main intention, misjudged by a crucial fraction of an inch. It was a mortal blow, but it did not kill the youth instantly, nor did it cut off his breath on the instant. The Zani's whole body convulsed, and as the shock of the pain went through him he gave vent to a cry which, though quickly strangled, was loud enough and anguished enough to wake at least one of the others.

Harmis came immediately to his feet and drew his sword.

The night was suddenly echoing with loud cries of anger and alarm. Three fighting men, he knew, would rise to their feet and come at him. A fourth might be dangerous, though his leg would not let him stand to take his place in a sword-fight. Even the burned man could not be left entirely out of account.

Harmis slashed at the nearest of the shadows which rose from the darkened ground to fight him, cutting low in order to immobilize the man because he could not be sure of hurting him badly.

His blade bit into flesh, but only the very tip penetrated, and the cry which came back at him in response was an ululating warcry and not a howl of pain. Such sudden yells could paralyze an unwary man with shock for half a second and more, but Harmis was a veteran of many a skirmish with the Zani and other fights with assorted goblin-kin, and he was proof against such tricks.

He thrust again, but the shadows were moving now in such confusion that it was very difficult to measure a blow. Such small advantage as the lantern gave was all to him, for he had no need to beware of striking out at the wrong shadow. But the enemy now had their weapons drawn, and he was still one man against a company.

The embers of the fire flared up again as one of the hill-men kicked at it, leaping over the spitting ashes with his sword licking out before him. As the blade came up and around Harmis saw that the man was a sweeper, not a stabber, and he leapt back to be clear of the horizontal arc that it would carve through the air. When the point was safely past, he lunged forward with desperate agility, striking for the base of the breast-bone.

He felt his thrust go solidly home, and heard the man let loose an awful choking sound. Instead of falling backwards, though, the dying man fell forwards, so that his weight became an inconvenient burden on the blade which had destroyed him. Harmis had to pull back with all his might lest he lose his weapon, but the dying hill-man still staggered on, pulled by the blade whose point was lodged in his chest.

Harmis had to move further back, urgently trying to recover his sword. If the man had actually fallen then, he might have forced Harmis down or ripped the sword from his grasp, but there was no strategy involved in his convulsive movements; it was an automatic defiance of the moment of death which kept the Zani on his feet and in motion. After one more lurching stride, Harmis gratefully pulled his weapon free, just in time to slap awkwardly sideways at another swordsman coming from the side.

Had this opponent been whole, he might have killed Harmis then, but he was one of the walking wounded, and pursued his quarry ineptly. Harmis met the initial challenge well enough to earn the time to move away – but then he had to face two challenges simultaneously as another came to join the fray and crowd him. There was no further advantage to be had from the dim light and the element of surprise; the Zani who were left knew now exactly what their situation was. Still, he fenced his two sluggish opponents off without having to draw on any exotic skills.

As the wounded man, who was very slow in his paces, tried to strike again, Harmis slashed sideways, and felt his blade bite into the man's midriff, putting him down. But that was the wrong man to hit first, for the other was more dangerous. That other cut at him furiously, and Harmis felt the blade collide with his left shoulder near the neck. He felt no pain, and the weapon rebounded as though it had only been the flat which had touched him and not the point, but still it was a blow, and it put him off balance for a moment or two.

A thrown dagger whistled by him, sparing him only by chance and not by any evasive skill of his own. He could not tell where it had come from, but his most urgent priority was perfectly clear: only one swordsman stood against him now, and he must surely have taken a blow or two at some time, in this melee or the last. Once this one was down, the others could be put to death with relative ease.

This last standing hillman had moved away from the confusion of his fallen kin, and was ready to fence, but as Harmis moved to follow his opponent into an uncluttered space his calf was gripped, angrily if not so very securely, by one of those who was fallen but had not been struck dead. Harmis dared not stab at him and leave himself open to a swordthrust, so he tried to kick out – but that did not work, and the grappling hands resisted well enough to make him stumble.

He had no alternative then, and was in any case in the grip of his fighting instincts. He passed his sword from right hand to left and cut viciously downwards at the man who held him. His right hand went like lightning to the scabbard behind his right shoulder, and as the remaining swordsman leapt forward, exulting prematurely over an easy kill, the heavy knife took him full in the chest and dropped him like a slaughtered aurochs bull.

Harmis did not relax. He looked fiercely about for any sign of movement, but saw none.

After a while, he touched his hand to the shoulder where he had been hit, and was distressed to feel blood freely flowing from a cut. Though the cut was not deep it was by no means trivial, and now that he was consciously aware of his hurt it began to pain him.

Suddenly, he felt desperately thirsty. Dizziness swirled in his head, and he had to make a very determined effort to take hold of himself. Though the pain and the thirst did not abate, his determination proved adequate to give him full command of his senses and his limbs. He went to the wagon where the lantern hung, and took it from its hook.

One by one, he began to inspect the stricken Zani, looking for any remaining signs of life.

He killed the man who had taken the belly wound in the earlier fight, and the burned man – both were too weak to know it was being done, let alone to resist. Only one of the others tried to raise a weapon against him, and that was a sword which he had not the strength to lift in any effective way; Harmis struck it callously aside and ran the man through. Then he stood back and took a deep breath. The stink of spilled blood and the other concomitants of sudden death had been in the camp before he came, but now it had become overpowering.

He coughed, and spat upon the ground. Then he sheathed his sword.

When he moved to one of the wagons, leaning on it for support, his attention was suddenly distracted by a noise from beyond the boundary of the camp, and he came immediately to the ready, clutching again at his sword-hilt. But it was Averil and Nicodemus, who had unwisely crept closer when they had heard the warcries of the Zani.

Harmis turned up the lantern, so that he could see them more clearly – and so that they could see him. Shock and horror were written plainly on their faces, though they had been through a fight only two days before which had seemed to Harmis more horrible by far. But on that occasion the bodies of the defeated attackers had been dragged into the tarn and out of sight; here the extent of the carnage was very evident indeed, with bodies lying everywhere and the air reeking.

Harmis knew by the way his uniform clung to his left side that he must be drenched in blood himself – but surely only a portion of it was his own. Though he knew that he was wounded, he thought that only a little of it could possibly be his – but when he touched his hand to his neck again, bringing forth another rush of belated pain, he was not so sure. The cut he had taken was still bleeding copiously.

The wound was high on the shoulder, at the base of the neck, and had not cut the artery, but it was a long cut, extending four full inches from back to front. The pain was unrelenting now, and it seemed to him that his every action or attentive thought increased its magnitude. The thought uppermost in his mind, though, was how exceedingly glad he was that the wound had not made him miss his throw with the knife which had put down and killed the last able-bodied hillman.

He went to recover that knife, but when he lowered the lantern over the man whose chest it had split he recoiled in surprise. The man's shirt was open at the neck, and beneath it he could see a stain of corruption which was visibly spreading. While he paused, disturbed into inaction by the unprecedented sight, the dark stain consumed the Zani's pain-racked face, so that the flesh seemed to crumble upon the skull, blackening as if to desiccated tar.

Averil caught his hand when he reached again for the knife, whose hilt was still dressed in a bandage which she had bound about it before replacing it in its scabbard while they were still in the house by the Black Tarn.

'Let me do it,' she said, in a low and slightly reproachful tone. 'Only hope that you have not used up all its virtue, for we might have found a far better use for its curse than this.'

'If you have cause to throw again,' said Nicodemus – who did not seem inclined to blame him for having been forced to throw the weapon at the Zan – 'use the same knife. Don't use the other, save in the direst extremity, for we may need it badly if and when we find the *katharos*.'

Harmis laughed drily, but he let Averil pull the dagger from the dead man's chest. He did not need to be told, though she instructed him anyway, not to touch the unnaturally rotting corpse.

He checked the other dead hillmen once more, to be quite certain that none was shamming. Then, and only then, did he think of going to the bodies of the two women the Zani had made captive, to see if either of them might still be alive.

Both had been badly stabbed and cut about while they had resisted the Zani, but the young one was still alive. When Harmis hung the lantern over her, she opened her eyes, which were very dazed but still seemed to Harmis to be full of pain and fear.

'Well, sir magician,' said Harmis to Nicodemus, hoarsely, 'is there aught you can do for *her*?'

Nicodemus was perfectly capable of inferring what had been done to the girl, and he did not have to inspect her wounds to see how much blood she had lost.

'No,' he said, in a whisper. 'Nothing at all.'

The girl struggled to speak, and Harmis had to kneel down in order to hear her, so faint was her voice. Though he listened as well as he could, he could not make out what words she was trying to say. He wondered whether she might be pleading for help, or to be put from her misery by a single clean blow; he could not believe that she only wanted to express her gratitude because he had exacted a violent vengeance for what the Zani had done to her kinfolk. She must know how badly she was cut about, and she probably knew that there was no way back from the brink of death to which she had been brought. All that remained to her was as easy a release as might be contrived, from a life which had been short and probably full enough of misery.

He could hardly bear to see her open eyes, knowing what intelligence and suffering was behind them. She was only a girl, on the very threshold of adulthood. He would have cut her throat to end her suffering, if that had been all that he could offer her – but this was one task he could legitimately hand on to another.

'Have you magic enough to send her quietly to sleep?' he demanded of Nicodemus, more aggressively than he intended. 'Can you at least spare her the agony, until she dies?'

Nicodemus hesitated, but then he sighed, and said: 'Aye. However weak I am, that I can do.'

Harmis turned away while the novice enchanter touched his fingers to the poor girl's eyes to close them, and when he turned again to look at her, she seemed lost in a happy dream, for her features were quite still and all serene.

Nicodemus was looking down at his hand, and Harmis felt that he could read the thought in the young man's mind. Nicodemus, he knew, was regretting the irony of magic, which would not give him the power to alter the world for the better, but only the power to soothe away a little of its pain.

'I killed her,' said Harmis, dully. 'Whatever they did to her, I could have prevented. I should have waited until the Zani were almost here, then charged into the fight while giving the alarm. *Then* they would have trusted me. At that particular moment, they would have accepted any ally, unquestioningly. Instead, I did nothing. I let her kinsmen die, and let them hurt her so badly that she had nothing left to do but die, and that in anguish – so that the odds might be more even when I came in my turn to slay the Zani.'

Nicodemus was standing up again by now, looking carefully at the wound on Harmis's shoulder. 'Don't waste time with futile regrets,' he said, rather bitterly. 'You can't afford the luxury of guilt. I'm very glad the odds were as even as they were, because you have come far too close to making a martyr of yourself – and I think you still don't fully realize how badly we need you alive, to fight the greater foe.'

'I realize how badly *I* would be inconvenienced were I to be killed,' retorted Harmis. 'You'll forgive me if I consider your half-formed plans a matter of somewhat less importance, for the moment.'

Averil returned with his knife, which she had laved once more in the dark water of Astyanax's tarn. She carried a bottle of the water with her, which she sprinkled on the cadaver of the man the knife had slain, covering him completely while being as frugal as she could. Harmis watched her, wondering at her restored calmness. There was no horror in her eyes now; she adapted quickly to circumstance.

The sight of the sprinkled liquid made him very conscious of his thirst, and he asked to take a draught from the bottle when she had finished. She handed it to him immediately, and he took a deep draught, which seemed to bathe his inner being in ice and fire but brought a grateful satisfaction in its wake.

Had the apprentices needed fresh blood for their secret rites and spells they could have collected a generous measure now – but neither Averil nor Nicodemus showed any clinical interest in the unrotted bodies. Harmis could only conclude that the rumours which said that all magicians were ever avid to have blood for their mysterious potions were only rumours after all.

Harmis cleaned his sword by driving it into the soft humus beneath an ancient tree, and wiping the higher part of the blade with moss. Then he said: 'We have an hour or two before dawn, and must try to sleep if we can. These may not be the last of those who'll come to pursue us, whether they were sent to do it or whether they merely came upon us by chance. We need whatever strength we can recover.'

The apprentices allowed themselves to be led back to their own horses – but though they laid down their heads, neither slept at all. Harmis knew it, because he could not sleep himself, and could not help but know how restless they were.

But when dawn came, they all rose promptly to make their preparations for the continuation of their journey.

CHAPTER NINE

THE NEW DAY was much cloudier than the previous one, and the cloud thickened as they rode, threatening rain.

The wound on Harmis's shoulder had become less painful during the night, and it had not made his arm as stiff as he had anticipated. But as they continued southwestwards in the morning light, the jarring caused by Sable's steady canter slowly made the pain build up, and caused it to spread from the immediate vicinity of the cut to his head, his upper arm and his side. It was not a sharp pain, and was by no means intolerable, but it nagged at him while he rode. Still his arm did not go stiff, but it began to feel peculiar and the lower part of it, including the hand, seemed dull and heavy.

Because he was a man-at-arms, a certain stoicism was required of him. He said nothing to his companions about his trouble and tried to put it out of his mind. It was not until they paused to eat, and Averil came of her own accord to look at the injury, that any of them became properly aware of what was happening.

The girl had no sooner pulled the torn and bloodstained collar of his shirt away from the wound than she muttered an arcane curse and called for Nicodemus. He came immediately, and Harmis helped them to remove his upper garments entirely, to expose the spreading discolouration which extended from his ear to his bottom-most rib, and from his right nipple to the tip of his scapula.

It was like nothing Harmis had ever seen before. The discolouration was neither blue like a fresh bruise nor brown like a fading one. Instead it was red and yellow, the two colours curving round in whirligig streaks like eerie flames.

'You didn't bathe the wound!' said Nicodemus to Averil, accusingly. 'You washed the knife, but didn't treat the cut!'

His tone was so sharp that the girl reacted angrily. 'It was a Zani sword which cut him,' she said, 'not a beastman's blade or a Lazarite's dart. How could I know?'

Nicodemus shook his head. 'My fault,' he said, angrily. 'Astyanax would have expected it, and so should I. When the Lazarite struck him down with his stare, the curse reached into his very soul to corrupt every fibre of his being. It needed only a wound – even a natural one – to set that corruption in motion.'

'Is it poisoned, then?' asked Harmis, still too mystified to be properly alarmed. He remembered, though, that he had touched the wound twice with the fingers of the hand which he had used to throw the tainted knife.

'A poison of an awful kind,' said Nicodemus. 'Though you did not touch that sorcerer you slew, he contrived to infect you with someting of the taint which he accepted in his own flesh when he made his pact with the daemon.'

'Can you draw it out?' asked Harmis, feeling suddenly dizzy and disturbed now that the nature of his predicament was clear. 'Can the dark water still heal me, and keep me safe?'

Averil had already run to one of the pack-horses, and returned forthwith, carrying one of the bottles of Astyanax's magical fluid. Having unstoppered it, she poured the tarnwine liberally on to a cloth and immediately began to bathe the discoloured flesh, beginning with the cut itself.

Harmis gasped, then had to grit his teeth against a sting far worse than any pain the wound itself had caused him. It felt as though he were being washed with vitriol, and he clenched his right fist convulsively. He looked down at his left arm as though he expected to see the flesh melting from the bone, as the sorcerer had seemed to melt when the dark water was poured on his corpse.

Harmis had seen a soldier once who had been vitriolized by a discarded mistress, and had thought the acid-burned flesh a more dreadful sight than any injury inflicted in battle. It had made him glad he had always cared so little for women that he had never given one cause to bear him a grudge. And though his own flesh did not, after all, melt from the bone – but only felt as if it would – he could not displace from his thoughts the image of that poor man's ruined face.

'Morr's ravens!' he said, when Averil paused in her work. 'The wound was but a little hurt compared with that! Your cure is harder to bear than the disease itself!' His voice was harsh and strained as he struggled against the residual pain; and when he saw that she was not finished, but intended to soak him once again with the fiery water, it took all his strength of mind to refrain from crying out in anguish.

He knew that he could not refuse her permission to do what she had to do, and that he must do his best not to flinch or weep.

He succeeded in this aim. He was a man-at-arms, and courage was his trade. Before an army physician he could have cursed and raved, but this was only a girl, and honour bound him to play a better kind of man. He gritted his teeth as hard as he could, and forced his jaws together while she tortured him again.

I have felt worse, he told himself, insistently. He could not tell whether it was true or not, for pain once soothed cannot properly be remembered – but he knew that he had once had a toothache which threatened to explode his head, and on another occasion he had wished devoutly that he was dead when bad meat set him to retching and retching until he was sure that he would vomit up his own guts. On both occasions, he had survived; the pain had come and gone.

He was puzzled by this effect of the dark water. He had been washed in it when he lay beside the tarn, and had drunk it often, without ever finding it hurtsome in spite of its fiery temperament. He felt resentful for a moment that the tarnwine seemed to have turned against him and become his enemy – but then he realized that it was not the water itself which hurt him but the corruption in his flesh, malevolently resisting the treatment which sought to drive it out, as though it were some kind of mindless daemon.

'Will he recover?' asked Nicodemus, very anxiously.

'I cannot tell,' answered Averil, complainingly. 'Why do you ask me, when you know so much more of these things than I?'

'Mine is the magic of wind and water,' he told her, 'when I have the strength for it. Astyanax was a master, who could turn his hand and mind to the tricks of other disciplines, but I'm nothing but an instrument unformed. We're not healers, not even of little things.'

'You're sparers of pain,' said Harmis, gruffly, 'as I saw last night. Can you not spare me this?'

But he knew they could not. To induce a sleep in order to procure an easeful death was one thing; this was something else. He must fight for his life against the pain, without easy release.

'We must trust the tarnwine,' said Averil to Nicodemus. 'It was for work such as this that Astyanax laboured so long to prepare it.' Then, to Harmis, she said: 'Can you ride?'

Harmis tried to laugh. Ride! he thought. Why, until you put that salve upon my skin I could have ridden all day – but now... but now...

Aloud, he said: 'I can ride. Sable has carried me before when I was ready to fall exhausted to the ground. While I can cling to the saddle, or be tied, I can ride.'

He was a man-at-arms, after all; pride and determination were a matter of duty for him.

'He can't ride far,' said Nicodemus. 'Not if he's to be given time to fight the curse. We must find a place to rest, no matter what delay it causes us. What will it profit us if he ails while I recover? There may be worse to come, and we must be ready to face it. We need a place to hide, at least for a while.'

Hide! thought Harmis. With the Zani warhorde to the north, perhaps to the west as well, and mysterious daemons stalking the land. Wait and hide!

The country they had come to now was not so wild, and there were villages close by, on the fringes of the land which was most fruitfully nourished by the Tana Dante – but there was no way to tell how long they could safely linger while the aurochs herds came inexorably southwards.

Nicodemus and Averil helped Harmis back into the saddle, where he managed to cling without being tied, with all the strength of his good right arm, and he was able to follow them as they took the lead, heading for the cultivated land and whatever civilization might be left in this part of Faramond's little empire.

Gently, the promised rain began to fall.

THE PLACE THEY eventually came to was little more than a roadside hamlet, hardly big enough to contain a public shrine. There were some thirty houses, and a burial-ground marked with Morr's dour portal, fringed with yew trees. Beside the burying ground there was an inn of sorts, where those field-hands who had no permanent home here could come to slake their thirst after a day's labour, and where travellers might lodge.

It was to the inn that Nicodemus and Averil brought Harmis Detz, but they found that the owner of the house had already fled, taking his family and what portion of his wealth he could conveniently carry. How the news of the Zani's coming had reached this isolated place there was no way to tell, but a warning had somehow blown in on an ominous wind, and the wisest of the people had run away as soon as they could, leaving behind those who could not or would not go.

The inn had been looted, but not destroyed. Its supplies of ale and mead had been carried off, but the thieves had behaved in a half-respectful manner, being careful not to do too much damage. A few of the seasonal labourers, who must have been very tired of sleeping in barns and under hedges, had moved into the building – and now, no doubt, regarded it as their own – but they made no immediate objection when the newcomers arrived in the innyard.

Harmis was barely able to dismount in order to walk to the doorway, but he managed to do so without overmuch support from Averil, while Nicodemus stabled the horses.

There were six people inside the inn. They crowded around uncertainly, not knowing how best to respond to the unexpected invasion. No doubt they were glad to see Khyprians instead of Zani, but they were not inclined to offer a warm welcome to anyone at all. When they saw the colours Harmis wore, and the weapons he had, they stifled any objection they might have raised, but there was as much greed as fear in the way they stared. Harmis watched their eyes as he collapsed on a wooden chair, and fancied that he could see the calculations their minds were carrying out: *Can still walk but looks bad; be friendly now, and offer help... but if he should weaken further...*

They did not look so very dangerous; only one was a man in the full flower of his strength, and he was young and callow; the other two men were old, at the very limit of active life. One of the women was old, too, and one was very young; the third, who was apparently in her thirties, was heavily pregnant.

Averil told them her name, and the names of her two companions, but said nothing about being a magician's apprentice. The villagers gave their names in their turn. The two old men were Cavel and Burkin, the younger one Tarik. The old woman, who was Tarik's mother, was Rosola; the pregnant woman was Minorca; the young one, who was Minorca's daughter, was Sanya.

No one offered a second name; for peasants, as for magicians and their apprentices, one name usually sufficed. No doubt the villagers were descended from immigrants from the Empire, or from other realms where it was customary to own a second name, but they would probably be hard-pressed to remember what their family names had been.

Nicodemus came in after the names had been given, but Averil remembered them all for him faultlessly, and pleased them a little with this feat of ready memory.

'We thank you for your hospitality,' said Nicodemus, judiciously. 'We are on the nation's business, and will be gone as soon as we can. We have little food or money, but will gladly pay what we can for our lodging, and whatever help you may be able to give.'

The occupants of the inn must have known how obvious it was that they had no right to be here, but they were glad to take part in the pretence.

The old men nodded, and the one called Burkin promptly appointed himself innkeeper and began to shoo the others away to give his new guests space in which to work.

The apprentices took Harmis's shirt and jerkin off – with difficulty, for both had been soaked by the soft but persistent rain. When the custodians of the inn saw his strange wound they exclaimed with horror and fear, and seemed glad that they had been forbidden to come too close to him.

Nicodemus looked about for a better place to go, and found a large back room which contained a good bed whose linen was not too filthy. Harmis could still walk, and with Averil's help he went slowly from his chair to the other room.

Tarik had been using the bed – in company with Sanya, to judge by appearances – and he was quick to protest against Harmis taking it once he saw that Burkin would not. It was not on his own account that he denied them, he said, but on behalf of Sanya's mother, who was very near her time.

Nicodemus told him firmly that Harmis's need was the greater for the time being, and when he found that no one else would take his side, Tarik backed down.

When Harmis was safely lodged, Nicodemus went out to begin the task of bringing their belongings into the room. With Averil's help, he completed that task, and then closed the door behind him.

'A nest of thieves,' he said, in a low tone. 'Perhaps we should have taken one of the other houses – there are sure to be some which are empty.'

'No matter,' said Averil. 'There are thieves everywhere, and the vultures here might help to keep their fellow carrion birds at bay, while we protect ourselves from them. I don't think they'll try to murder us, for they have still a little common decency alloyed with their fear.'

'But we mustn't linger too long,' said Nicodemus. 'How long will it be before he can ride again?'

'There's no way to tell,' she answered, dully. 'But we have a choice in the matter. One of us might ride alone to Alynda, and bring Ritandyr here – or to some other meeting-place.'

'It would be dangerous,' said Nicodemus. 'This isn't a safe place to stay, even for the three of us. And one man alone on the road – with an unhealed arm – would also offer a ready target.'

'But we haven't time to waste,' she said, 'when every day might be vital.'

Nicodemus said nothing, but he bit his lip nervously as he weighed the alternatives in the balance. 'If we could find a cart,' he said, 'then we might lie him in it.'

'That would force us to remain on the road,' Harmis intervened. 'We might lose more time that way than by waiting. Perhaps tomorrow... if all else fails, I can be tied to my horse. I am a man-at-arms...'

'No,' said Nicodemus, sharply. 'We need you. Astyanax gave us firm instructions. You must rest until the curse within you is defeated, or made very quiet. Averil is right. She or I must ride to Alynda, as quickly as it can be done, to find Ritandyr. He has more power to call upon than either of us, and knows more than we do about the daemonkin who seek to destroy the realm. We must all agree to come together at a suitable place.'

'It's you who must go,' said Averil, 'and very soon.'

Nicodemus did not quarrel with her determination to stay. It would be out of the question for a woman as young as she to ride alone with the order of things breaking down around her. A man with a wounded arm would be vulnerable, but while he had a blade and could conceal the extent of his injury robbers would surely think twice before attacking him – a young girl, even in man's attire, would seem too tempting a target.

'You might be no safer here,' said Nicodemus, pensively. 'If you keep the larger part of our packs... could you defend them against that crew outside?'

'I'm not helpless,' she said. 'And they're not so very fearsome.'

Harmis struggled to sit up, intending to declare that he was no useless slab of meat to be talked over and about, but he could not rise. His right arm was still good and strong, though, and he gestured sternly with his index finger.

'I can fight,' he said, albeit in a croaky way. 'No one will hurt her. Change...'

Weakness made him pause, but neither of them could complete the thought for him, and they had to wait until he could continue.

'Change clothes,' he whispered, finally. 'Take my livery, so that you may display Faramond's colours.' He felt dizzy, and in some strange way the dizziness was worse than the pain – worse, at least, than the ordinary pain which he had when he was not being bathed in that scalding elixir.

Averil nodded to indicate her approval. 'It might keep you safe on the way,' she said to Nicodemus. 'And the roads may not be passable for long. While we come southwards, the Zani will be following behind us, and perhaps moving in from the west also. If we follow, when Harmis has recovered from his hurt, we'll find it easy enough to meet – as long as the Zani can't catch us.'

'Aye,' said Harmis, weakly. 'Where the river bends, there's a town called Cavanal. It has a good broad bridge and many boats, and might be our best chance of crossing over. If we must part now, that's the place to…' Again he could not sustain his speech to the end, but this time it was not necessary.

'They must break that bridge,' muttered Nicodemus. 'But…' Not pain, but uncertainty made his words trail off. Harmis knew well enough what possibilities the youth must have to consider. Suppose Harmis did *not* recover? Did they really need him at all, or could they take his enchanted knives and use the weapons themselves? Dare they mention such a possibility to him?

But it seemed they did not have a clear enough idea of what Ritandyr might require of them to know how badly they might need Harmis – and since he had been bathed in the magical water, the fiery discolouration had ceased to spread. If he was no better, at least he was no worse.

'Take my colours,' said Harmis, again. 'Go to your friend with all possible speed. If we can meet you in Cavanal…'

'And if we cannot,' said Averil, 'then we'll wait here, until the Zani come. If you and Ritandyr can find us, well and good… if not, you must do what you can with what you have.'

There were other things she left unsaid. In the final analysis, she and Harmis might both be reckoned expendable. The apprentices must, after all, count it to their good fortune that either of them was still alive after what had happened at the tarn. Harmis's twin knives were weapons they had not expected to gain, and whose value could not be taken entirely for granted.

'Go,' said Averil. 'Go now, without delay. Take two horses, and a light pack, and change from one to the other as each one tires. You will make better speed alone than the three of us could together. You must find Ritandyr; above all else, you must carry word of Astyanax's fate to Ritandyr, and add your strength to his in whatever magic he can make against the *katharos*.'

Nicodemus bowed to the pressure of her insistence. Nodding his head, he moved towards the door. He knelt down and proceeded to make up a pack from the contents of the two which he had laid in the corner, while Averil gathered all the emblems of Harmis's service for her fellow apprentice to wear.

When Nicodemus was ready, he took off his own jerkin and hose, and put on the bloodstained livery. He took Harmis's sword, and left the shorter blade which was his own. Averil hung the twin knives, in their leather scabbards, from the bed-head.

When Nicodemus had gone, curious faces peered in through the doorway, and Sanya came in to ask if they needed bread and hot tea. Averil said that they did – though they still had a little food of their own – and the girl brought it, though the bread was stale and the tea barely lukewarm.

Harmis contrived to eat one-handed, refusing help from Averil.

When they had finished, Averil bathed his unnatural wound again, and the bathing hurt as badly it had before. Still, he did not cry out – and he told himself sternly that he must not let the villagers know how weak he was, lest they should be encouraged to become troublesome.

Though the pain was very bad while the washing lasted, the relative peace which followed it was soothing, now that he was lying down and did not have to ride. Stillness brought a certain comfort, and Harmis became optimistic that in fact he would soon recover from the awful wound, despite the curse which had been put upon him by the Lazarite's evil eye.

How can I die, he asked himself, in a way as cheering as he could manage? Am I not a hero and slayer of daemon-kin? Are not the good gods too fond of me now to let me perish so simply?

He was a man-at-arms, and knew the ways of the world. He had known other men who believed that there must be a kind of balance between pleasure and pain, and between good and evil, which the gods held firm in answer to some principle of justice, but he could not share that belief. In his opinion, there could be no such balance – for how could the small pleasure which the hawk had in eating be balanced against the mortal agony of the mouse which was its prey? Mercy, as he knew only too well, was far rarer than cruelty, and friendship far less easily discovered than malice. And yet, there *was* mercy in the world, and friendship, and though there was no balance in the order of things, still there was hope.

Whatever troubles the viler gods might heap upon the unlucky world, still there were means to oppose them, and to hurt their malicious servants.

And so, while the pain ebbed away to leave him numb, and the dizziness left him room to think, he said again to himself: I am a slayer of the daemon-kin, and fate has conscripted me for better things than this. I will live.

I will live. I will live…

Sanya came in again, no doubt driven by the urgings of her companions as well her own curiosity, to ask how he was. She had a prettier face than Averil, but her prettiness was masked by anxiety and fear of the enemy's approach. She knew that none was left who could properly protect her.

Averil told her that Harmis was not badly hurt, and would recover.

Minorca and Rosola came in then, curiosity giving them the courage to pry. Minorca had the same cast of features as her daughter, but whatever prettiness she had once had was long since overlain by the marks of strife and strain. Despite her pregnancy her face seemed thin and gaunt, and Harmis guessed that not an hour passed when she did not curse her condition. Khypris was now unfit for the bearing of children. Rosola might conceivably have been pretty once as well, but there was no way now to tell. To imagine her youthful appearance was beyond Harmis's talents, and her face presented itself to him now as a death-mask mounted on a tired frame. No doubt she had been frugal in her living, but life had used her up just the same.

'Where do you come from?' asked Rosola, not looking at either of them when she posed the question.

'Vimera,' replied Averil. 'I am apprentice to Astyanax of Violtis, the greatest wizard in the realm. Nicodemus and I are about his work, which is also Prince Faramond's, and this fighting-man was assigned to help us.' It was not a dishonest answer, but it was a little economical with the truth. It had the desired effect, for Harmis saw the eyes of the two women widen in alarm when Averil named herself a wizard's apprentice.

'I'm from the northlands too,' said the old woman, tentatively. 'Tarik is a good son, who takes good care of me.'

'But I'll need the bed,' said Minorca, very faintly, 'when my time comes, for there are no others left.'

'It's a big bed,' said Rosola. 'I slept in a bed like that when I was younger, with only three others to share.'

'You never slept in such a bed!' Minorca contradicted her. 'On a pallet of straw, more like – that's the best bed in all the town, and the innkeeper wept when he couldn't take it, for he and his sons had never, never slept on the floor.'

'Harmis will be better soon,' said Averil, authoritatively. 'Tomorrow or the next day, he'll be able to ride again, and you'll have your bed to lie on – but in the meantime, I will curse the bones of anyone who lifts a hand against us.'

The two women left, in a hurry, to carry this message back to all those for whom the girl had intended it.

'Perhaps I shouldn't have sent Nicodemus away,' she said, biting her lip. 'Was I wrong, do you think?'

'No,' said Harmis, wanly. 'You were right. He'll find Ritandyr, and we'll meet him in Cavanal. Only pray that Ritandyr will know what to do, for I certainly don't – and nor, I suspect, do you.'

'Perhaps there's nothing to be done,' she whispered, 'now that Astyanax is dead. I should have cleaned your wound last night. I'm too poor a thing to do what's required of me.'

Though his left arm was nearer to her he could not lift it at all, so he reached over with his right to take her head in his worn and horny hand.

'Fear not,' he said. 'If we can but stay alive, we're winners in this deadly game, and if we die... well, we've done what we can, and the Lazarite at least was slain.'

He did not try to stop her when she began to cry, but he clutched her to him so that the sound of her sobbing would not be heard by any other.

An ounce of kindness, he thought, and a cupful of affection. No whore is this, but a white witch without a wrathful bone in her body.

Eventually, she went to sleep, and so did he.

CHAPTER TEN

SLEEP GAVE HARMIS some release from his discomforts, but when he awoke, Averil was ready again with the dark water to bathe his wound. He protested that he did not need it, and that he had taken only the slightest of cuts from the Zani's blade, but he knew as well as she did that the metamorphosis of his flesh would not heal of its own accord.

To make matters worse, he craved the tarnwine more desperately with every day that passed, and though it required only a few drops to be poured down his throat for the need to be eased, it was a need he did not like to have.

'If you can outlast this curse which is upon you,' she told him, when he complained about his condition, 'then you'll no longer thirst so desperately for the tarnwine.'

'And is outlasting all that's required?' he demanded to know. 'Will time alone heal me?'

She shook her head, more in uncertainty than denial. 'I cannot tell,' she said. 'It may be that the curse must unwind to some conclusion of its own. There's a bond, as Astyanax told you, between yourself and the daemon

which commanded the Lazarite; it's possible that the
curse can't be ended until you have faced that creature,
and brought a climax to its time on earth.'

'Ah!' he said, softly. 'Is *that* all I must do, to become
again what I was before. The sorcerer is dead, and now I
must slay its master – and must I then, perchance, take
arms against the wrathful god himself, by whose permission this daemon roams the earth?'

'Do you think it's easy to be a hero?' she said to him. 'Do
you think you can carry daemon-slaying knives without
cost? Do you think that the curse with which the Lazarite
tried to damn your soul is an untroublesome thing to bear,
to be shrugged off like a little scratch? Harmis Detz, this
entire nation is under a curse, and will fall to the forces of
Chaos and the foul breath of plague unless we can save it.
Khypris cannot be saved without pain, and nor can you –
but you can be saved, and so can Khypris, if only you and
the nation can bear what must be done to cauterize the
wounds which Chaos inflicts.'

It was the longest speech he had heard from her, and he
liked her fierceness – though it seemed somehow incon-
gruous in one so round and dull of face. He resolved to put
his complaints away, and bear his burden patiently.

'How did you come to be apprenticed to the wizard?' he
asked. 'It's an odd calling for a daughter of the northlands.'

'My mother was unwed,' she said, simply. 'I was a burden
to her, and she abandoned me in Aldium, to be indentured as a pauper serving-girl. When I was old enough to
work I was sold to a pharmacist, who taught me to find
and mix his potions – but most of his potions had no
other power save to make men drunk, and he was a besot-
ted slave to his own medicines. Astyanax knew him, and
thought that I was nimble enough in the mind and the fingers to be useful. When my first master drank himself to
death, Astyanax took me in. He was a kinder master by far
than the other, and I only wish that I had been a better
pupil. Nicodemus was a better pupil – but then, he was
better born than I, and knew his father's name.'

Remembrance brought tears to her eyes, and Harmis felt sorry for her.

'I had a brother,' he said. 'I had a father and a mother too, but I was not the best of sons. My brother and I were born in Faramond's service, and I'll die surely in it as he did. But Faramond is not a bad master, as masters go, and if a man is fated to be a servant – especially a man-at-arms – then it's best to have a master who stands above all others. In Khypris, there are no better colours to wear than claret-and-gold.'

'There are magician's colours,' she answered, softly. 'In the Empire, it is said, they have wizards who display their calling and prowess in costumes of every glorious hue. Astyanax always spoke of them as though he didn't approve of the custom, but I don't know why.'

'One day you might go to the Empire,' he told her. 'You're not bound, as I am, to Khypris. When this mission is complete, you'll be Ritandyr's apprentice. From Alynda it's easy to see the peaks of the Black Mountains, beyond which the southern reaches of the Empire lie.'

'It has always been easy for me to see the peaks of the Black Mountains,' she reminded him. 'They stood all too clear upon the horizon when I looked out from my room in the house beside the tarn.'

She had stifled her tears, but still she felt compelled to go away, so that she need not face him and let him see how weak she was. He wanted to tell her that he understood her distress, and that he had faith in her courage and her fortitude, but he did not know how to talk to a woman in such a confidential fashion, and so he said nothing at all.

More than once that day the fiery application of the tarn-wine to his wound brought Harmis near to weeping himself, and it was all he could do to avoid surrender to the racking sobs which threatened to overtake him. He could feel the sweat standing out on his face at such times; and when each laving was over he felt that his soul had turned to ash and ember, blackened and enfeebled inside him.

But every time the pain passed, he could feel more strength returning to his body, and he mustered the conviction that he would soon be whole again, and well. And when the night came, he slept.

HE WAS NOT awake when they brought Minorca in to lie beside him on the bed. Nightmares had him in their teasing grip, and when he woke, blinking against the lamplight, to see her there beside him – with the sweat standing on her face as it had earlier stood on his – he thought at first that she was some illusory grinning daemon sent to taunt him.

Then Averil spoke to him, from where she stood with Sanya and Rosola, saying: 'I couldn't deny her, Harmis, for the birth seems set to be difficult. But you must stay where you are. It's a big bed, and there's room for you both.'

Harmis did not want to stay in the bed, for there was something strangely disturbing about the prospect of the woman giving birth beside him. He felt well enough, though weak, and immediately tried to rise – but the witch-girl commanded him to be still, and he contented himself with making as much room as he could for Minorca.

The woman smiled at him, though it required an effort for her to do it. Harmis took heart from that, for it seemed that she shared his burden, and the burden of his duty to the nation – which, in a way, she did, for though Faramond's soldiers were the armour of the princedom, mothers of all classes were its beating heart.

Rosola and Sanya fluttered about the room like moths, but it was Averil who took the lead in tending the pregnant woman. In these backward lands all midwives were suspected of being witch-women, and hence all witch-women were expected to be midwives. Rosola and Sanya expected it of Averil, and Averil expected it of herself, though Harmis was sure that she could never have attended at a birth before.

How much time passed while Minorca lay beside him Harmis could not tell. It was a time of waiting, while he was still disturbed by his wound and its violent treatment, and he could not measure it well. He might have slept again, briefly, while lamplight was replaced by daylight, and he remembered that at one point Averil gave him bread to eat, but for the most part he simply lay still and watched Minorca racked by the stresses and strains of her child's passage from womb to world.

At last, Averil said: 'Now!' and Harmis saw Sanya and Rosola crowd in close to see. Averil bent down, and Harmis – overcome by sudden curiosity – tried to prop himself up on his elbows.

All Minorca's effort was concentrated on expelling the child; she sucked in air desperately and blew it out explosively. Harmis felt nauseous as he tried to rise, and lay back again before the infant's head made its appearance.

Time seemed distorted while the next few seconds elapsed. It was Rosola's reaction which first told Harmis that something was wrong, for the horror came upon her while Sanya's face was still blank and uncomprehending – but all the old woman did was gasp and turn away.

Then Sanya screamed.

Harmis sat up quickly, ignoring the wave of dizziness which swept through him.

Averil was holding the infant in her arms, having lifted it from the bed. She was staring at it as though numbed by shock. It was very red in colour, and unquestionably alive, but its head was deformed – more ratlike than rounded – and its flailing upper limbs were more like paddles than arms. As Sanya's scream died away the child began to whimper plaintively, and Averil laid it down beside its snaky afterbirth.

Minorca was bleeding heavily, and Harmis saw her face whiten with a relief which was altogether too extreme.

'You did it!' screeched Rosola, stabbing a bony finger at Averil. 'You cursed her, witch-woman! You cursed her child!'

'No,' said Averil, softly but urgently. 'You don't understand! I didn't do anything.'

Harmis shoved himself along the bed, knowing that the situation was out of control. He had heard Averil threaten them, to make them afraid of her, and he knew that she had succeeded only too well. Though the monster had been in Minorca's womb for months, it had been born into Averil's hands, and the blame for its deformity had come with it. Rosola and Sanya were not capable of a considered reaction; they only knew that Averil had threatened to curse them, and they believed that now they were accursed.

The door had opened and Harmis could see Cavel and Burkin in the background, curious to understand the screaming but by no means anxious to come forward. Tarik was not so reluctant, and when he saw the condition of his mother and the horror-stricken Sanya his expression became ugly. He took Sanya by the shoulders as if to draw her away, but he did not take her out. His eyes were fixed on the child.

Harmis was standing by now, coming between Rosola and Averil. He met the old woman's wrath with his own, commanding her to be silent and to get out. Rosola could not continue her tirade, and stepped back as fear displaced her anger. It was all absurd, for if Averil had been guilty of that of which they accused her, they could only attract more damage to themselves by loud complaints and intemperate threats – but the fear which had been building in them since the other villagers ran away was bursting forth now like a volcanic eruption, and they no longer had control of themselves.

Harmis turned abruptly to Tarik, and told him to take Sanya away – and though the youth scowled, he backed away with his mother.

Harmis felt so weak that he had to support himself by leaning on the bed, but he knew that his presence was still menacing. On the other hand, his own sense of horror had been awakened too, and he took care to keep his distance from the partly-human child, whose whimpering was dying now.

Minorca was already unconscious, her white face bearing a ghostly smile. Her blood was soaking the mattress profusely, and Harmis knew that she was dying with her offspring. He looked back at the others, who were still in retreat, and while he stared at them as balefully as he could they withdrew, and allowed him to close the door.

'It was no fault of mine!' said Averil, faintly.

'No one was at fault,' he answered, roughly. 'No one. But we can't stay here now. We must ride after Nicodemus, or to Cavanal. We must make ready.'

But when he had said it, he found that he was no longer strong enough to stand, and though he did not want to, he sat down again upon the bed, bemoaning his affliction.

'Lie down,' she commanded him. 'I'll do what must be done.'

He did not lie down, but he let her go from the room alone, and he sat as if drugged while she brought Cavel and Rosola back in. She gave them orders sternly, and they obeyed – not because she was a magician who might hurt them, but because they did not know what else to do, and were content to be told.

They took the child away. Then, when they were sure that she was dead, they took Minorca too.

Averil spread a blanket over the vast bloodstain, as though by hiding it she could blot out the memory of what had happened. Then she instructed Harmis to lie down again and rest.

He continued to fight against sleep, determined that he must maintain his vigilance while the danger lasted, and quite certain that the danger would remain until they were away from this place. Averil tried to reassure him, telling him at intervals that Tarik was quietly digging a grave; that the two old men had gone scavenging for food; and that all was quiet and mended.

Darkness came again, and dawn followed so very smoothly that he knew his resolve must have betrayed him, and that he had slept – but he felt all the stronger for it, and when Averil looked at his wound she said that it

was healing normally now, and that the curse had been
defeated for the time being; there need be no further pur-
gation by the fiery water, and no more pain.

He ate ravenously of the bread which Averil gave him,
and drank some water which was sweeter by far than the
magical water of the tarn – though he had to take his
ration of the latter too.

By noon he could stand with ease, and he put all his
clothes on, including his sword-belt and the harness in
which his knives were carried. Averil called to Tarik, asking
him to help her load the horses, but he refused.

When Harmis and Averil carried out the first of their
packs between them, Harmis saw that the young man was
still in a poor temper; he was whispering in conspiratory
fashion with his mother. Nevertheless, they both seemed
to be glad that their unwelcome guests were leaving.

Cavel and Burkin were nowhere to be seen, and nor was
Sanya at first, but when Harmis and Averil came back from
the stable a second time, in order to collect the remainder
of their belongings, the girl was standing on the stairway
which led to the upper part of the house. She had evidently just come down from above. She stared at them, her
eyes full of hate – and Harmis could see that while Rosola
had forgotten the accusation which she had flung at Averil,
Sanya had not. While Rosola had seen the sense of waiting
quietly until Harmis and the magician's apprentice left,
Sanya's wrath had seethed and festered like a wound gone
bad.

'Witch!' cried the girl. 'Do you take your evil elsewhere
now? Or will your master-daemon be content for now
with the blood which you have paid to him, and with my
mother's soul?'

'I have no pact with any daemon,' said Averil, quietly,
'and your mother died, in the end, at peace. The curse
which was upon her came from another source, and one
whose enemy I am.'

'Liar!' said Sanya. 'Until you came here, all was well –
and all would have been well still, had you not put your

stricken lover in my mother's birthing-bed, and bought his life with another.'

'It's not true,' said Harmis. 'It's not true, and you mustn't think it.'

Sanya was further enraged by these denials. 'I know it!' she shouted. 'If I had any power to curse, I would curse you both! Were there any god who would avenge my mother's fate, I'd call upon his wrath, and bid him make you suffer as you made her suffer when you spoiled the child which was waiting in her womb.'

The colour drained from Averil's face as this was said, and Harmis saw that she was genuinely afraid.

'You must not call upon such gods as those,' he said, harshly, 'for you cannot tell what the consequence of such an invitation might be.'

But this served only to heighten Sanya's vengeful madness. The girl leapt from the stair and flew at Averil, determined to strike her about the face. Averil had to put down the saddle she carried, and grab the girl's wrists – but she rendered the blows quite impotent by virtue of her superior strength.

After only a few moments of struggling, Averil hurled Sanya away from her, making her fall.

'Little fool!' hissed the witch-girl. 'You know nothing! There are daemons in Khypris, to be sure, but you must not call upon them, lest they answer your call and steal your very soul away!'

Tarik left his mother then, and went to Sanya instead, picking her up from where she had fallen. Harmis did not know, at first, whether he simply intended to help her up, or to hold her back from further foolishness. Whatever he intended he only succeeded in providing an easier target for her pent-up anger, for she lashed out at him as fiercely as if he had been the murderer of her mother instead of her friend.

Astonished by her reaction, Tarik hit back, more brutally than was necessary, and split her lip badly. Then he turned to Averil, drawing the dagger from his belt.

Harmis immediately dropped all that he was carrying, and drew the short sword which Nicodemus had left him in place of his own, stepping in front of Averil as he did so.

For a moment, the youth and the soldier stared one another in the eye. Harmis made no move to attack, but simply waited.

Tarik must have known that he had no chance at all in combat with a trained swordsman – even one enfeebled by a wound. His own small blade was ridiculous even in the face of Harmis's half-sized weapon, and with a sword of his own he could only have proved himself clumsy and inept.

'Drop it,' said Harmis, quietly – and when Tarik reluctantly obeyed, Harmis took the dagger up and hurled it through the open doorway, as far as he could. 'The Zani are coming,' he said, 'from the north, and perhaps from the west. You have enemies enough, without expending your fury on those who would do you no harm. Hide if you can from those who come behind us, and pray to the best gods, not the worst.'

Sanya's anger at last gave out, and she fell to crying bitter tears.

'Go!' said Tarik, bitterly. 'Go, and be saved or damned as the gods decide. What difference do you think there is to the likes of us, between one master and another, one god or another? Leave us alone, so that we may play the part of innkeeper's guests, until your friends arrive to fire the fields, or your enemies to harass us for what little plunder we have taken from the ruins.'

Harmis put the sword back into its scabbard, and picked up the things he had dropped. Was this, he wondered, how heroes were always received in the world which they set out to save?

Outside, the sun was very bright and the air was much cleaner. The day was hot and still, and that cold and clammy night when the uncanny mists had sheltered the mutants in their work of slaughter seemed very distant, as though those events had taken place in another world.

Harmis mounted Sable, not without difficulty, and immediately wheeled her around to face the afternoon sun.

'Let's ride,' he said to Averil, gritting his teeth against the sickness which still had not been completely banished from his body. 'Let's do what work we can to save this good and grateful world from the evil which intends to claim it.'

'I would have saved her if I could,' said Averil, bitterly, 'and would have made her child perfect, had I that kind of magic and that kind of power. But my magic is of another sort, and unimproved by learning or long practice.'

'Aye,' said Harmis, 'I know it. The world is full of wizards who would set it to rights if they could, but the weight of the curses which have been visited upon it by bad and reckless men is beyond any power of healing. I don't doubt that magic is an awesome power, but neither can I doubt that I was wise to follow the profession of arms, and put such trust as I have in the power of the arrow and the blade.'

This speech annoyed her, and she changed her tune. 'You don't know what power the best magic has,' she told him, darkly. 'And though doubtless you think me very feeble, and Nicodemus too, we have our own part to play in what will come.'

'I'll be glad to see it played,' replied Harmis, shouting now because Sable was cantering and her mount was hurrying to keep up. If she made any reply, it was lost in the rush of their progress, as they rode towards their rendezvous in Cavanal.

CHAPTER ELEVEN

As DUSK FELL Harmis and Averil were ascending to the top of a long ridge which cut across the moorland like a huge natural wall, running from north-west to south-east. From the crest of the ridge they could look northwards across the hills to a more distant horizon than any they had seen since they quit the crags around the tarn.

The northern horizon was shrouded in what seemed to be a thick mist which caught the red rays of the setting sun and shone in an oddly metallic way, grey and purple.

'Is it the smoke from fires?' asked Averil. 'Have they begun to burn the fields?'

Harmis looked to the east, towards the great north road which ran from Khypris to Aldium. There a few thin plumes of smoke could be seen, but nothing to indicate that any large-scale burning was as yet underway.

'Aurochs again,' said Harmis. 'The herds of the Zani. Hundreds of thousands of beasts, hurrying towards Cavanal. Their keepers have spread them out into a broad host, but its centre is directly behind us. We've lost what time we had to spare, thanks to my wound. They'll reach the banks of the Tana Dante no more than two days behind us. Even if the burning were to begin tomorrow, and even if tomorrow were as bright and hot as today, the fields are too green to be easily destroyed. The beasts will have plenty to eat, while their masters try to make a bridge-head for themselves.'

She did not react at all to this news, but urged her horse forward again on to the downward slope, intending to make good use of whatever twilight there was. Harmis followed her meekly, and was content to let her find a spot to rest for the night. When he finally tumbled from the saddle he felt utterly exhausted, but not sick. The wound in his shoulder no longer gave him much pain, even when it had to be bathed in the tarnwine.

Averil did not make a fire for fear of attracting unwelcome attention, but they were able to eat a little from their dwindling store, and to drink fresh water from a stream. They each slept for a while, one after the other, but woke with the first light of dawn and made haste to resume their journey.

In the valley below they forded a tributary of the great river, and followed its course for a while until they came to farmlands, and to another village little different from the one where they had stayed. Here they saw how much their delay had cost them. Like the other, the village had been abandoned by most of its inhabitants, but a Zani warband had already been here to attack those who had stayed behind, and to carry off what loot there was.

From some distance away Harmis could see that there were dead horses and dead men in the streets. When he had come a little closer, he was able to confirm what he had immediately suspected; many of the dead were liveried as he had been in the Prince's claret-and-gold. One of the first and least battles of the war had been fought here, and his own side had got by far the worst of it.

Harmis urged Sable forward, but looked about him anxiously as he went, lest the Zani should still be about. When he reached the first corpse, he was able to see that the man had probably been killed during the night. Like those he had attacked in the gypsy camp, the Zani who had done this had come a long way ahead of their herds – and having met armed opposition must have gone swiftly back to safer ground.

Harmis looked for the inn which would be the centre of the village. Thought of the sad band of scavengers he had found in the last place made him unenthusiastic, but duty impelled him to discover whether any of the Prince's men-at-arms had survived, and to offer such help as he could. He also wanted to be sure that Nicodemus was not among the slain, for the apprentice had surely come this way, and might not have had time to pass through before the fighting broke out.

The innyard was littered with bodies, and it was obvious that this was where the fiercest defence had been mounted. There were no horses left in the stables, and Harmis judged from this that the survivors had gone on their way – but even while he looked he heard a voice calling to him from inside. He drew his sword, but put it away again when the door opened and a liveried man appeared there, bandaged about the head and raggedly wounded in the right arm.

'Who are you?' demanded the wounded man, made bad-tempered by his injuries.

'Harmis Detz,' replied Harmis. 'Once of the Border Guard, now appointed to special duties.'

'Special duties be damned,' said the other, now looking past Harmis at Averil, who had ridden up behind him with the pack-horse. 'A deserter with a pretty whore, more like. But I'm extremely glad to see you, my friend, however you came to cast off your colours, for there are others wounded within and we have no horse to put between the shafts of a cart. We must reach Cavanal by tomorrow, or we'll never get across the Tana Dante.'

Harmis dismounted, and went to the doorway where the other man stood waiting. He looked back at Averil, who had remained on her horse. She wore a deep frown, and he

knew that she did not want him to give up their one spare
horse to haul a cart for the wounded soldiers.

The soldier looked at the cut on Harmis's neck, which
was still ugly although the flesh around it was no longer
spoiled.

'You've met the Zani yourself, I see,' he said, in a more
amiable tone. 'I'm Garin Sarkar, of Captain Byrin's command. The man on the couch is Malo Hauser; the one in
the chair is Gotthard Meriden. The sister of mercy who
tended our wounds is named Asmunda.'

It was so gloomy within that Harmis could not see at first
what Sarkar meant by a 'sister of mercy,' but then someone
moved from the shadows behind the couch on which lay a
man with a badly wounded leg. She had silky black hair
and tanned skin which was almost lustrous in the thin ray
of sunlight that played upon it as she passed by the cur-
tained window. She was very beautiful, but seemed
extremely tired. She smiled at Harmis, rather wanly.

'We have only the one horse unridden,' said Harmis,
'and our mission is urgent.'

Sarkar scowled, and said: 'The saving of our lives is no
less urgent – and a good deal more than that to us. Cavanal
is only one day's ride from here, and if your duty is as special as you think, Byrin or any other captain will give you
new mounts. You cannot leave three comrades-in-arms and
an innocent girl for the Zani horde to find.'

'Your companions left you,' Harmis pointed out.

'They rode north,' countered the wounded man. 'They
have duties to perform which are not so very special, and
from which they will likely not return. They would have
given us a horse, had they one unridden. I do not care how
fully-laden your pack-horse is – you cannot leave us here.'

It was true, and Harmis knew it. He could not abandon
these men to certain death while he had a horse that might
draw their cart. They wore the same colours as he, and had
he been in their situation, he would expect no less – even
from a man in plain dress, who had a paper warrant to set
him above the common run of his kind.

Averil had dismounted by now, and she came to stand in the doorway behind them while Harmis moved forward to look at the two men who could not walk. Both would live, if they could get to Cavanal in time to be taken over the river, by whatever means were to hand. Harmis looked each of them up and down, feeling their anxious eyes upon him and Sarkar scowled again, more angrily than before.

'Oh, measure us all,' he said. 'With my head cut and my sword-arm slashed, I can do you no harm – and these two haven't the legs to chase you if you decide to run away. We cannot fight you for your horses, but are entirely at your mercy. Nevertheless, you know that if you left us here, it would be murder.'

Harmis knew that there was no point in protesting that others might come this way before the enemy. He had already estimated that the Zani herds could not be more than two days away. But he did say: 'Even if you can reach Cavanal, you may not be able to cross the river, for the order has already gone forth to break the bridge.'

'There are boats,' retorted Sarkar. 'And if I know my captain, he'll leave the breaking of the bridge until the Zani are near enough to cross swords.'

Harmis shook his head. 'They'll not wait,' he said. 'Not this time. But you're right, there are boats. And Cavanal must be defended, by every man who can get there in time to take a hand. Averil – unload the horse, and keep only what we need most desperately, in packs which we can fit behind our saddles.'

'We cannot tarry long,' she said, very uneasily. He could tell that she wanted to say no, but he knew that she dared not say it aloud, with the eyes of the wounded men upon her. She could not reckon the pressure of her own duty in the same way that Harmis reckoned his, but even a magician's apprentice could not ignore the demands of common humanity.

'Do it,' said Harmis, firmly. Then, to Sarkar, he said: 'We can't stay to help you. You and the girl must lift the others to the cart, and see to the horse's harness. I would give you what protection I could, if I had the choice, but I have orders from the commander in Aldium, and must ride on ahead as quickly as I can. I hope I'll see you in Cavanal, if I'm still there when you arrive.'

Sarkar semed unsure as to whether to protest that this generosity fell short of the mark he desired, or to be grateful for what he had. In the end, he said: 'Very well. I hope that we'll meet again. At least we have Asmunda, and though we're too lame to use her as we might, she is a better sight to look upon than your own whore – and I don't think she likes us well enough to stay behind, had you offered to take her with you, in place of your plain companion.'

Harmis looked grimly back at him, and replied: 'Averil is apprentice to the wizard Astyanax, not a whore. Nor does your sister of mercy have the appearance of a whore, unless she's a lady of the court, for she has none of the scars of humble birth.'

Sarkar only scowled, as though determined to pay his benefactor back for the poor quality of the generosity he had received.

But Asmunda, who had heard the exchange, put out a hand to soothe and restrain the injured man. She looked straight into Harmis's eyes, and smiled at him, in gratitude for his defence of her character. For a moment, he thought that she was offering herself in the exchange which Sarkar had mentioned, trying to tempt him; but then she lowered her eyes again and made him ashamed to have thought it.

'Don't worry,' she said. 'I can hitch the horse to the cart, and get these men aboard it. I'll get them to Cavanal, if I can. You have our gratitude, for you have given us all a chance to live.'

Her thanks were a heavier burden on his conscience than Sarkar's evident bitterness. Had she pleaded with him to stay and lend assistance, he would have found it difficult to refuse.

'The Zani herds are only three days from Cavanal,' he said. 'The hillmen must know now that their way is clear. I doubt that other raiders will come on ahead, for their war-lords will be intent on gathering them together, to fight a fierce battle along the river's shore.'

'I hope you're right,' said the girl. 'I'll get these men to Cavanal if I can – you may depend on it.'

Sarkar stood by, with a suspicion of a sneer upon his lips, while Harmis bowed and turned away.

Averil was waiting outside, ready to mount her own horse. She had loaded Sable with as much as the mare could carry, and her own animal likewise. Parts of their pack were strewn about the yard, but none of the tarnwine had been set aside. The unladen horse was tethered to a water-pump.

'We may see a thousand people yet to whom we can give no help,' she said, calmly. 'Do you think that man would have hesitated to kill us if he could, so that he might take our horses by force?'

'I'm sure that he would hesitate,' said Harmis, dourly. It was true – but he did not doubt that after hesitating, a man like Sarkar might act. He looked uneasily back at the windows of the inn, fearing to see an arrow aimed at his heart. But there was no evident threat, and in a few moments Asmunda came to the door alone, to watch them depart.

'Good luck to you,' said Harmis, ignoring Averil's disapproval. 'I hope they'll take you across the river, with the soldiers.'

'I think they will,' she said. 'I have something which might persuade them.' The smile she flashed at him made him think that she meant to barter her body for a passage, but then she laughed.

'Money,' she said, by way of explanation, and showed him what she had clutched in her right hand. There were several coins there, which glittered in the light as if they had been freshly minted. They were Imperial coins, not the poor debased things stamped out in Khypris, and they gave every appearance of being gold.

An ounce of gold, thought Harmis, and a cupful of blood. If this is in fact a whore, she is one of very high price, for what she holds in her hand is very much more than an ounce.

'I would have bought your horse,' said Asmunda, 'had you not offered to give it freely. But I may need this gold if I'm to get across the Tana Dante and make my way to Khypris, for if I know Captain Byrin, the price of a ferryman will be very high by now. If you intend to cross the river, I wish you luck.'

'We have all that we need to see us both across,' said Averil, coldly, 'and our horse would not have been for sale, had we not been ready to part with it for mercy's sake.'

But Asmunda only laughed again at that, very prettily, and looked at Harmis as if to say that he might easily have been persuaded, by one such as she. Harmis did not attempt to deny it. There was, he thought, something of a plain girl's mean-spirited jealousy of a beauty in the way that Averil addressed Asmunda – and it was surely out of place, given that Asmunda, whether or not she was a whore, had pledged herself to rescue the three wounded men.

Harmis was suddenly conscious, though, that he had no more than a few copper coins in his own pouch – hardly enough to buy a flagon of ale. He did not think Averil had much more. Would his paper warrant, he wondered, be enough to get the two of them safe and speedy passage across the river?

Averil was already turning her horse away, and Harmis – with one last salute to the lovely Asmunda – was about to follow her example when the girl suddenly ran forward. She did not call out, but only flung something through the air, which he caught in his left hand with an ease which surprised him, in view of his recent troubles.

It was a single gold coin.

He looked back at her in astonishment, but she only smiled again, and turned to stroke the horse which he had left behind. She patted it gently on the neck; then she gave

Harmis one last wave of thanks, before he had to follow
the wizard's apprentice, who had not looked back.

Although Sable was more heavily burdened now,
Harmis urged her into a canter. In the course of their journey they had used up most of their food and a good deal
of the water from the tarn, so the pack behind his saddle
was not so very large – and when they reached Cavanal,
Sable would have every opportunity to rest. It did not take
him long to catch up with his companion.

Paradoxically, the gold which he had not asked for – and
which he would probably have refused, had she offered it
in exchange for the horse – made him feel even better
about having done his duty to his brothers-in-arms; somehow, he felt sure that they would all reach Cavanal in
safety, and that Khypris itself might yet be saved.

THEY HAD NOT gone much further when they began to catch
up with the crowds hurrying towards Cavanal. Although
they tried to keep clear of the road there was no way they
could avoid continual meetings with the southward flock-
ing refugees, who were all afoot and all made desperate by
their determination to carry what they could of their possessions. Sarkar's was only the first of many pleas for help
they heard that day, but they had no alternative now but to
be deaf to them all, and to make haste to reach the place
appointed for their meeting with Nicodemus and Ritandyr.

They had not quite reached the town before nightfall.
Averil consented to break her resentful silence long
enough to tell Harmis that they must not stop now, for fear
of being attacked and robbed, but must press on until they
reached a safe haven. Harmis guessed that the time was
rapidly approaching when she might be very glad to have
the means to hire a ferryman, but he did not tell her about
the gold he had acquired, and listened patiently while she
said they must continue to ride by the light of lanterns –
and when he said that they had but one, because
Nicodemus had taken the other, she replied that he must
take it and share out its light as best he could.

He tried to do it, but the lantern was too feeble to light their way efficiently, and she was forced at last to give him proof that she had some power in the Arts Magical. She took a small crystal rod from her reduced belongings, and held it in her hand until its tip glowed very brightly – and this she used to let the horses find their way.

Harmis was glad when they were forced to find and take the road. There were many others camped along its length, some of whom had lit lanterns of their own. There were doubtless many robbers and vagabonds mixed in with the folk who had no other thought than to preserve their lives, but he did not think it was dangerous for him to travel this way, even though he had no colours, and had gold in his pocket and a young woman in his charge. There were many others who offered safer and more obvious targets to those of predatory inclination.

When they reached the town at last they found it very crowded; though the hour was such that the streets should have been at peace, they were in turmoil. There were soldiers everywhere, and their presence was sufficient to maintain a sullen and resentful kind of order, but the noise of countless fearful arguments was in the air.

By far the greater part of Cavanal was on the other shore of the river, but the northern sector was by no means tiny, and nearly a thousand people must have lived here before the refugees began to flood in from elsewhere. Though many must have crossed the river when the first rumours of danger came, that number had been replaced sixfold in the meantime.

Harmis did not delay at all once they had reached their goal, and he spurred Sable through the streets despite that she was tired enough to drop. He had to force her through the crowds, who were by no means inclined to let him pass while he was not in the Prince's colours, but when he called out to the patrolling soldiers that he had a message for Captain Byrin, and waved his paper in the air, they were quick to make a way for him. Paper had a power of its own which even claret-and-gold could not possess.

When they finally reached the bank of the river Harmis thought for one moment that the bridge still stood unbroken, and he knew from Averil's gasp that she thought the same. Then he realized that there were men at work on the business of demolition even while he watched. The arch which extended from the further shore to the first of the four great stone columns set in the river's bed had been removed already, and now the men were working on the second arch, breaking the stone with hammers and picks and tumbling the debris into the river.

And yet the bridge was not entirely closed – for in place of the broad span which had been broken there now extended a thinner bridge made of rope and logs, and across that narrow passage went a steady stream of men and horses. On the part of the bridge which remained there was a great and very quarrelsome crowd, many of them protesting that they had carts to take over, while others screeched about the toll which was being asked of those admitted to the slender walkway.

'They have disobeyed the order!' wailed Averil. 'What fools they are!'

Harmis could not share her opinion – indeed, he thought that the captain in charge of the bridge must be an exceedingly clever fellow, to keep the bridge open to his own folk while making ready to frustrate the enemy.

'They've obeyed it,' he contradicted her, 'in the best way they could. If it's not what Astyanax wanted, I'm sorry – but I don't think we could expect anything more of these people than they have done. We're a long way from Khypris, and Byrin's men owe a loyalty to others as well as Faramond.'

There was plenty of light near the approach to the bridge, but the crowds were so thick that they could not get closer. Harmis had to dismount, and ask a soldier where Captain Byrin was to be found. He was glad when the man pointed away from the melee at the bridgehead, towards a warehouse which had been commandeered for temporary headquarters.

'Let's pray that he can read, or can find a scrivener to read the paper to him,' Harmis said to Averil, 'for the man in charge of all this will certainly have no patience to spare, and won't be readily persuaded of our need to cross.'

'Perhaps we shouldn't go to the southern shore,' said Averil, 'for it will be far more difficult than I'd anticipated to discover Nicodemus and Ritandyr in a crowd like this, and we can't be sure that Ritandyr will succeed in making the crossing.'

'It'll not be safe to stay on this side if we can get across tonight,' said Harmis, anxiously. 'And what if Nicodemus has crossed already? He and Ritandyr might be waiting on the other shore.'

'Can we get across the bridge tonight?' asked Averil, who seemed to be in doubt as to whether she would rather be told that it was possible or not.

'Aye,' said Harmis. 'We may have to wait a little while for our turn, but when we've shown the paper which the commander at Aldium gave me, we'll be allowed to cross before the greater number of these people.'

Averil was still uncertain, but they had reached Byrin's headquarters by now and Harmis dismounted, showing his paper to the sentries at the door. He was allowed to go inside, and the fact that he had orders from Aldium moved him quickly past a throng of excited civilians, every one of whom was desperate to place some kind of petition before the captain. Averil followed him.

Byrin proved to be a much younger man than Harmis had expected, and it was obvious that he was the son of one of Faramond's most favoured nobles; he wore red-and-white in place of claret-and-gold, and was very handsomely armoured, though he seemed near to exhaustion from strain and lack of sleep. Somewhat to Harmis's surprise, the young man took the warrant from him immediately and held it to the light, muttering something about a 'foul hand.'

When Byrin had read the paper, his reaction was not what Harmis had expected or hoped. 'There are two named here who are supposedly in your charge,' said the captain, sharply. 'Where's the other?'

'He went on ahead when I was wounded,' answered Harmis. 'He took my livery and my helmet to keep him safe. We're supposed to meet him here, when he comes from Alynda with the wizard Ritandyr. We don't know whether they've already crossed the bridge.'

'They have not,' snapped Byrin, thrusting the paper back at him with a carelessness which only a literate man could have achieved. 'Your orders say that I may not use you to defend Cavanal, but they say nothing about pandering to your craving for personal safety. If your duty is to defend two people, it demands that you wait for the second, not flee with one. I have horses and fighting-men to move across the bridge, and a town to defend. I can only say to you what I say to all: if you join the line you may have your chance to cross when your turn comes, tomorrow or the next day.'

Harmis opened his mouth to protest, but was not given the opportunity. The captain had not time for argument, and he had guards to make sure that no man could over-stay his welcome. Harmis found himself escorted away, not roughly but insistently.

Averil was not so displeased; she merely allowed the captain's order to confirm her half-conviction that it would be best to remain on the northern shore while they waited for Nicodemus and Ritandyr. When Harmis reminded her that the Zani were little more than two days away she simply shrugged.

'Perhaps,' said Harmis dourly, 'we'd better pray that your friend knows a spell which will allow us to walk on water.'

'We didn't come here to escape the Zani,' she answered, 'but in the hope of finding a way to oppose the *katharos*.'

'I fear,' said Harmis, 'that unless we accomplish the first, we may not have a chance to attempt the other.'

They made their slow way back to the main road which led to the bridge, and there consented to be assigned a place among those who desired to cross to the heartland by the soldiers whose task it was to keep discipline in the crowd. There was a great deal of noise about them, but not – as yet – any real challege to that discipline, for if the soldiers were too sorely annoyed they simply took those who annoyed them from their places in the queue and moved them to the rear.

No matter how fretful the waiting people had become, they still had faith at this point in time that waiting would see them through. Not until that faith began to wane would there be any serious threat to the army's authority – and even then, if the people were wise, they would submit to that authority, for the order which the army kept was much to be preferred to a violent anarchy which might see the rope bridge cut and every available boat requisitioned for the soldiers' use.

'We must search for Nicodemus,' said Averil, impatiently. 'We'll have no need of a place here, if we can't find him.'

'In the morning,' said Harmis, 'I'll go abroad to look for Nicodemus while you remain to keep our place. In the meantime, we'll stay where we are, and be grateful for what we have. We must try to sleep – or at least to rest.'

With that, the witch-girl had to be content, for Harmis was determined that although he would do whatever his duty demanded of him, he would make every possible effort to cross the river as well.

He saw no other hope of staying alive.

CHAPTER TWELVE

WHEN MORNING CAME, Harmis firmly instructed Averil to remain in the place which had been given to them, with their belongings and the two horses. There were numerous men-at-arms assigned to the business of keeping order, and he judged that she would be as safe there as anywhere – but he showed them his paper, to make certain they would remember him.

'I'll search the throng from one end to the other,' he assured the girl. 'If Nicodemus is here, I'll find him.'

He was as good as his word. He went to the bridge again, waving his paper imperiously at any who challenged him, and then made his way back along the road very carefully, scanning the crowd for the young man's face. When he had reached the point at which he started he did not pause, but continued on, looking at all those who had taken their places in the later hours of darkness. There were more of these than he had expected, but Nicodemus was not among them. Only one familiar face was among those still trickling into the outskirts of the town, and that was Asmunda's.

She was on foot; there was no sign of the horse he had given to her, or of Garin Sarkar and his lame companions. She greeted him warmly, before he could speak for himself, and said: 'Are there boats to carry us across? What price do they ask?'

'Byrin has put up a bridge of rope and wooden beams,' he told her. 'He says we'll be allowed to cross over today, though his first priority is to move his fighting men across.'

She laughed, in a way which was ironic but not unpleasant. 'Promises,' she said. 'How many people are waiting?'

He shrugged, and said: 'Not too many for the bridge to bear – provided that the Zani will allow us one more day. But if five hundred more should come, and another troop of soldiers... I would gladly take you into the place we have in the line, but if others protested, the soldiers would order you back.'

'It's not necessary,' she told him, lightly. 'I have gold enough to get a better position than the one you would gladly give me. I shall cross before noon – you may depend on it.'

Conscious that part of her little hoard of gold was in his pouch, Harmis could only shrug his shoulders again.

'Will it take you all the way to Khypris?' he asked.

'Oh yes,' she assured him. 'Even in times like this, a handful of gold may obtain almost any objective. I'll reach Khypris sooner than any of *these* people.'

He did not doubt it. 'Where is Sarkar?' he asked. 'Did he bring his companions safely back?'

'He did,' she assured him. 'All three of them are here, and alive. They too will be taken across the river as soon as possible.'

'I'm glad to hear it,' he said. He spoke awkwardly, feeling that he ought to be about his business, yet not wanting to go. She was a remarkably pretty woman, and he felt drawn to her in a way which he did not quite understand. He saw little enough of women, except for whores, and in spite of the way that this one looked him frankly in the eye, and smiled so freely, he could not believe that she was a common whore.

'How did you come to be in that village where we found you?' he asked. 'By your appearance you are well-born, and your accent is that of the Khyprian gentlefolk. How did you come to be playing ministering angel to three wounded soldiers?'

'I had travelled from the north,' she said. 'I fear that I am not so nobly born as you suppose – my father is only a leather-merchant, though he sought to take advantage of my comeliness to make an advantageous marriage for me, and had me carefully educated in the manners of our betters. I begged him to take me with him when he went to Aldium to see to his business there – my brother was with him too. He sent us both south when the rumours of invasion first began, but we were attacked by the Zani who had fought the soldiers in the village, and would both have been killed but for the fact that the hillmen were weakened and pursued.

'My brother died defending me, but our horses were driven off. The soldiers who chased the Zani away told me to go to the village where they had left their wounded comrades, there to await their return. But Sarkar, as you saw, became impatient.'

'We've come from Aldium ourselves,' said Harmis. 'I'm a soldier in the Border Guard – I survived when mutants slew my friends, and followed them to the house of Astyanax, where I fell in with the magician's two apprentices. Averil is one – the other we hope to meet here.'

'I have heard of Astyanax,' said Asmunda. 'He was said to be a good wizard, and an enemy of the darker gods.' Her eyes were still on him, the pupils huge and dark; there was something slightly teasing about the smile which played upon her lips.

'He was,' answered Harmis, bleakly. 'But the darker gods have crushed him now, and seem set to crush all Khypris. I don't know what mere mortals can do to stay the hands of those which now oppose us, but I can only suppose that evil and the forces which Astyanax called Chaos are somehow limited in their power to do us harm, else Hell would have claimed the world long before you or I could be born into it.'

'Aye,' she said. 'there is an equilibrium of some sort in the nature of things, which has not yet been tipped – just as order has so far been preserved in this crowd whose members long for the safety of the other shore. But when hope runs out, order must be lost... and Chaos, in the end, cannot be kept at bay.'

Her expression was very serious as she spoke, and the way in which she looked at him seemed somehow more important than anything she might say. 'You mustn't be anxious,' he told her. 'The real heart of Khypris has never yet been conquered by the likes of the Zani – who are after all only barbarians. When you get there, you'll certainly be safe. But I beg you to be cautious in letting others know that you have so much gold, for if you're right, and the order of society does break down, there are many here who would kill you for a single coin.'

'Only barbarians,' she echoed, in a soft voice – made soft by tiredness, he assumed. 'Yes, they are, after all, only that. And Faramond is very different, is he not? His men-at-arms are braver by far, with the discipline of their colours to guide them and the cause of civilization to defend. It is good to know that the city of my birth is quite impregnable, and I thank you for the help you have given me in reaching it. I will see you again in unfallen Khypris, Harmis Detz, when all that is fated has come to pass.'

She walked away from him, heading for the river. Harmis did not doubt that she would find a way across, by one means or another. If there were many who would kill for her gold, there were at least a few who might do as much for the favour of her smile. If any of those who were in Cavanal today were to reach Khypris and safety, Harmis thought, then she would surely be among them.

He continued his search for half an hour more, but there was no sign of Nicodemus and Ritandyr, and he returned in the end to Averil.

WHILE THEY CONTINUED to wait, Harmis was approached more than once by groups of Faramond's men, who were enthusiastic to impress him into the army. Everyone knew that a considerable battle must soon be fought, and the soldiers were anxious to recruit every able-bodied man they could find. On each occasion, though, he kept them at bay by showing the paper he had been given in Aldium. Though neither he nor they could read it, it was accepted immediately as a justification of his separate destiny.

It was, as Harmis once remarked to Averil, an interesting proof of the magical power of inscription. Could she, he wondered aloud, have made a spell to give them any better protection from interference?

She did not deign to dignify this question with an answer. In his turn, he did not deign to tell her that he had seen Asmunda again, or that the other woman had such powerful enchantments in her appearance and her purse that she would surely fly over all the obstacles in her path to reach her destination. He had not the slightest doubt that the dull-faced Averil had no spell in her repertoire which could do the same for her.

Harmis proposed that they should make a frugal meal from the last of their food, and that afterwards he would go again to the outskirts of the town to search for Nicodemus. She agreed, though she seemed frustrated by the fact that there was nothing else to be done but wait.

This time Harmis took Sable with him, thinking he would have a better view of the crowds from horseback. He found that the throng had increased considerably since he had spoken to Asmunda, but there was no sign of Nicodemus among the newcomers. He rode around the western boundary of the town, to come back by way of the river bank, but Nicodemus could not be found there either.

The second broad span of the bridge had now been destroyed and a slender thing of wood and rope installed in its place. The trickle of people and animals crossing over was slow, for the makeshift bridge was very precarious, but the flow seemed steady enough to Harmis. All those allowed on to the span by Byrin's men – and they were not all soldiers, by any means – hurried as fast as they could, while those behind them grew increasingly impatient.

He could see no ferrymen plying for hire; it seemed that every boat on this stretch of the river had been taken by the army, partly to serve their own purposes, but also to ensure that they should not fall into Zani hands. He supposed that civilians would be allowed to use the boats in much the same way that they were being allowed to use the bridge – provided only that they could make out a case for their privilege, with or without the aid of gold.

When dusk fell, Harmis sat down with Averil, and told her to go to sleep. Although they had nothing left to eat he had not attempted to use his gold coin to purchase food; he knew that it might still be necesssary to get them across the river. His intention was to keep watch all night – for as panic gradually increased, as it surely would, their situation would become more hazardous.

His belly did not feel as empty as it might have done, for the dark water which he continued to take in order to slake his curious thirst seemed to ease his hunger pangs.

Though he kept to himself and did not join in the clamorous babble which was all about him, Harmis could not help but hear every rumour which passed through the crowd: the Zani were less than a day away; the Zani had turned east to skirt the Caracasana and would not come to Cavanal at all; a second horde had been sighted in the west; a battle had been fought in Nyrcos or Meloya or Hivari and had resulted in a victory or a stalemate or a defeat.

All of these rumours save one fluttered briefly about and were lost, mere fancies and falsehoods born of hope or fear; but one remained, spoken again and again in a grimmer tone. And though he ignored it when first he heard it, he paid more attention when it was repeated again and again.

It was said that there was plague in the town.

Harmis told himself, uneasily, that it was inevitable that such a whisper should go abroad, for there were always diseases aplenty in waterfront towns, and such diseases inevitably called more attention to themselves when the town was full of strangers and everyone was in a hurry to be gone. In ordinary times, people were patient with sickness in themselves and in others; in times of crisis, everything distressing became a sign and symptom of impending doom.

The third time he heard it, though, there was an added detail which gave him extra cause for concern. Among the first victims of the plague, it was said, had been three wounded soldiers who had been brought to Cavanal aboard a cart after a skirmish with the Zani. He knew, after all, that such a cart had recently arrived – and he knew also that those three men had been given a horse by one who had only recently recovered from the effects of a corruption in his flesh. He still had the tarnwine to help him, but they had not.

Was it possible, Harmis wondered, that he himself might be the source of this plague?

He could not help but remember something Astyanax had said: that he who had been touched by Chaos must beware, lest he become the instrument of Chaos. Astyanax and his apprentices had insisted, also, that the true enemy of Khypris was not to be found among the Zani, but was instead a servant of a loathsome god.

Is it possible, he thought, that this strange daemon is within me? Am I possessed, and doomed to carry corruption into the heartland of the empire?

And if this was not frightening enough, he had to wonder whether he might also have inflicted the plague on the beautiful Asmunda, who had shown him such kindness and goodwill.

He tried to put these fears away, telling himself that they were childish nightmares born of an unease which was unfitting in a man-at-arms. He reminded himself sternly that Astyanax of Violtis himself had trusted him with this mission, and that to him alone had been given the true name of the *katharos*, that he might destroy it. It was surely unthinkable that he might harbour the daemon unwittingly.

But there came another thought to disturb him in its turn, which was that if the plague was truly in Cavanal, and if the *katharos* had brought it, then the daemon might have crossed the Tana Dante already. If so, then Ritandyr, if he arrived at all, would come too late to save the heartland from its ravages.

Harmis found himself looking very frequently at his own hands, then running those hands over his body, or tenderly pressing the wound in his neck, searching for signs of renewed sickness – but the curse of the Lazarite seemed still to be held in check by the black water. For the time being, at least, he was free of any supernatural decay.

The crowd in the streets was a little thinner by night, and as time went by it became thinner still. Every breath of rumour, substantial or not, weakened the resolve of some of those who were waiting, and some were fleeing east or west along the shore, in the hope of finding a better place to cross or of avoiding the Zani hordes. Harmis remained in his place, but was forced to consider all his options. He decided that if it should transpire that Nicodemus and Ritandyr never did arrive, he must take Averil across the river, and then must play his part in the defence of Cavanal against the Zani.

In the morning, when Averil woke, he told her about the rumours of plague.

'They have not understood,' she said, in a defeated voice. 'They didn't break the bridge as they were commanded to do, and now I fear that it may be too late. If they've let the *katharos* cross their foolish span of wood and rope, then all Astyanax's efforts have been for nothing.'

'Even if there were no bridge,' said Harmis, tiredly, 'there would still be boats plying for hire. And if there were no boats – can your daemon not fly, or swim? I know little of magic, but what I know suggests that magic cannot be confined, save by stronger magic. Evil gods are surely not confounded by mere rivers, no matter how fervently we might wish that they could be.'

'I know too little myself,' she told him, 'but I suspect that there's an order in the nature of things which is not so easily disturbed by the forces of Chaos. Where time and space are not warped to their convenience they are apt to decay and be dissolved. I cannot say how the *katharos* maintains its presence in our world instead of returning to its own place, but I do know that a powerful illusion is not maintained without cost and compromise – and because of this, it might be more easily confounded than you suppose, if only we had Ritandyr's magic to aid us. Even now, it may not be too late to act.'

Harmis shrugged his shoulders. 'All I know,' he said, 'is that I know too little. What skill and strength I have, I use – and where less honest power is concerned, I must trust to the luck which the gods award me. I'm not fit for this work which I've been appointed to do.'

He turned then because he heard the noise of a commotion in the distance, where the rearmost end of the great queue was.

'Stay here,' he said to Averil, and then went on foot to see what was happening.

He found a group of half a dozen men-at-arms – four in the red-and-white which marked them as servants of Byrin's family, two in Faramond's claret-and-gold – faced by an ugly crowd of men armed with swords, axes and pitchforks. He guessed immediately what had happened. A large group of farmers and their labourers had arrived all at once, intent on crossing the river with the least possible delay. They had arrived with the determination that they would not be conscripted to the defence of Cavanal, and hence ready to quarrel with the soldiers. On finding such a huge throng waiting patiently to cross the makeshift bridge they had quickly become fearful that they might have no choice but to defend the town, because they would still be here when the Zani vanguard arrived in all its force and fury.

The leader of this gang was a big and burly man, who put Harmis very much in mind of the bully-boys who had caught and hanged Rolf Humbold. This red-faced pillar of wrath was brandishing a heavy sword, in a fashion made all the more intimidating by the fact that he towered above the short-statured men-at-arms who had interrupted him.

It was obvious that it would require a man of courage to stand toe-to-toe with the giant – and it was not at all obvious that the six men-at-arms had one such among their number. The soldiers were moving as if to share the burden of confrontation, falling back to form a semicircle. Harmis could see at a glance that this was the wrong strategy, for such a ragged line could easily be broken and overwhelmed by a surge. Once the farmers had thrust down the bearers of Faramond's authority they might easily be joined by a hundred others who, until now, had been prepared to wait patiently in line.

If Byrin or one of his tougher sergeants had been here, they could certainly have controlled the ugly situation – but the six who were here instead were only youths, at least half of whom had only recently been given arms.

Harmis paused for only a moment to regret that he no longer had his colours on, and his own strong sword in place of the little one which Nicodemus had left in its place. Then he strode forward, drawing the sword he had and taking his warrant from his shirt in order that it might exercise what magical power it could. He went to stand before the leader of the unruly crew, and looked him in the eye as contemptuously as he could.

'What treason is this?' he asked, very coldly.

'No treason at all,' said the big man loudly, 'but a claiming of our rights. We labour for Khypris, and pay taxes to Faramond. Now we demand that protection which is ours in return, and we intend to have it. None has the right to deny it to us.'

Harmis showed him the paper, and said: 'This is the only right which has force today. It is a warrant which commands the instant execution of anyone who defies Captain Byrin's authority. To defy it is treason. If you lift a hand against any of those whose duty it is to stand and die in the coming battle against the Zani you will declare your allegiance to the hillmen's cause, and every loyal citizen of Khypris will demand your death.' He looked around as he said it, implying with his eyes that the crowd was full of loyal citizens, and that the newcomers had far more to face than six callow men-at-arms and one bold Harmis Detz.

Harmis thought for a few seconds that his ploy had worked, and a grim smile of triumph had already begun to catch his lips. Then the pent-up wrath of the red-faced man overwhelmed what intelligence and discretion he might have had, and he raised his sword to strike Harmis down.

Harmis knew, as he raised his own weapon to parry the blow, that the light blade was inadequate to the task. He tried to move back to give himself space, but the men-at-arms had huddled too close behind him and there was not enough room to allow him to dodge the sweep of the giant's sword. Had the blow fallen, it would have knocked him bleeding to the ground, where a single thrust could have finished him off.

But the blow did not fall. As the blade tipped backwards, while the big man gathered his strength to deliver his rude answer to Harmis's challenge, its point somehow came into contact with the tip of a carved wooden staff which had been thrust out deftly from one side. Though the touch was momentary, and very light, it seemed that a weird light sprang from the end of the staff to possess the iron blade, which glittered very strangely.

The big man screamed in agony, and instantly let go of the sword, which clattered harmlessly to the ground. He grasped his right hand in his left as though it had been stung by some monstrous wasp, and fell instantly to his knees. In that position he was by no means so intimidating, and the tears which coursed down his cheeks gave him the aspect of an absurdly bloated infant.

The crowd which had gathered behind the belligerent giant suddenly thinned out as everyone in it took a step backwards. All the cudgels and pitchforks which had been raised in threat were lowered now, and in an instant the situation had been transformed. The men-at-arms were back in control.

Harmis looked wonderingly at the owner of the staff, who had lowered it again and now leaned upon it, almost as if he needed its support. He did not recognize the man himself, but he knew who it must be by virtue of the fact that the man who stood beside him, as proud and upright as a man might be with one arm bandaged, was Nicodemus.

'We are not barbarians,' said Ritandyr, intending his words for the entire crowd, although he was looking at Harmis Detz. 'You are right to say that any man who takes up arms against his own people at a time like this is the foulest of traitors. But there is no other here who would do such a thing, for we are all men of Khypris, who understand the meaning of duty, and loyalty to our prince.'

When Harmis looked around, he saw that the saying of such words was enough to make them true, and was very glad of it. He sheathed the sword which he had not been forced to use, and extended his hand to his deliverer.

'I am Harmis Detz,' he said, 'And I am very glad to see you, master wizard.'

'No more glad than I am to see you,' replied Ritandyr.

Ritandyr was not as Harmis had imagined him. He was neither tall nor venerable, neither white of hair nor sharp of eye, nor was he robed in any fine or unusual way. He was small and fat and had the kind of face which would normally seem naturally cheerful – though he was at present unsmiling. But he did have the intricately carved staff, which was clearly invested with significant power, and his eyes were grey and quizzical, as though the mind behind them was privy to mysteries which ordinary men could never penetrate.

Harmis greeted Nicodemus too, and led them back to the place which Averil was keeping for them. While Harmis and Ritandyr studied one another further the younger man caught hold of his fellow apprentice and embraced her. His arm was so nearly mended that he was able to hug her firmly – but his face was lined by strain, and it seemed to Harmis that the dark water had left a shadowy mark upon him as the price for its healing work. Harmis wondered if he had been similarly marked.

Ritandyr was distressed to hear that the bridge was still open – which was the first news that Averil took care to tell him – and when she then told him how rumour of plague had gone abroad he became more anxious still, saying that events must have moved faster in their course than he could have wished.

'They must still move on,' said Harmis, 'and quickly too. Have you food and money? If we're to cross the river, we must do it today, and if you have the means to obtain an early passage, I wish that you would use them.'

The spellcaster studied him for a moment or two, and then said: 'You are right, my friend. If events move rapidly, then so must we. If the *katharos* has crossed the river, then so must we. In answer to your questions, we have only a little food, and only a little money – but the most vital of our resources is not to be so easily counted. We must take proper stock of our situation as soon as we have crossed to the southern shore.'

Mindful of what Byrin had said to him when he had first arrived, Harmis now felt able to go once again to the bridge with his warrant in his hand. This time, it proved effective – though that may have had as much to do with the authority of Ritandyr's staff as the power of the paper. For whatever reason, though, they were allowed on to the makeshift bridge within the hour, with all their horses and their packs. Asmunda's gold coin still rested unused in Harmis's pouch.

Harmis saw Captain Byrin watching while they were installed in their place of privilege, but the young man offered him no salute as he led Sable carefully across the swaying planks.

CHAPTER THIRTEEN

IT WAS EASIER than Harmis had expected to find lodgings on the far side of the river. Many of those who lived here, and most of the civilians who had earlier crossed the river, had already fled the town. When it had become clear that the Zani were bringing their herds this way, it had also become clear that Cavanal would be a city under siege, and that everything of use would be requisitioned by the army. Many of the loyal citizens had preferred to flee with their goods before the burden of their loyalty could become too much to bear.

Harmis and his companions had no difficulty in finding an inn which had rooms to spare, and they hired two of them at a moderate cost.

This made Harmis feel a good deal less anxious, and gave him more faith than he had managed to raise before in the possibility that Ritandyr might be capable of some achievement. Indeed, he felt relieved to find that Ritandyr was a man whose authority might be trusted, and to whom he might defer without the sense of awkwardness and foreboding which had made him reluctant to take instruction from Nicodemus and Averil.

For the first time, as he climbed the staircase to his room, Harmis began to believe that he might survive this awful adventure, and that in spite of the rumours of plague, all might somehow be set to rights.

Once they had taken possession of their rooms there was no further delay. Nicodemus and Ritandyr were very tired, having ridden hard through the night in order to reach Cavanal, but they dared not allow themselves the luxury of a pause for rest and recuperation.

'Our first task,' said Ritandyr, 'is to try to discover the whereabouts of the *katharos*. We must ascertain, if we can, whether it has already passed through Cavanal, and how long ago. The divining spell is a petty one, but it is not without risk, because if the daemon is indeed nearby, it may be given the opportunity to strike back at us.'

'And if you can discover where the daemon is,' said Harmis, 'will you be able to prevent it doing further harm?'

'I cannot tell,' said Ritandyr, frankly. 'Astyanax, who was a greater wizard than I, has already been destroyed by the forces of evil which threaten Khypris. I expect to be tested to the limits of my skill and strength, and it is possible that I will prove inadequate to the task before me. Nevertheless, I must try – for I have given my solemn word that I will do my utmost to oppose the forces which threaten Khypris and the greater world of men.'

Although this speech was by no means optimistic, it did not discourage Harmis. He was glad to find that Ritandyr was so frank and honest, and was ready to believe that if the *katharos* could be destroyed, here was the man who could discover a way to do it.

'If you need my help,' said Harmis, 'you have it. Only tell me what I must do.'

Ritandyr merely nodded. 'First,' he said, 'we must try to find our enemy. After that, we will be in a better position to decide what can and must be done. First of all, Harmis, you must find food for us, if you can – for wizards need their bodily strength as much as any man. What Nicodemus and I have to do will require an effort of will, and we will not be ready for a while; we will be all the better prepared if you can find us a good meal. You must take such coin as I have in order to buy it.'

Harmis was not displeased by the modesty of this request, though it was not what he had expected. He knew that he could be of little use in matters of magical ritual, and he found a certain relief in being given a task which was within his compass. When Ritandyr offered him money it was on the tip of his tongue to tell them about Asmunda's gift, but he kept silent, telling himself that the gold might be better held for future use.

Though the task was simple enough, it was not so very easy to carry out. All the shops in the town were closed, and the soldiers had requisitioned what they could for their own supply. There was not a loaf of bread or a cabbage to be found on open sale, and those traders who had contrived to hide their goods from the army were forced to deal covertly in back alleys. There they found customers aplenty, and Harmis heard it whispered that a man who had but a single cheese to sell might become rich if only he could keep it safe from thieves.

Harmis had not yet taken the trouble to recover his own livery from Nicodemus, but he soon wished that he had. He was stopped by soldiers several times, who demanded to know who he was and where he was staying, and what weapons he had apart from those he was carrying. He was forbidden to leave the town, and told that the only reason he was allowed to keep his weapons about him was that Byrin would require his arms to wield them as well as the blades themselves. From this he judged the Zani were coming quickly enough to cause great consternation. Once, he asked a sergeant about the rumours of plague, but the question was contemptuously dismissed.

After much searching, Harmis managed to buy some meat of dubious provenance and some old bread, for whose purchase Ritandyr's money proved barely adequate.

These items he carried furtively back to the inn. The absurdity of having to hide them brought home to him how desperate the situation had become. Nevertheless, the prospect of a host of barbarian warriors descending upon the town was somehow less fearful than it might have been. Warfare, after all, was something he understood; mere murder, even on a massive scale, was ordinary. Curses and daemons were a very different matter.

By the time he returned with the meagre meal, Ritandyr and the two apprentices had set up the apparatus they required for the first of their spells, and were composing themselves for the performance. A shallow bowl had been set in the centre of the table-top, surrounded by curious squat candles.

As soon as they had eaten, Ritandyr began rummaging among the bottles and jars which Averil had carried. He took some of their dwindling stock of the tarn water and poured it into the bowl, then added some droplets of a paler liquid from another phial. When he lit the candles they quickly filled the room with a strange vapour which Harmis did not like. Then, while Harmis watched from a distance, Ritandyr required Averil and Nicodemus to join hands with him, and all three proceeded to mutter in some arcane language, imploring help from the enchanted water.

It was the first time that Harmis had ever seen spellcasters of this kind at work, but it seemed to him a business hardly less dull than the routines of religious practice with which he was familiar. Though Ritandyr seemed somehow to stand taller than he had before, and though he spoke in a deep and sonorous fashion, he was no more imposing than a priest of Myrmidia whom Harmis had once seen at work in Khypris. Ritandyr was obviously a man of greater power than the young apprentices, but he had not yet acquired the kind of awesome presence which Astyanax must have had before he was struck down.

The working of the spell brought a strange kind of thrill to the air, and Harmis found himself shivering. He felt a

sudden pang of that unnatural thirst which he had for the
dark water, and a dizziness which recalled the macabre
fantasy that he might somehow be unwitting host to the
daemon they sought.

The water in the bowl began to swirl in an agitated manner, stirred by the power of Ritandyr's command. Harmis
moved closer, so that he might see what image the water
came to contain, but to him it was all meaningless confusion.

'There is something,' murmured Ritandyr, his face still
ruddy and sweat-stained, his cheeks blown out with the
effort of his concentration. 'There is something *near* – why,
I can feel a presence so close at hand that it might be in the
room! Can the *katharos* be lodged in this very inn?'

Harmis felt an icy alarm strike at his soul when Ritandyr
said this, for the words reawoke the full measure of those
fears that had visited him during the sleepless night. What
if it were true that the *katharos* had possessed him? What
would become of him, if a battle of magicians had to be
fought in this very room, with himself at its centre?

'I can see nothing!' complained Averil – but Ritandyr
clenched his fleshy hand about her smaller one, commanding her to be silent.

'Something most strange,' he said, his voice full of stress
and strain. 'Something evil. Something in our very midst...'

'What you sense is the knives on Harmis's back!' said
Nicodemus, suddenly. 'They took the life of the Lazarite,
and are marked by it. It is those whose nearness you sense,
not the *katharos* at all.'

Harmis felt like crying with delight. Of course, it must be
true! Of course he was not possessed!

For a second or two, Ritandyr seemed to believe it – but
then he shook his head violently, and that shaking was
reflected in the swirling water which bubbled and foamed
as it thrashed about in the bowl.

'Not honest iron,' he said. 'No weapon at all, but something treacherous. Something touched by the *katharos*,
which retains the taint of evil. The seeds of plague are here

– what have you found or bought since you came to Cavanal?'

'Nothing that you have not seen and touched,' replied Averil, in perplexity. 'We have but paid for the hire of the room, and for the food which we have just consumed...'

That thought obviously frightened her, and she turned to Harmis. She looked at him very darkly, as though accusing him of buying tainted meat, dressed with the seeds of plague. Harmis met her gaze for a moment or two, fearfully – but Ritandyr was still shaking his head.

'No, no,' said the stout man, perspiring so freely that he seemed almost to be melting away. 'Something small, something hard, something bright… something *gold*...'

Harmis felt his heart lurch.

'No!' he said, breathlessly, 'It cannot be the gold. It cannot be.'

Averil's eyes were still upon him, uncomprehending now but still somehow accusing. He felt sweat on his own brow.

'What gold?' whispered Nicodemus.

'Take out the coin,' whispered Ritandyr, with a groan. 'Take out the coin, and throw it in the bowl.'

Harmis snatched the coin from his pouch, and stared down at it in bewilderment. He could not throw it immediately, because it seemed to cling to his palm, as though it did not want to be thrown. It was small and very bright, as if newly minted. He thought of Asmunda, her shining hair and her lustrous skin, and wondered how blind a man might be.

Then, with a convulsive thrust, he threw the coin into the dark water, which boiled and seethed about it in a most extraordinary way.

On the palm of his hand, where the coin had rested, there was a dark spot, as though the flesh had turned to sticky tar.

'Damnation!' said Ritandyr. 'Poor fool – you have carried the plague in your own pouch! Were you not steeped in the water of the tarn you'd be a rotting corpse by now – and the daemon must have known it! It has used your strength against you, sought out your company, mocked you with its gift. This creature plays with us, and makes us the target of its malevolent jests.'

Staring at the black spot on his palm, Harmis whispered: 'Asmunda – the *katharos*!'

It was then, and only then, that Averil realized what had happened.

'You gave it the means to come here!' she said. 'You offered it a horse, and it paid for its safe conduct with accursed coin!'

Not for the first time, Harmis heard Astyanax's dying words echoing in his soul: *He who is touched by Chaos may harm Chaos... but must always beware, lest he become the instrument of Chaos instead of its destroyer.*

'That is not the only such coin in Cavanal,' said Ritandyr, staring dolefully down at the feverish water while he supported himself by leaning on the table's edge. 'You may be sure that the daemon will find many who are eager to accept such payments between here and Khypris. It will use the greed and desperation of men to spread its poison.'

Nicodemus came away from the table to look at the mark on Harmis's palm. Harmis made no objection when the young man took up a bottle of the tarnwine; he knew what must be done, and he knew that there would be a price to pay in pain. Even so, when the water washed over the ruined flesh, he could not help but cry out in anguish and agony.

It was all over in a matter of seconds; the black stain was wiped out as though it had been no more than an illusion – but Harmis knew only too well what had been done to him.

The *katharos* had come to him, bearing a false name in place of its true one, and a false appearance too; it had toyed with him, confused him, seduced him, using his own avarice to make him a partner in its project. It could not have been necessary for the daemon to do that; as Ritandyr had said, it had done it as a kind of cruel jest, an insult to himself and all his kind.

'It is why they are called the Pure Ones,' said Ritandyr, softly, when he fully understood what had happened. 'They hide their foulness with amazing skill, masking that which is most hateful with the power of illusion. Do not blame yourself, Harmis.'

Harmis read disgust as well as dismay in Averil's stare. She had tried to prevent his generous action; she had silently opposed his decision to offer Asmunda and the wounded men-at-arms a horse. At the time, he had thought it a lack of mercy, a lack of any spirit of fellowship; now her reluctance had been transformed by circumstance into forlorn wisdom. But it had not been wisdom really, for Averil had no more seen what Asmunda truly was than he had.

'I'm a common fighting-man,' Harmis said to her, bitterly. 'If you were blind, how might I have seen?'

'Recrimination can serve no purpose,' said Ritandyr. 'The point is to discover where the *katharos* is now, for I was blinded by the nearness of the tainted gold, and could see nothing more.'

'Gone,' said Harmis. 'I saw her yesterday in Cavanal. She was on her way to the bridge, to obtain an immediate passage by bribery. She has gone to Khypris, and she has a full day's start. We must warn Faramond!'

'She will move too swiftly to be caught,' said Ritandyr bitterly. 'And if there were carrier birds kept in Cavanal, they are already on the wing carrying news of the Zani's impending attack. Whatever gold the daemon left behind is doing evil as it moves from hand to hand, with every one of its owners anxious to hide and protect it. We must get word to Byrin – but it will do no good, for we have been outplayed.'

It was easy enough to guess how widely the gold which Asmunda had brought to Cavanal might now be scattered. Some at least must have found its way into the pouches of the soldiers guarding the bridge. How many would agree to give it up or throw it away, Harmis wondered, if Byrin broadcast the news that it was tainted? In all the world there was only one thing more powerful than fear, and that was greed. Perhaps Byrin was already sickening himself, and half his subordinate commanders with him. How could Cavanal now be defended against the Zani?

'What can we do?' he asked, in a horrified whisper. 'Have you any means at all to counter this magic?'

The wizard looked up at him, all too frail and human in appearance, with no answer ready on his lips.

The water in the bowl ceased its seething and became still; the coin still glittered beneath the shadowed surface, as if the kindly darkness in the water could not quite contrive to smother its evil radiance.

'There is one thing which we might try,' said Ritandyr, speculatively. 'It is a difficult spell which will drain us of all the power we have, and I do not know how far its virtue will extend, but it may be our only hope. If we do it tonight, we might yet nip this evil in the bud – but if we fail, we will have exhausted our resources. And the *katharos* will certainly strike back at us, if we try to recall the deadly coins by magic.'

'The breaking of the bridge has failed,' said Nicodemus sourly, 'and this evil is already in the heartland of the nation. Delay after delay has cost us dear. If we do not risk all, then all is lost.'

Ritandyr took the coin from the bowl, and held it out to Harmis. 'It is safe now,' he said. 'You may keep it, or throw it in the river, as you choose, but I beg you to take it away from here. Do not be hard with yourself, Harmis, for the daemon has made a victim of you in the hope of making you regret your courage. You must take word to Byrin now, telling him what has happened here, but I doubt that there is anything he can do.

'It will take us two hours and more to prepare the spell which we must try. When that time comes you must leave us, for the sake of your own safety. So far, you are the only one who has struck a firm blow against these monstrous invaders, and you may still have power and opportunity to strike another while you have that knife upon your back and the name which Astyanax gave you in your memory. Whatever happens here, you must go on – that is your duty, as I think you understand.'

'Aye,' said Harmis, dully. 'If there's one thing in all of this which I do understand, it's my duty. If all else fails, I'll try to find that thing which posed as the lovely Asmunda, for I know now that Lavarock my brother still cries in the eternal night for full and proper vengeance.'

He paused only to demand the return of his helmet, his colours and his sword from Nicodemus. Having recovered these things, he left the three of them to do their part of that work which remained to be done.

He took his message to the bridge – but there he found another bearer of the red-and-white in charge, who told him brusquely that he had no time to listen to tales of tainted gold, and that he must make ready to face the Zani horde, which was already massing for the assault upon the town.

As HARMIS MADE his way back to the inn to report his failure, heavy clouds were forming in the sky. There was a sultry warmth in the air which made it seem tangible, and Harmis judged that a storm was brewing.

All through the afternoon the town had been emptying of people. Four out of every five who still remained were men-at-arms, though not all wore livery and few could have had experience in fighting the hillmen. The rope bridge had been closed to all but the military since noon, but so far as Harmis could judge there had been no riots in the smaller part of the town – those who could not or would not bear arms had been left to flee along either bank in the hope of discovering hiding-places in which they could wait out the impending battle. Many would have been forced by extremity to abandon their possessions – some would undoubtedly try to cross the river on makeshift rafts or by swimming, while the majority who had never taken the trouble to learn to swim would curse their lack of foresight while they ran.

While Ritandyr and the apprentices made ready for the casting of their spell, Harmis went up to a small attic under the eaves, whose gable window was high enough to allow him to look out over the river and watch what was happening on the bridge.

The soldiers were bringing horses and men across in a steady stream, ready to make their defence on this shore. Though the bridge was broken and as many boats as the soldiers could secure had been made safe, it would not be easy to stop the Zani crossing over in force. What the army had done with ropes and logs the Zani could do too, if they were allowed the opportunity – and half of the bridge still stood, jutting out into the river from the far bank to narrow the gap which would have to be closed.

When it was nearly dark, Averil came to see him. He lit a lantern, so that he could see her accusing face.

'The hillmen will arrive before morning,' he said. 'They've driven themselves and their herds harder than I'd have believed possible. It's as if they knew that the plague had come among us to weaken our resistance and resolve. We have a great many men here, but they'll be ready to flee if the fight seems to go badly – and though no one will say so, I believe that Byrin has already fallen sick.'

'The god of plague has whispered in the dreams of every shaman in the horde,' she said. 'They don't know what it is that has inspired them to begin this war, but they're intoxicated with promises of victory. They would be more fortunate, I think, were they to be turned back. If they succeed in crossing into the heartland, they may share the fate of those they come to destroy. The whole population of the nation is on the move, and I doubt there's any way that the plague can now be confined.'

'Unless your magic can turn the tide,' he said – but he could not bring himself to sound hopeful.

'We will do what we can,' she said. 'But even if we succeed, the best we can achieve is to soften the blow which this daemon has struck.'

'What is your plan?' he asked her. 'What kind of spell is Ritandyr preparing?'

'Ours is the magic of the elements,' she told him. 'We aspire to mastery of wind and water, earth and fire. Astynanax spent his life by the tarn whose waters he sought to remake for his ends, and he taught both Ritandyr and Nicodemus something of the art of that command. We must use the water of the tarn as best we can.'

'But the tarn is hundreds of miles away,' said Harmis, bitterly. 'And the meagre remains of what we brought with us would hardly fill a basin.' While he said it, he could feel the thirst building in him again, and he feared the time when it would have to be allowed to build unchecked, because there would be no more of the elixir to drink.

'True,' she said. 'But the water of the tarn, like any other water, feeds the clouds which roam the skies above the Border Princes – and that grey mass which fills the sky even now has some of the virtuous water in it. Ritandyr and Nicodemus will try to take possession of these clouds, and bring to life such healing powers as are in them, so that the rain which falls might exert some force against the ravages of the *katharos*. We can't hope to obliterate the plague, but we might ameliorate its effects, so that a far greater number of those who are stricken might survive and recover.'

'It sounds simple enough,' he said.

'But by no means easy,' she told him, soberly. 'Many glorious tales are told of magicians who have commanded storms, and I'm told that in Sigmar's Empire they keep whole legions of wizards who use storms as weapons of war; but such a spell is difficult to work at the best of times. Wind is always unruly and lightning is very dangerous. To make things worst, we may not be the only magicians trying to command the storm. Faramond's battle-wizards, such as they are, are cowering in Khypris, but the shamans who have travelled with the Zani horde may well be ambi-

tious to try their powers in this way, and though they're
mostly uneducated charlatans, some of them will have a
measure of raw power to draw upon.

'Ritandyr has gathered his strength most carefully for
many years, but he has never attempted such a bold spell
as this. The help Nicodemus can give him will not be very
great, for his strength is only recently returned, and he's
still frail. Their difficulties are further compounded by the
fact that they must simultaneously try to seize and render
harmless the tainted coins which the *katharos* has used as
agents of contagion.'

Harmis looked up at the sky, which was heavy and star-
less. There had been precious little twilight, and now the
black of night was upon them. 'The cloud seems to cover
all the land,' he said. 'I grant you that the nation will take
a soaking tonight – but I fear the waters of the Black Tarn
will be lost within such a deluge, adding no more than a
single drop in every million. Still – that's your business,
not mine.'

There was a moment's uncomfortable silence, and then
she said: 'Ritandyr is right. You mustn't reproach yourself
about the *katharos*. It was I who should have known her for
what she was. I was unready, and like you I saw only a
seductive face. When I was angry with you because you
gave the wounded men a horse, it wasn't because I thought
she was dangerous, but only because I thought you weak
to be swayed by her appearance.'

'Many a sickness is spread by seduction,' he told her. 'I
was glad, in my prideful fashion, that you were jealous.
Had she been only what I thought she was, I could not
claim to be blameless.'

'Such blame does not matter,' she assured him. 'Men are
not to blame for the way their desires are shaped by the
gods which make and move them. But if you see her again,
remember what she really is, and what she has done to this
realm. This daemon is of the company which murdered
your brother, and it has become very promiscuous in
killing brothers and sisters and wives and children. Only

keep your left-hand dagger safe, and pray that something
might yet be saved of Faramond's nation.'

'I'll remember,' he said, awkwardly. 'And for what it may
be worth, I'll add my prayers to yours.'

'We must begin the incantation soon,' she said, as she
turned to go. 'Ritandyr asks that you leave the house. If you
must take part in the battle, I wish you the best of luck
with bow and sword.'

Harmis nodded, and came down with her to fetch the
bow and the quiver of arrows which Nicodemus had
brought from the Black Tarn, and to put on his armoured
coat. Then he went down to the waterfront, to take his
stand with the soldiers who were there. The captain who
was organizing the defenders – not Byrin – must have recognized him as the man with the mysterious paper, but
said nothing to him. Harmis said nothing either, but only
took up a place behind a barricade, in company with half
a dozen archers. The rope bridge was down, and the far
shore seemed utterly deserted.

There was fear in the humid air, which seemed in consequence to be doubly saturated. Harmis looked about him
at his comrades-in-arms, but even those who wore the
same colours as he lacked the carriage or the attitude of
fighting-men. He felt very much alone, and wished that he
had men of the Border Guard to stand at his shoulders –
men who were long used to the sight of the savage hillmen, and knew how to kill them. Most of all, he wished
that Lavarock was with him, to joke with him and share
the dreadful burden of the waiting. But Lavarock was gone,
the darkness all about him was empty and desolate of
everything but brooding storm-clouds and the threat of
violent death.

He and his unknown, unnamed companions had been
waiting for barely an hour when the first arrows began to
sing through the air.

The assault of the Zani had begun.

CHAPTER FOURTEEN

IT WAS IMPOSSIBLE at first to see what was happening on the far shore, because the few lamps which had been left on that side by the retreating soldiers had gone out or had been extinguished. The only clue to the number of hillmen who were massing there was the number of arrows which soared over the river, and they constituted a gesture of defiance rather than a serious menace.

The hillmen, by contrast, would have little difficulty in assessing the strength of the force facing them, for the southern shore was very well-lit, though not in such a way as to make the defenders clear targets. There were lanterns hung from the bridgework and from the piers, so that the water was illuminated; when swimmers tried to cross, as they surely would, they would be seen as they tried to scramble up on to the shore.

But the darkness on the other shore did not last long; the hillmen were methodically setting alight the buildings, almost all of which had abundant wood in them. As the flames spread the mounted Zani who were clustered on the shore became visible in silhouette – it was as though they wished to show themselves, to make a parade before their enemies. It was obvious that there had been little or no fighting on the far bank; the Zani had met no substantial resistance there.

Some of the Khyprian bowmen began to shoot as soon as the enemy was visible, but Harmis had no confidence in his ability to hit a target so far away – his eyes were on the stone spur which still extended to the bridge's second arch.

He could hear splashing sounds in the water, and knew that swimmers were trying to carry ropes across the river, intent on securing them so that they might serve to guide and help support those who would come after. Still he kept his eyes on the bridge. Only when shadows finally became visible at the broken edge, where crouching Zani bowmen had taken their position, did he finally let fly.

Others did likewise, and the air seemed suddenly to be full of arrows flying this way and that. Each time Harmis discharged his weapon he would turn and drop behind the barricade until another arrow was properly notched – he would rise up only to fire it. Those who were with him were glad to recognize a seasoned fighter, and they copied him assiduously – but not one in three had any skill in aiming, or sufficient steadiness of hand to make their arrows fly true.

The experienced men-at-arms behind the barricades sent young boys running hither and yon to collect the enemy arrows which fell uselessly upon the wharf, bringing them to their own bowmen so that they might be sent back whence they came – but many shafts broke and some of the points embedded themselves too deeply in the barricade, so the supply was all too quickly reduced.

Zani warriors soon began to climb up the struts supporting the piers, fastening ropes with a quick twist and moving on as soon as they were able. The first half dozen were all shot, and fell back into the water. Harmis was astonished by the number which came, sometimes in twos and threes, to replace them. These were the youngest of the enemy warriors, emboldened by panic or liquor; they hurled themselves foolishly against the massed ranks of their enemies, mad with courage. Few had swords to brandish; most had only knives which they had carried clenched in their teeth while they climbed.

However uneducated the Zani shamans were, Harmis thought, they had certainly brought their men to a fine fighting frenzy. Faramond's army had its own spellcasters to raise morale, but civilized men had a different attitude to magic, and could not be brought thereby to such reckless madness as this. In tactical terms, superior discipline and superior weaponry should be more than a match for the wasteful fury of the fur-clad barbarians, but in the darkness of night the fervour of the attackers was very frightening. The defenders were labouring under the additional handicap of rumours which said – probably truthfully – that plague had already decimated the ranks of their commanders, and that many here were doomed to die even if the battle could be won.

It was not only swimmers who came so recklessly across the river to join the fight at close quarters, for the Zani had at least a few boats which they had seized from rivermen in the north. Some of these were large enough to hold twenty or thirty crouching men, and *these* warriors were not without good swords and bows.

Harmis quickly realized that the defence of Cavanal would not be as straightforward as he had earlier thought. Although the commander had placed a considerable force near to the broken bridge he must have been well aware of the necessity of guarding every mile of the shore, and a part of his forces had to be spread thinly on either side of the town. The Zani were under no such obligation to spread out, and could pick and choose where to concentrate their forces. It soon became clear that the Zani intended to hurl their warriors forward as rapidly as they could, hoping to overcome their positional disadvantage by sheer weight of numbers. The exchange of arrows was quickly abandoned as enemy warriors plunged into the water in hundreds.

When the shower of arrows died away the men of Harmis's contingent were ordered to draw their swords, and they were pushed forward over the barricade, to cut the Zani down as they came up out of the water. Some were reluctant to go, but Harmis went boldly enough, and no one was allowed to stay behind.

The work was childishly easy, to begin with.

Harmis found at first that he had all the time in the world to thrust with his sword at the hillmen who were trying to come up at him from below. They could not strike back with equal alacrity while their heavy garments were clogged with muddy water.

He cut where he must, but much of the time he was able to lash out with his booted foot, sending men crashing back into the water. Most of those would come again, but in the meantime they impeded one another and made things more difficult for themselves. In any case, it was impossible to cut them all, for there were simply too many of them.

The soldiers to either side of him thrust and kicked in similar fashion, laughing as though they were having a fine time of it. But the Zani archers had not entirely ceased their work, and the group on the lip of the broken bridge was replenished as often as its members fell to Khyprian arrows. There were archers in the river, too, firing while they trod water – and though they found it very difficult to aim, the lights on the shore made the soldiers into tempting targets.

The sergeants howled orders, trying to regroup their men in order to concentrate them in the places where the Zani were climbing up – but the attackers constantly shifted their assaults in a ceaseless attempt to evade the heaviest resistance, and confusion spread rapidly among the defenders as their discipline began to dissolve in the heat of the battle. The barricades which had sheltered the Khyprian forces from arrows began to be pulled down by

Zani warriors coming up beneath them, shielded by them from sword-thrusts and bowshots alike.

Harmis knew that the Tana Dante must be running red with blood beneath the cloak of darkness which turned its waters black.

The Zani were dying in hundreds – but such was the weight and ferocity of their attack that they were making significant progress. Now, he saw, they had brought great logs forward in order to span the gaps left by the fallen arches of the bridge, and with the aid of the ropes which their swimmers and boatmen were securing they seemed unstoppable, despite the Khyprian archers who harried their efforts with deadly arrows.

The defending line on the river's edge was still holding firm despite all the confusion, and Harmis still had allies to either side of him while he thrust at the heads and hands which appeared over the edge of the wharf. But many of the lanterns had been kicked over by now, or pulled back into the water, and it would soon be very difficult to tell friend from foe, or to see where danger might be coming from.

Rain began to fall, huge drops splashing upon the stones of the wharf in great profusion. Harmis looked up with a sudden thrill of anticipation – for was this not the sign which he had been promised, to mark the working of Ritandyr's spell? But his enthusiasm quickly died, for it was only rain after all. So heavy had the clouds become that it would surely have taken a spell of mighty power to hold the raindrops back.

The rain felt like any ordinary rain upon his helmet and his face, and the droplets did not taste of tarnwine when he touched his tongue to his lips. The deluge had no effect upon the Zani, who were wet enough already, but he could see that those who fought on either side of him did not welcome it at all.

The man to his right was suddenly gone – not slain but moved away – and Harmis began to back away from the water's edge, feeling that he was too exposed. But still the

Zani were coming, and still he had to thrust out with his sword, trying to send them tumbling back into the river. He tried to keep moving, dancing and swaying so as not to provide a tempting target for archers, screwing up his eyes in the hope of seeing more clearly what he needed to see. In that matter the rain was not helping him, for the lanterns were still going out, one by one, and the lowering clouds seemed to be choking the lightless sky.

The rain fell even more heavily, and began to blind him as it ran from his hair into his eyes. He tried to clear his face with his sleeve, but it was useless.

A bolt of lightning flared across the sky to the west, illuminating the figures moving along the waterfront, and he was astonished to see how many there were – but which were Khyprians and which were Zani it was well-nigh impossible to tell.

Someone not so very far away was howling an order to retreat into the buildings. It was all that could be done, for without light and shelter the attempt to fight must become ludicrous – but as the archers retreated from the barricades the remnants of the stone bridge were surrendered entirely to the Zani, who would certainly soon succeed in erecting some kind of link between the shores, across which men could come and horses too.

Harmis backed into a warehouse where two dozen soldiers were regrouping. Two lanterns were already lit, casting great looming shadows over the filthy walls, but the first invaders were already hurling themselves at the Khyprians with the same reckless fervour as those who had come before them and died. Harmis knew that their disregard for mortal danger would strike despair into the hearts of many of the the defenders, whose reason was no match for such furious ferocity. He joined with the others in cutting them down, but he could not help sharing their anxiety as he did so. He had not expected so furious an assault, and it was all too obvious that those of Faramond's captains who were still able to fight did not know how to cope with it.

One of the lanterns was tumbled over as a soldier lashed out at a Zani swordsman, and a cascade of burning oil was launched across the warehouse floor. Part of the floor was littered with straw, which caught alight – and though it was too thinly scattered to pose much danger, it added to the panic the defenders felt.

Outside, there was another flash of lightning and a great roll of thunder. Harmis shivered, feeling that the air had suddenly become taut, and that something other than thunder was trying to take possession of the sky.

Magic! he thought, again – but this time he was certain. This time, it was Ritandyr's spell, bidding to control the angry elements and to recruit them to the cause of virtue and cleanness.

Then, as if some dreadful madness had been let loose in the air, there came a veritable fusillade of lightning-bolts – five or six of them, following one after another so closely as to seem mere facets of a single explosive display. Brilliant light split the northern sky again and again, and illuminated the whole battle for two or three full seconds.

After the lightning came the thunder, which seemed to rage about the sky from horizon to horizon, echoing back and forth as if it would not consent to be stilled.

There was a strange pause while this remarkable coincidence of shocks lasted. As the flickering light played over the roiling river Harmis could not help but wonder whether this was the proper culmination of Ritandyr's spell, or whether the power which he had invested in it had been wrenched altogether out of his control. It was easy to believe that the power of a wizard's magic was too feeble to control something as vast and heavy as the thunderstorm, and that all a human being might contrive to do was to unleash its own inherent fury, setting the thunder and the lightning free to run riot in the air.

The thunder went on and on... and on. Though the lightning had died quickly enough when its brief flashing was done, the noise could not be stilled so easily. Harmis had never heard anything like it, and could not help asking

himself whether the sky itself might be cracking into frag-
ments. Could this, he wondered, be the oft-prophesied
end of the world of men?

What had started in the sky seemed to descend to the
earth, and Harmis became convinced that Ritandyr had
overstretched himself, releasing a flock of angry elementals
who would wreak all the malicious havoc that they could
in the interval of their freedom.

The flames which were consuming the buildings across
the river seemed to leap more excitedly into the air despite
the deluge that fell upon them, and it seemed as though
the whole world was in upheaval, shaking with uncanny
laughter.

Still the thunder went on, and on...

Harmis saw by the light of the fire which burned near his
feet a single Zani warrior, caught hesitantly in the doorway.
He could see the expression on the other man's face, in the
wide eyes and the soaking hair of brows and beard.
Mirrored there was all his own uncertainty, and his own
fear that the order of things had somehow collapsed
before the assaults of the lightning-strikes.

Then he saw something else – another anxious thought,
brightly captured by the startled eyes of his enemy.

It was some frightful realization. The Zani *knew* something, which gave him cause for horror.

When he saw that the Zani had perceived something to
fill him with awful terror, Harmis was immediately able to
guess for himself what must have happened. The thunder
was still building in its long-delayed crescendo, rolling on
and on and unnaturally on. The ground beneath his feet
seemed all atremble... and Harmis knew that although the
thunder in the sky had died away as it should, it had been
replenished and replaced by a very different thunder upon
the surface of the earth.

In the meagre pasturelands to the north of Cavanal the
Zani had abandoned their herds. The warhost had come
on ahead, leaving the tired and hard-driven animals to rest
and graze. But those five lightning-bolts so close together,

and the thunder which had bellowed across the sky thereafter, had frightened the beasts so badly that they had begun to run excitedly in the grip of panic.

They were stampeding southwards – and they would not stop until they reached the bank of the Tana Dante, where tens of thousands of their herdsmen were gathered, waiting for the bridge to be remade so that they might cross.

Harmis saw, written in the Zani's wide eyes, what the terror-stricken man had deduced from that dreadful sound. Unless the entire force committed itelf to the waters of the river, the Zani warriors would die where they were. That bridge whose rebuilding had seemed inevitable could not now serve its purpose, for there was no longer time enough to use it.

There was no time at all!

With an ululating cry of triumph Harmis Detz hurled himself forward at his enemy, and wheeled his sword so mightily round his head that he nearly severed the Zani's head with the extravagant stroke.

The Zani went crashing down – and with him, it seemed, went all the hopes his people had raised that for once the Tana Dante could not be held, and that Khypris itself would be theirs to sack and plunder.

With the Zani felled, Harmis could see clearly enough what was happening on the far side of the river, by the light of the fires which burned there. The Zani were in flight, riding pell mell along the shore on mounts which must be every bit as terror-stricken as the aurochs thundering towards them.

The marauders fled one way or the other quite without discrimination, just as the crowds which their advance had displaced from the farms and villages had fled when the bridge was closed. In but a single instant their whole campaign had been rendered hopeless, and had been abandoned. More than that – their horde and their herds would be scattered so widely that they would take home far fewer beasts than they had brought, and would be condemned to wait for many generations before they could dare to think of assaulting the lowlands again.

The hillmen in the water and on the bridge were there to be slaughtered now by the ebullient defenders, no matter that there were hundreds of them, or even thousands. The aurochs could not cross the river, and nothing on the far bank could possibly withstand the power of their panic-stricken charge; there was no retreat for the Zani who were already committed to the fight.

The battle of Cavanal was won, and the heartland of Khypris had been miraculously saved from invasion.

Whether it could yet be saved from its subtler enemies, time alone would tell.

CHAPTER FIFTEEN

HARMIS RETURNED TO the inn soon after dawn. The first light of day had confirmed that the battle of Cavanal was over, and won. The Zani were gone and their herds had been scattered. The northern shore of the town had been turned into a wasteland by burning and trampling, and that wasteland was deserted now.

He came into the room in a state of some excitement, exultant with the happy result of the magicians' work; but his excitement died very quickly when he saw how things stood.

Ritandyr's body lay in the centre of the pentacle which had been inscribed on the floor of the room. There was so little flesh left on the bones that it had the appearance of a bundle of damp rags. His broken staff lay beside him and the shards of several shattered bottles were scattered about the room.

Nicodemus was still alive, but he had not survived unscathed. He lay in a corner of the room, as though he had been contemptuously hurled there. He was conscious now, and a cloak had been draped over his shoulders to warm him, but he was as yet unable to rise. Averil was with him, mopping his face with a soft leather cloth.

Among the debris, five gold coins gleamed brightly, as though radiant with evil. Only five – though Harmis knew, having once seen what Asmunda had clutched in her hand, that there ought to have been more.

'What happened?' asked Harmis. He put out a hand to support himself against the doorpost. He felt suddenly exhausted, as though all the strength which had been taut within his body had unwound. He was soaked to the skin, and the rainwater was leadenly heavy in his clothes, cold and unrefreshing.

'Revenge,' replied Averil, with a tremor in her voice. 'Revenge for what you did to the Lazarite – but more than that by far. I saw his face – the Lazarite's. All twisted, corrupted flesh... with the worms feeding. And I saw the *katharos*, in its human guise, possessed by furious laughter. It knew what we would try to do, and it was ready. Nor has it finished with us yet.'

'The Lazarite is dead,' said Harmis, dully.

'The dead can return,' she told him, 'when the order of things is disturbed and distorted. As the spell came to its culmination – when all of Ritandyr's effort and the entire strength of his soul were taking command of the clouds – the air opened around him; space itself was split and from that rent such foul things looked out... when two spells collide, there is such a flood of force... Ritandyr was weaker. The *katharos* knows where we are... it knew what we would do... and the water of the Black Tarn could not destroy it... could not, in the end, hold it at bay.'

Harmis could hear the accusation in her voice again. It was *his* fault that he had welcomed the angel of death into their company. It was his fault that he had let her touch him.

It was his fault that he had taken tainted gold.

He looked down at the five coins, hurled here by some derisory miracle, to add insult to injury.

Was it his fault, he complained silently, that a role had been thrust upon him which he was not fitted to play? Was it his fault that the servants of the dark god of plague sought to sport with him?

He struggled to find what comfort he could in the face of the tragedy. 'Though Ritandyr is dead,' he said, hoarsely, 'he did not die in vain. When his spell was wrecked, the flood of power which was unleashed sent the aurochs stampeding, and drove the Zani away. Perhaps the *katharos*, too, did not escape without injury.'

Averil shook her head. 'The *katharos* is more powerful than that,' she said. 'It will be weaker now, for all magic is effortful, but it will not weaken itself much further as it carries the plague to Khypris, for that is a slow and smouldering spell, which will continue to do its work until the tainted gold has exhausted its evil. The daemon will save strength enough to meet us in Khypris, for its vengeance is not yet complete. It will not let us go, now that it has deigned to be playful with our destiny.'

It was a prophecy which made Harmis shiver. 'Then we're beaten,' he said. 'Khypris is lost and we must fight for our own safety.'

Nicodemus struggled to rise then, and said: 'No!'

Harmis went to help the youth, and found him not so badly hurt as he had at first appeared to be.

Ritandyr alone had taken the full force of the perverted spell – perhaps deliberately, conscious that he might shield his assistant. They would never know exactly what kind of hero had lurked behind those fleshy cheeks and watery eyes.

'This is an unending war,' said Nicodemus, when he was on his feet and standing unsupported. 'The god of plague cannot build an empire or recognize surrender, nor is the utter extermination of a race to be counted by him as a victory. Where he rules there must be misery and fear, not universal death – and what he thrives on most of all are loud despair and lamentation, and the mad merriment of hopelessness. The plague may kill two in three, or three in four, but still the survivors would stand in need of salvation.'

Nicodemus paused to cough convulsively, and the spasm brought tears to his tired eyes. But then he continued. 'It is imperative still that we go to Khypris. Every life we can save from his predatory glee... every soul we may save from the abandonment which is his worship... is a tiny victory, and not to be despised. We must find the *katharos* and destroy it. That's the task for which the kinder gods have appointed you, Harmis Detz, and never say that all is lost while it can still be done.'

'But has Averil not told me, just now, that this is what the *katharos* intends we should do?' asked Harmis, incredulously.

'That's not important,' answered Nicodemus. 'It's what we *must* do, whatever the daemon may intend.'

Harmis suppressed an urge to laugh. Despite all the blood and hurt he felt that this adventure had become a macabre comedy, in which a tide of absurdity would carry him on to some silly, stupid death he had not deserved. But was it not the same for everyone else? Lavarock was dead, and the entire nation which Faramond ruled was dying in its turn. Even the schemes of the invading Zani had been aborted by their own startled herds, which must have slaughtered their erstwhile masters with their trampling feet – and would now provide good meat for whatever survivors there were in the derelict northlands.

What sport the gods must have, in watching the frantic stirrings of the human ants'-nest! What tides of helpless laughter must stir the cold grey depths of the sea of souls!

'Well,' he said, dourly, 'if ride we must, then ride we shall. To the fortified city which is the beating heart of the realm – bearing the wondrous news that the Zani are scattered and the princedom saved from all but the enemy within.'

They collected what they could of what they had owned. The five gold pieces tossed to them by the wrathful daemon were sealed by Nicodemus in a small stone jar with a measure of that dark water which had not quite suppressed the curse which was upon them; this they threw into the muddied and bloodied river by the broken bridge. But Harmis kept the single coin which Asmunda had thrown to him with such cunning contempt, accepting that the chance might yet come to fling it back at her.

Later that day, they left Cavanal to its brave defenders, and took the road which led to Khypris.

At first, the road was all but deserted, for those who had fled Cavanal before the Zani came had felt a keen necessity to take themselves away as quickly as they possibly could. But in the evening they began to catch up with those who had fled on foot – and they began to see what swift and hungry work the tainted coins had done as they had passed so furtively from hand to hand.

The villages to which they came were swollen with people. Every house or encampment or wagon that had come this way had been touched by sickness, and every man, woman or child who still could walk had become a beggar on behalf of those who could not. Wherever people gathered, there were crowds of fearful people, crying out for help to all who were not yet taken ill. They were as desperate for water and food as they were for curative magic and healing hope.

Those of the sick who had been forced to travel alone had none to beg for them and none to take them in; a great many simply lay beside the road, where they had fallen when they were no longer able to go on. Others, who had taken shelter in inns or farmhouses before falling sick, had been brought quickly forth from their temporary havens and abandoned by their frightened hosts. These had usually been placed in such a way as to catch the attention of passing travellers.

'See,' said Nicodemus to Harmis, in a low tone, 'how the hypocritical conscience is inclined to work. It whispers to those who find themselves endangered: cast the sick man out, for thine own protection – but place him where others may see him, so that they too must accept their share of the guilt of his abandonment.'

But Harmis only shrugged, knowing full well that he would have done the same, in similar circumstances.

Harmis was a strong man, and his feelings had been numbed by what had happened in the days since the evil mist had come to Vimera; he felt hardly a qualm when he rode by old men and old women crying feebly for his help; but he could hardly bear to look at the children, for fear that the desperation in their frightened eyes might break his heart.

It did no good to tell himself that there was nothing he or any other man could do – or that if there was an end to be achieved, it could only be accomplished by riding by, in relentless pursuit of the evil daemon which had stricken the princedom with disease and anguish. All of that was true, but it did no good to know it, for the horror that was in the children's eyes could not be properly answered by the truth, but only by a charity which must be as boundless as it was reckless and hopeless.

Harmis could not bear to look at the little children, because he was not that kind of hero.

He took stock of himself when they stopped to rest for the night, as far away as possible from the anguished cries of the sick and the dying. He had not been cut at all in the defence of Cavanal's waterfront, and his body was as numb as his feelings, sustained by the magical care of the tarnwine which he craved, and by the strength of his determination.

He no longer ached, or felt fatigued in any physical way. Perversely, though, there was an unquiet yearning in his limbs for sensation – even such cruel sensation as the dark water had brought when it did its harshest healing work. In one part of his being he wanted desperately to feel, even if all that he could feel was pain, for the whole world seemed to him to be in pain, and he was part of the world, and did not want to shirk its burdens. But that was only a part of him. The rest of him was desolate, quiescent, patient... waiting to confront again the thing which had pretended to be a pretty woman, and had named itself Asmunda.

Harmis Detz knew its true name, and its true nature, and when the next morning came, and they rode on again towards Khypris he came to feel, for the first time, that what Astyanax of Violtis had told him must indeed be the truth. He, Harmis Detz, was a champion appointed by fate, thrown up by the uncoiling thread of circumstance to succeed or fail in one of the very many quests which men must pursue in trying to save their world from spoliation and make it better than it was.

During the following night, when they camped in another desolate spot, Harmis heard Nicodemus and Averil making love to one another. They had not done so before while he was with them and he felt oddly annoyed that they had chosen to do it now. It seemed to him as though it was a deliberate act of exclusion, intended by Averil to make him feel more lonely than he was, or to punish him for having paid such futile and fruitless attention to her prettier rival while she waited, patiently and unsuspectingly, among the crowd at Cavanal. But he was able to put it from his mind, telling himself that he must not begrudge his friends what comfort they had because he had none of his own.

He slept very deeply, in spite of all the anxieties which conspired to haunt and harry him, and he dreamed of his brother Lavarock and peaceful times when they had both been young.

THE NEXT DAY they came within sight of Khypris, seeing it first from the crest of a rise.

It was at once a city and a citadel, its great grey walls sprawling over the slopes of a hill in most ungainly fashion. It had always seemed to Harmis a very grand place, within whose cradle all that was best and cleverest in the nation was nurtured and nourished, but it did not seem so grand now. Its high walls no longer marked a boundary of safety and seclusion, but rather a cold and impotent barrier against a mighty legion of the poor, who had fled to it expecting succour, and found none.

He had never seen so many people as were gathered in the shadow of those walls. It was an incredible crowd, and though he could not begin to count it he could easily have believed that the whole nation had somehow crawled here to die.

In fact, he realized eventually, the crowd was not packed as densely as he had at first assumed. There were wagons and crude wooden shelters in great profusion, but they were not huddled together as one might have expected had they been gathered by fear of an approaching enemy. These people knew that whether the Zani warlord and his host would come or not, they had an enemy in their midst which was not one whit less malevolent. The plague was among them, and was running its virulent course, reducing three in every five of those who had come here to a shabby and rheumy wreck, besoiled and besored.

How many of the plague's victims might ultimately recover Harmis could not yet begin to guess – but he knew that everyone who was weak of constitution, very old or very young, or already afflicted by any one of the myriad woes which harried mankind even in the best of times, must hear the wings of Morr's dark ravens hovering near.

The makeshift city-without-a-city which had grown around the walls of Khypris was the saddest sight Harmis had ever seen; he could not help but offer up a prayer that he would never see a sadder one. There was an awesome, terrible quiet in the vast encampment, which could not have contrasted more absolutely with the noise and urgency agitating the lesser crowds which had gathered on the approach to Cavanal. The people in those smaller crowds had been desperate to be on the move, avid to run; the people here had reached their destination – or had come as close to it as they were allowed. There was nothing left for them to do but pray for deliverance, and wait for the judgment of the gods to be passed upon their unlucky lives and hapless souls.

Still there were beggars lining the road, but their voices were not clamorous or hopeful; these wrecks of men and women had been reduced by constant failure to mere automata, their calls as lifeless as the keening of the wind upon the stony hills.

Wherever there were no beggars there were corpses instead, laid out in the glaring light of the hot high sun. There were flies everywhere, and rats swarming in plain sight; many of the dead had been ravaged by the teeth of tiny predators. But there were dead rats to be seen too, claimed in their turn by the omnivorous blight which the daemonic angel of death had bought with her treacherous coin.

Break the bridges *now*, Astyanax had ordered. Harmis had not understood why at the time, but now he saw the logic of the case all too clearly. The gathering of this crowd was what Astyanax had sought to prevent, or at least to minimize. But Faramond and his functionaries had not properly understood; they had not seen the necessity to do other than their ancestors had done; forewarned by magic though they were, they had not seen the urgency of the task before them. Whatever had been done had been done half-heartedly and too late. The crowd had gathered, its members huddling like a herd of docile beasts for mutual comfort and protection, not knowing that they had come to the slaughterhouse, and that corruption would pass among them as swiftly and as surely as an ugly rumour.

Harmis still could not bear to look from side to side, lest he meet the hollow eyes of little children. He kept his eyes fixed on the city's western gate, which was closed and list-lessly guarded.

When they reached the gate, Harmis gave their names to the guardsmen and showed the captain of the guard the paper which he carried. The captain could not read, but he was a very dutiful man, and he called for a scrivener or a scholar to be brought, who could tell him exactly what the warrant said.

'Faramond has magicians aplenty in his court,' growled the captain, scanning Nicodemus and Averil without enthusiasm. 'Or had – for they say that his chambers have fallen as silent as the rest, and such orders as we have come from the seneschal. 'Tis treason to say that the prince might be dead, so loyalty commands that he be hale and hearty, but don't expect a warm welcome when you go to his palace, or to any other part of the town. The dead can't answer you when you knock, and the living will not.'

'If the plague is already in the city,' said Harmis, 'why do you close and guard the gate? How can it matter who goes in and who comes out?'

'The order of things must be maintained as best we can,' said the captain, darkly. 'If it should transpire that so many die within the walls that the food which is stored there is too abundant to be used, no doubt they will send some out to these unhappy beggar-folk, to lend a little strength to those whose task it will be to make bonfires of the legions of the dead.'

'The order of things,' echoed Harmis. 'Order must be maintained. I beg your pardon, sir, for I had quite forgotten it.'

It was insolence of a kind, but the captain only grinned. Whatever discipline still held together the ranks of the claret-and-gold, it was not fear of punishment and the wrath of captains. Nor, it seemed, was the order of things too rigidly maintained, for when the word came back that not a scribe or scholar could be found, the captain instructed that the gate should be opened anyhow.

'I can't read your paper,' he said, 'but we wear the same colours, and so I take your word that it entitles you to enter. Perhaps there's no longer any man alive in Khypris who can read it, so that its meaning will be forever lost. I trust you, because it can't matter whether I trust you or not, and if you've made a fool of me in order to trick your way into this great grey charnel-house, I wish you well of my foolishness.'

Harmis saluted the man, and moved on through the open gate – which, when the last of their horses had passed through, was carefully closed again, in the interests of maintaining order.

There was a striking contrast between the road outside and the streets of the city. Whereas the former had been lined with people, the latter were almost deserted. Here, the dying had homes to die in, and those who were left to care for the sick had pallets on which to place them.

There were death-carts abroad in the city's streets, where the rotting and the dying were not allowed to lie. But there were men-at-arms patrolling, in ones and twos, wearing claret-and-gold or red-and-white or blue-and-grey as their allegiance commanded.

It seemed that every window in the city was shuttered and secured, and that every door was bolted. The city had ceased to be a place where every man, woman and child was constantly part of a jostling crowd, and had become instead a thing of walls and barriers – a huge maze of lonely vaults and tombs.

When they passed the square where executions took place, with its scaffolds and gibbets, they saw that the traditional emblems of the old authority were still maintained, for there were hanged men swinging from three of the gibbets, to demonstrate the follies of dishonesty. There was also something not quite human and not quite dead which had been roughly nailed by its wrists, knees and ankles to a wooden stake. The sewers of Khypris were said to be home to fugitive goblins and ghouls, and here was proof of it, put on exhibition for all to see.

'How will we find the *katharos*?' asked Harmis. 'Khypris is very full of narrow lanes and alleys, and its houses have many rooms and cellars. It might take a year to find her if she's cunning enough, though none who have seen her is likely to have forgotten her.'

'I don't think that it will hide,' said Nicodemus. 'It knows what happened to Ritandyr, and it could have killed me with him had it not elected to preserve me for a later death. It is not afraid of us, because it knows and savours the memory of the ways in which it has deceived and used us in the past. Now that it has done its work, it is free to turn its attention to our destruction, and will seek to be amused in accomplishing that end.'

It was not a comforting thought, but Harmis believed he was beyond fear now – he wanted only to see this adventure ended. If all that was left to be salvaged was a hot moment of revenge, then he would have it; and if it transpired that he should die in trying to achieve it, so be it. There was nothing to be gained by turning back.

'We'll go to the palace,' he said. 'To Faramond's inner sanctum, if we can. If my prince is still alive, I'll give him a full account of what has happened to the land he ruled. If he is not, then I'll ask for help from the steward who rules in his name. If anyone knows where the woman is, the prince's steward will find out for us.'

'It's not a woman,' said Averil, harshly. 'You should have learned the error of that way of thinking, and shouldn't speak of it thus. It's a daemon, whose true nature is very horrible indeed.'

'It'll make no difference when I face her,' said Harmis, flatly. 'No difference at all.'

CHAPTER SIXTEEN

FARAMOND'S PALACE WAS a citadel-within-a-citadel, and its doors were by no means as huge as the gates which controlled the flow of people in and out of Khypris; they were not wide enough to allow the passage of carts.

These doors were made of a dark wood, of a mass and solidity very rarely seen in the timber-poor land; all were usually guarded from within, by militiamen who would peer out at anyone who knocked through small rectangular holes faced with iron grilles.

Faramond liked to be thought of as a popular prince, and he was not quite as fervently hated as some of his ancestors had been, but he was a firm believer in that wisdom of princes which places more trust in the protection of strong walls than the good opinion of the lower orders.

Perhaps, thought Harmis Detz, the character of the realm could be read in the fact that the palace was more secure from invasion from the city than the city was against invasion from the heartland, just as the heartland's security against invasion from the lands beyond the Tana Dante was greater by far than the security of the north-lands and westlands from the hillmen of the Zani.

When Harmis knocked on the first door he came to, no one answered him, and though he hammered with the hilt of his sword when he was tired of banging with his fist, still he had no reply but booming echoes.

'They must have have sealed the palace,' said Nicodemus, 'in an attempt to keep the plague at bay. While his people die like flies, Faramond and his retinue are determined to be safe. It's only to be expected.'

'Perhaps,' said Harmis. 'But the guardsmen at the gate must still receive their orders. It may be that these doors were sealed too late, and that the plague has run a more furious riot within than without.'

'Do you think so?' asked Averil. 'Can the *katharos* possibly be lodged within?'

'They couldn't seal the palace before they'd provisioned it,' said Harmis, drily. 'If such a decision was taken, they would have held the doors open while a flood of food and wine came in – and there are many inside who'd think of pretty women as provisions too. A sick man or a starving child would be turned away without a second glance, but a winsome whore would find a different welcome. A woman like Asmunda might have won her way to Faramond's own bed.'

'If that's true,' said Nicodemus, 'the prince and his courtiers may have paid a dreadful price for their pleasure.'

'No meagre ounce of gold,' answered Harmis, pensively, 'nor any mere cupful of blood.'

They did not know quite what he meant, and he was glad of it.

'We must go to another gate,' he said. 'It's possible there's such sickness among the guardsmen that only one or two of the doors can be watched.'

With this in mind, they made their way around the perimeter of the high grey wall which bounded the core of Farmamond's domain. As they came in turn to each of the doors they repeated their hammering, but with the same result.

At one of the doors, a poor man squatting nearby in the gutter called out to them that none had passed that way for two days and more – and when Nicodemus tried to give him a copper coin by way of thankful recognition he refused, saying that he no longer had need of it, having passed beyond the reach of hunger or hope.

'What can we do but go away?' asked Averil. 'We've done what we could.'

'Perhaps we should find lodging for the night,' admitted Nicodemus, 'and come again in the morning.'

'If it's a matter of duty,' said Harmis, hollowly, 'then it's a matter of duty. What safe lodging can we find, in a city of the dying and the dead? If the *katharos* has grown wings and taken flight, then all is done and finished; but if it's still within the citadel – within these walls which seek to keep us out – then we must try to get in. If we can't have the bolts withdrawn by hammering, then we must have them withdrawn by magic. Is it not a petty spell, to open a sealed door?'

'Aye,' said Nicodemus, grudgingly. 'If there are only bolts to hold it, a petty spell will draw them back.'

'Why *if*?' demanded Harmis, who had grown impatient with the reluctance of these novices to use their skills.

'The prince has magicians in his court,' said Averil, 'and the means to block achievement is ever easier to come by than the power of accomplishment. If these doors have magical barriers about them as well as bolts, Nicodemus won't be able to get through them, and might hurt himself by trying.'

Harmis felt an urge to laugh. 'I understand,' he answered, ironically. 'Although we walk through the streets of a dying city, where the plague-stricken beggars are too polite to take his coin... although he's had his arm broken by a Lazarite's anger, and his head spun by wild lightning... he must beware of hurting himself in trying to open a wooden door.'

'You do *not* understand!' objected Averil. 'Indeed you do not. You don't know what kind of world this really is, or what traps and curses abound within it. You believe our magic is at best a wayward thing which we haven't learned to use, and at worst mere charlatanry. But you don't understand what power is truly set free in this land, or what hazards there are in trying to draw upon it fruitfully, and channel it to better ends. But even you, poor soldier that you are, must know how much easier it is to destroy than it is to build... how much easier it is to kill than it is to preserve.'

'Enough!' said Nicodemus, tiredly. 'The man is right. If they will not let us through, then I must try the door with magic. He has the truth of it when he says that it's a matter of duty.'

While Harmis and Averil stood back, therefore, Nicodemus began to test the dark wood of the door with his artful fingers, as if trying to trace invisible contours within its substance.

After a few minutes of careful exploration, he placed both hands, with fingers splayed and thumbs just touching, along a line which Harmis judged to be that of the upper bolt. Then he murmured an incantation as quickly and indistinctly as he might have intoned a casual prayer in a temple.

Harmis heard the sound of an iron bolt drawn slowly back in its bed – but when Nicodemus turned to look at him, there was sweat on the boy's face, and far more distress than had seemed likely.

'The protective spell is weak,' said the young magician. 'It's not like one of those curses which gains in power with the passing of time, and is opposable by brute willpower – but it is an effort, nevertheless. Alas, the *katharos* left me very weak when it condescended not to kill me.'

'I'll help,' said Averil, stepping promptly forward.

But Nicodemus shook his head, saying: 'A proper combination of wills is too difficult – had it been easier, I think I would have been dead with Ritandyr.'

Harmis took Averil by the arm, and pulled her away as Nicodemus crouched, then knelt to place his hands along the line of the second bolt. Again there was the sound of the hurried incantation, followed by the scraping sound of the bolt laboriously drawing back.

Then Nicodemus wiped his brow on his sleeve, and quivered as though an icy blast had passed through him. 'The palace is open to us,' he said. 'I only pray that what we seek is to be found within.'

When they had come through the door, bringing their horses with them, Harmis drew the bolts again to secure it. It was such a little thing, requiring hardly any strength at all – but he had a hand and a muscled arm to use, while Nicodemus had been forced to use the sinews of thought and desire.

Within the covered coutyard, which was lit by a single lantern, three dead men could be seen, lying by the wall. All wore uniforms; all were badly bloodied by rat-bites. There were dead rats beside one of the corpses, which the rats had attacked just a little too soon, while the man could still make some defence with his dagger.

Harmis looked around, at the inner doors which gave access to the main part of the building. There were three, the two to either side giving access to rounded towers, the middle one to a hall beneath the sleeping-quarters of the noblemen.

He had been here before, but not for some time. He could find his way to the prince's audience-chamber, where Faramond played judge and counsellor from the high station of his wooden throne, and to the barracks where the guard was lodged, but those were the only places he knew tolerably well, save for the labyrinthine warren of the prince's stables where he had been born and raised.

Harmis looked about, half expecting that now he was within the palace, someone would come to ask what he wanted – but the place was so silent that his last doubts melted away. The plague had come like a well-aimed arrow

to the very heart of Khypris, and had wrought its worst
destruction here. That had always been the daemon's first
intention, and neither Astyanax's foresight nor Ritandyr's
spell, nor even the combined might of Faramond's armies,
had contrived to deflect or interrupt it.

What was there left to do now, but make sure – if he
could – that the reign of the *katharos* in Khypris would be
as short as possible?

There was a slight sound then – the sound, perhaps, of a
wooden shoe upon a stone stair. It came from the door to
the right, which led into a tower where Harmis had never
been. It made up his mind for him, and he allowed himself to be drawn by it, abandoning the horses in the yard.
Nicodemus and Averil followed him.

He quickly found the stone stairway, which led downwards into the cellars beneath the tower, but he hesitated
to descend because of the darkness awaiting him. Averil
did not wait to be asked; she took from her cloak the crystal rod which she always carried with her, and coaxed from
its depths a cold white radiance to light their way.

Harmis went down, pausing briefly before the doors of
three or four rooms, and looking along the single side corridor which he passed – but each time he heard another
faint noise it came from below.

The staircase spiralled twice, then ended in a stone corridor whose walls wept with slime. There was a stink of rot
and excrement, and Harmis remembered again the stories
about ghouls which lived in caves beneath the city, emerg-
ing by night to hunt their human prey in the alleys and
lanes.

He moved along the corridor. The floor was very wet,
and the water flowing there was discoloured. There was
fungus growing abundantly in the angles where the walls
met the floor and the ceiling.

There were doors at regular intervals along the corridor,
each of which had two bolts on the outside. These were the
dungeons of Faramond's little realm-within-the-realm. But
at the end of the corridor there was a different kind of

door, which had no bolts, but only a catch, and was constructed out of iron bars, not made of wood. It was very rusty, and it stood ajar.

While he approached it, Harmis made every effort to walk quietly, though he knew that he and his companions had made noise enough when they came down the stone stair. If there was really someone to follow, that person must be aware that he – or she – was pursued.

When he reached the door, he looked in furtively, to see if anyone was there. Averil was still close behind him, holding her steady light so that he could see.

Beyond the iron door was a round, high-ceilinged chamber. In the centre of the room was a wrought-iron cage suspended a foot or two above the floor. It was far too small to hold a man comfortably – but its intention was clearly to hold a man as uncomfortably as possible. It was empty now. There was a firepit set beneath it, which could be used to make the bars of the cage red-hot, or to roast alive the prisoner placed within it.

One section of the curving wall was hung with neatly-arrayed iron tools of various kinds; another had several sets of manacles. Set before a third section was a curious construction whose horizontal wooden frame had two rectangular slots in it, which served as beds for the ends of a metal band that curved between them like an arch. Under this half-hoop there was a metal device with a screw-thread and a winding-handle, which could be used to increase or decrease the radius of the arch. At either end of the wooden table were catchments for wrists and ankles.

Unlike the cage, this curious stretching-rack was inhabited. Extended across the arch was the emaciated body of a man. His eyes were open, but he had long since passed beyond the power of any torturer to hurt him.

Behind this device, watching Harmis over the stretched corpse, was the creature which had seemed to him a beautiful and vulnerable woman: Asmunda, the angel of death. The expression on her face was unfathomable.

'It is my eager would-be lover,' she said, in her curiously husky voice, as though to mock him with pretended surprise. 'You are very welcome here, for now that my work is done I will be pleased to tarry a while with you, and make up for that opportunity which was missed.'

Harmis stepped into the room, cautiously. Averil came in behind him, and Nicodemus too.

'But you are not alone,' said the *katharos*, reproachfully. 'I wish that you would send your friends away, for we do not need them at all.'

'You led us here,' said Harmis, accusingly. 'You were not fleeing from us – you led us here, intending to confront us. Why did you do that?'

'Why,' she said, 'to show you the underbelly of that world of which you are so proud and carefully protective. I am disappointed, I confess, to find it as empty as this. I had hoped to find those special fruits which ripen here clustered more abundantly upon the bough. But you are not without imagination, Harmis Detz, and you know what this place is, and what is done here.'

'I know,' said Harmis, 'but what of it?'

'Oh Harmis, I thought better of you than that. This is the very centre of your prince's empire, which you have come too late to save. It is but a single dismal chamber, with only a single sad and sorry corpse to decorate it, but it is your whole and entire world writ small. This is what men make of themselves, and one another, when they have the power to do it. It has ever been the business of men to vent their violent wrath, not only in killing, but in the patient excruciation of their kin. Men are great visitors of pain and death upon their own kind, Harmis – is it any wonder that my master has so many secret worshippers?'

'Kill her,' said Averil, softly. 'Do not listen to her, or look at her. Kill her now.'

Her! thought Harmis. Does she call it *her*, now that she can see it, and fear it honestly?

The creature which had called itself Asmunda laughed. 'Do you truly think that he has come to kill me?' she asked.

'Do you truly think that I will consent to be killed? Why, child, he has come to seal the bargain which he made with me, and offer himself to my master, to become a lord of plague!'

'Bargain!' said Harmis, angrily. 'Though I took your coin, all unsuspecting, I made no bargain!'

'Have you not, my sweetheart?' replied the daemon. 'Have you never looked about you, at your tawdry world and its wretched people, and said: let there be a curse upon them all, save only me; let them all be destroyed, for there is none but I worth saving! Come, have you not said it, time and time again?'

'No,' said Harmis, stolidly. 'I never have.'

'You cannot say so to *me*,' countered the daemon. 'To your fellow men, you may present a false face, but I am servant to a master which knows your inmost and very secret thoughts – who knows the real nature of your wrathful heart and your corrupted soul. You must not think that he does not like you, Harmis Detz, because you slew his Lazarite. The gods do not bear grudges of that mean and manly sort.

'The Lazarite looked deep into your being before he died and the knives which you bear on your back are anointed with his blood. You have been touched by Chaos, Harmis, but you need not fear that touch, if it does not make you foolish. Become my master's champion and not his foe, and you will have the kind of power that those who built this little world have only dreamed of.

'My master is the lord of pain and anguish, who scorns such petty things as racks and pincers and red-hot cages. You are a soldier, Harmis, and you know what it is to hunt and kill. The soldiers of my master, I vow, are the greatest hunters and killers of all, and you cannot begin to imagine what rewards he offers to those who serve him well!'

'Kill her!' screamed Averil – and before Harmis could react, she snatched the dagger from the sheath upon his back that was nearest to her, and hurled the weapon with all her might.

But the *katharos* was not in the least alarmed and the knife embedded itself in the unfeeling corpse of the man arched across the iron rack.

'Fool!' cried Harmis – and even Nicodemus seized Averil by the arm, very fearfully.

The *katharos* laughed again, and said: 'You cannot hurt me, little witch. You cannot hurt me at all, for I need not even exert myself to melt into these walls or to hurl myself in flight into the empty air in order to return to a place where I am beyond the reach of any weapon which you can throw. There is nothing you can do – nothing at all. And I need only extend my arm, thus, to blot you utterly from existence.'

And as the creature said it, as casually as though it intended only to show how a finger must be straightened, it pointed at Nicodemus. But there was more involved than mere demonstration, for the youth was instantly seized by some invisible hand about his throat, which choked him.

'Stop!' shouted Harmis.

And, to his surprise, the *katharos* stopped. Nicodemus gagged and retched, but it was clear that the constricting force had been removed from his throat.

The *katharos* was still smiling.

'Belated mercy?' asked Harmis, bitterly. 'Or mere delay?'

'Mere delay,' replied the other, with a curious chuckle. 'Damned or doomed you are, but I had rather offer you both the choice. He is a wizard of sorts, after all, and my master can find uses for such servants as he – and you are a fighting man, who understands duty and the hunger which fierce men have to be avenged on those who have hurt them. But I will not take the girl, for she is so very plain!'

The contempt in her voice was almost tangible.

'Though you have touched me,' said Harmis, 'still I am not stricken with the plague. I have the protection of the water from the Black Tarn, as have we all. And I have the second knife upon my back, which is the one which has not been drawn since Astyanax bid me keep it safe. I think I had rather test its worth than sell myself to a master such as yours. That is what my hunger for vengeance, which you so admire, bids me to do.'

Then, for the first time, the *katharos* seemed near to anger.

'Poor fool,' it said, disdainfully. 'You little know what a thirst you will begin to feel when the last of that vile water is used up. But do not trouble to draw your knife, for I shall not tarry here if that is your answer to my promise.'

The thing which looked like a beautiful woman raised its arms and its form began to blur.

Averil cried: 'Kill her!' yet again, but Harmis did not draw his knife, because he knew that there was not time enough for it to fly through the air.

Instead, he struck a magician's pose himself, and cried as thunderously as he could: 'Stay, I command thee!'

And when the daemon began to laugh at his absurd presumption, he howled with all his might: 'I name thee YSTARETH, and with that name I bind thee to the earth!'

All of a sudden, the beautiful mask which the daemon had worn began to dissolve, and it let out such a dreadful shriek that his ears were hurt by it, and his head began to spin. Harmis recoiled beneath the uncanny fury of that scream, and he saw in what had been dark but human eyes a glare and a gleam which he had not seen since the Lazarite had cursed him.

He tried to shield his eyes, but could not do it, and again he felt the force of that stare moving in and through him, balefully staring into the very depths of his soul – a soul which had been much teased and tormented, which was subject still to a frightful taint.

He could not draw breath, and felt that he was overwhelmed by hopelessness and despair... but against the weight of that despair he fought, and in the deepest silence of his own being the voice of his thoughts cried out again: 'Ystareth! Ystareth!'

* * *

THE LIGHT WHICH Averil still carried, held aloft by her left hand, suddenly went out.

The darkness seemed utterly lonely, and very cold. Harmis felt that he was falling, but not to the floor of the torture-chamber. He felt that he was descending through the earth itself, mile after mile, deep into the solid rock. He moved, it seemed, towards the womb of space and time, where the gods played dice and fought their silly duels, with the souls of men and elves and dwarfs and goblins for their petty prizes.

In what he thought must be his moment of death, he screamed in rage and pain against the ignominy of it all – and thrust against the curse which caged his soul with all the pent-up fury of his righteous wrath.

CHAPTER SEVENTEEN

THE UNDERWORLD BENEATH the earth was all fire and confusion, and so vast that the awesome sublimity of it overwhelmed his simple terror – and that terror did not return to possess him even when he saw the face of the dead Lazarite engraved upon the unfolding record of eternity. The curse which the sorcerer had put upon him was cancelled out, obliterated by the merciful magic of the tarnwine – but his account was not yet settled, for there remained the tainted coin which he had unwittingly accepted from the *katharos*.

He saw another face then, which filled his sight and excluded all else: the face of Asmunda, whose true name was Ystareth. He looked into her dark and wonderful eyes, and saw behind them clouds of memory.

This daemon, Astyanax had told him, had once been a human being, who had entered voluntarily into the service of a Power of Chaos to become an eager and worthy champion of plague and pestilence. Harmis had assumed – as perhaps even Astyanax had assumed – that the champion had been a man. In fact, it had been a woman.

Harmis saw in those numinous clouds of memory the motives which had made the woman become what she now was, and knew that chief among them was that hunger for revenge which she had seen in his own soul. She too had once had a brother... a brother she had loved far more than Harmis had ever loved Lavarock... a brother who had been treacherously killed. He had died in Faramond's torture chamber, in that awful cage above the firepit... murdered by false accusations, born of greed for gold.

Harmis could not see within the cloud the face of the man who had brought those false accusations, for the dead man's sister had not held any single man to blame. She, in her wild and bitter generosity, had blamed the nation whole and entire, and if there was one particular thing upon which her hatred fixed itself it was not a man at all – not even Faramond – but an emblem of power: the claret-and-gold colours which were the symbol of Faramond's authority.

Harmis could not help but wonder whether fate had selected him to warn Astyanax of danger, and then to slay the Lazarite, not because there was a hero inside his livery, but simply because he wore the claret-and-gold. And if that was so, what loyalty did he owe to the fate which had selected him, and what trust could he put in destiny? Why should he not, after all, turn traitor to those who had only sought to use him as a catspaw, and accept the bargain which was offered to him now by a master more powerful by far? Had he not said, himself, that if a man must be a servant, it was best to serve the most powerful master he could find? Why not become a champion of a dark god, if that god could give him the power to wreak such angry vengeance on the world that even the fiercest of men must be more than content with it?

But Harmis had seen the working of that vengeance which Ystareth had taken, in the awful extremity of her bitter wrath.

He had seen Astyanax and Ritandyr, dead and daemon-rent.

He had seen the dying man who had refused a coin.

He had seen the miserable wrecks cast down at the roadside by those who would not keep them in their homes.

He had seen the faces of the little children, crying out for help and hope in a world from which all help and hope was banished.

Those were *his* most bitter memories, and while they possessed him he could not be tempted by what Ystareth and her leprous overlord had to offer him.

He was not that kind of hero.

And so he shut his eyes against that wrathful face and its skin-deep mask of beauty, and prayed to Shallya, Myrmidia and Morr that he might be given back the armour of his flesh, so that he might seek a rightful vengeance in his own measured way – and might then be released from the fierceness which howled in his soul, to be at peace again with the world and destiny.

HARMIS AWOKE TO pain, but it was a cleansing pain which he had grown to know well enough. Averil was bathing him yet again with the strange dark wine of Astyanax's mysterious tarn.

The *katharos* was nowhere to be seen.

Nicodemus was holding Averil's crystal rod, but it seemed that the extent of his weakness was reflected in the sickly yellow glow which it gave off.

Harmis groaned, and said: 'So this magic too has failed us! The last breath of Astyanax, as feeble in the face of this dire daemon as anything else we have done.'

'Not so,' said Nicodemus. The apprentice was leaning against the wall for support, breathing harshly, but his tone was not defeated or despairing. 'You've bound the daemon to the earth, and it must stay to face us again. It went from this room, but it can't go from the city, nor even from the palace. That thread which has connected you to it since you slew its servant is tightly-reeled, now that you have used its name to claim it – but I bid you beware, Harmis, for it still has magic to use, and though we have the dark water for armour against its blights and curses, it will not die easily.'

Harmis came slowly to his feet, and he knew that part of it, at least, was true. Somehow, he was connected to the *katharos*, whether by his act in slaying its human minion, or by some spell which Astyanax had placed upon him. But that bond could tug in either direction, as the daemon had known when it tried to tempt him.

Something dark and wild had entered into his soul, and there was something of Chaos within him still. It would be there until this business was finished, once and for all.

They returned along the gloomy corridor, lit for them again by Averil's magic – but instead of taking them back to the courtyard Harmis led them by another way into the main part of the building, through the great hall where great oaken tables were set out.

The remains of the final banquet Faramond had enjoyed with his lords and ladies was still upon the tables, left for the rats which were scampering hither and thither upon the embroidered cloth, bickering over crusts and crumbs.

A dozen of the dead were still positioned at the table, never having risen from that meal. The greedy rats had eaten their fingers and their faces.

Harmis drew his sword.

In this great vault of a room there would have been no need of Averil's magic light by day, but it was night-time now and the starlight which came through the high, narrow windows was very weak indeed. The radiance of the wand was still feeble and discoloured, and there were shadows everywhere, ominous and menacing. But there was nothing in the hall to threaten them, save for the rats which had been emboldened by their meal of human flesh.

Harmis went through the hall and out again by another door, looking for a place he knew: the audience-chamber, where Faramond's throne was.

Though he had to go slowly, struggling to remember the way, his instinctive sense of direction drew him on, so that he came at last to its door, and pushed it open.

Here too there were high windows to let in the light by day, but now the darkness seemed absolute, until Averil came forward to stand with him, and lifted up her magic crystal.

Before the throne which faced the door a man's handsomely costumed body lay. The rats had not touched it, though it seemed that it might have lain there for many hours. The man lay on his back, with arms outstretched, and his face was oddly like the long-dead Lazarite's, its flesh all stirred and ravaged as if by a malevolent hot hand whose one intention had been to wreak unpretty havoc.

Harmis could never have recognized the face, but the clothes the corpse still wore gave ample evidence of the man's high station. This had been Faramond, Prince of Khypris. He had been brutally cast down from his hard-held throne.

Harmis did not waste time studying his dead liege-lord. He looked instead at the creature which now sat nakedly upon that throne.

Its features were those it had worn before, but they seemed magnified now – as, indeed, its entire frame seemed magnified. The full lips were very red, and the soulful eyes seemed to promise an infinity of tenderness and love. Before, it had worn the beauty of a supernally pretty woman; now it wore that same beauty differently, as a goddess might wear it, with a pride of which no human – not even the greatest queen who ever sat upon an empire's throne – could ever have been capable.

'There is your nation,' said the *katharos* to Harmis Detz. 'There is your petty princedom, and the vain fool who sought to command it. Know, Harmis, that every nation of the earth is but appearance and illusion, and that the power which kings and princes have is but a shabby shadow of the *real* power which stands astride the world. Your rulers are but puppet clowns, dancing on the strings which gods and daemons tug for their own amusement. This world is but an eddy of dust in the whirlwind of eternity, infinitesimal in the eye of time. What do you think it can signify, to save a nation? What do you think it can matter to the masters of Chaos, if a world such as yours were here, or gone, or never here at all, when there are so very many worlds in the universe of stars?'

'I do not believe that there are masters of Chaos,' Harmis replied, as steadily as he could. 'Not even those who style themselves its gods. And I do not care at all what matters to them, or to you, or to all your monstrous kind. I care about what matters to me – which is this world, this nation and my friends. You have murdered my brother, and thousands of our kin, but you still have me to face, and in the power which Astyanax and fate have given me you will meet your last reckoning. Come down from the throne, Ystareth, for it is I who am the judge here, not you.'

And when he said *Come down from the throne*, the daemon came – and as it came, it lost the semblance which it had worn so proudly, for the illusion of purity was stripped from it now, and he saw it as it really was: twice as tall as he, with a huge head and but a single glaring eye, with great pointed ears and a lipless mouth full of horridly rotten teeth. It was green and grey, with its skin so marked with ulcers and lacerations that he could see through a dozen ragged slits to the pink and pulsing flesh inside.

And the monster – which was a *katharos* no more, but only an Unclean Champion of Chaos – roared like the thunder, and its foul breath caught Harmis in the face like a wind from the grave; and when he felt that foetor upon his flesh, it seemed that he lost all control over his own living body.

He had already planned his move; he knew that he must transfer the sword which he carried in his right hand into his left, while his right hand reached over his left shoulder to snatch out the dagger which had not yet been drawn, and hurl it at the daemon's heart. But the scourge of that withering breath changed everything, and it hurled him back like a rag doll, as though he were indeed a puppet jester, whose strings had instantly been cut.

He saw, from the corner of his eye, what the blast did to his two companions.

He saw the crystal rod plucked from Averil's grasping hands, and knew that its sickly yellow light was turned to vivid green as the instrument spun eerily about, dancing upon the air.

He saw poor Nicodemus snatched from his feet as though consumed by a vortex of corruption, and heard his desperate attempt to pronounce the words of power which might protect him.

He saw the girl – that poor, plain girl who had detested the appearance of Asmunda for all the wrong reasons – seized about the face as if by a wicked hand intent on serving her as cruelly as it had served the mighty Faramond.

In his desperation, he tried to speak, to shout aloud as he had done before the name by which this vileness might be commanded to desist; but when he drew air into his lungs to form the shout, that air was full of corruption and cloying contagion, which rebelled against his will and would not form the syllables he required.

He felt consumed by weakness, as though no possible effort of his dying frame could force his arm to move or his hand to grip. He was tumbled back against the door, pinned down to the stone floor by the awful weight of the hatred emitted by the dark angel of death.

He saw Nicodemus consumed by the blast of hatred, so completely that his flesh withered on his bones. The young man's terrorized cry of pain dissolved with horrific smoothness into the desolate empty grin of a fleshless skull – but even as death claimed him Nicodemus reached out his hand to seize Averil's wrist. Averil, meanwhile, was struggling with all her might against the invisible hand which sought to tear her face apart, and destroy whatever fugitive beauty there yet might be within her – but when she felt the touch of her fellow apprentice's fingers, she reached out too, towards Harmis's empty left hand.

Harmis took her hand in his, and felt a curious surge of strength pass from Nicodemus to Averil, and from Averil to himself. In the ritual of their hopeful clasp a spell was worked, and though it was fuelled by desperation rather than power, and by hope rather than wisdom, still it was a spell which worked against the daemon's horrid breath. *This* was the last legacy of Astyanax's teaching – teaching which had encompassed duty and affection as well as ritual and conjuration.

There built a cold and reasoning fury in the soul of Harmis Detz – the same cold and reasoning fury which had saved him in the dungeon and in his dream of the centre of the earth; a fury which said, *this will not be so!*

All the brave words Harmis Detz had spoken, and all the bitter tears he ever had shed, were suddenly within him, forming strange sinews and cords by which his nerveless body could be moved again. Though life was draining from the fibres of his body, there was something in him still which could resist the claw of corruption gripping his soul.

Chaos had touched him, but it had not claimed his heart.

He still had his sword in his right hand, and now he thrust it at the daemon, as he would have thrust it at a Zani marauder or a malevolent goblin. And the sword ripped the belly of the monster open, so that black blood and entrails came spilling out, with a cataract of noxious fluid.

The daemon screamed; although it was a daemon, which could easily survive such terrible hurts, still it could be hurt. An iron blade was not without virtue in the fight against Chaos and its champions, and a swordsman's skill was not to be despised.

But when Harmis came to his feet, releasing Averil's hand as he rose, it was the injured daemon which still had the advantage. It thrust out with its great hand, whose fingers were webbed like a frog's and very slimy, and threw him back against the wall so powerfully that his spine was badly jarred and the sword was jolted from his hand.

Then the monster howled in triumph, not caring at all that its guts were trailing from the cut in its belly, and took a step towards him, avid to rend him limb from limb.

No magic now could flow into him from his fallen companions; he was alone in the reeking storm of the monster's odious breath. He had nothing to draw upon but the vestiges of his own strength.

One thought – one supremely strange and unexpected thought – gave his hand the motive power which it needed to snatch the dagger from its scabbard.

He could not bear to look at the hollow eyes of the little children! He could not bear to see what had been done to them!

He was not that kind of hero.

This was the kind of hero that he was.

He hurled the knife with all his might, and saw as it flew that it was as true a throw as he had ever made. The virtuous blade sped like an arrow to the centre of a gaping sore in the daemon's mighty chest, through which a beating heart could be clearly seen.

The blow was precise, and awesome in its power.

The daemon screamed again, more loudly than before; but its scream did not last long, for like the body which it had worn and the evil wind which was its breath, the sound was snatched out of space and time, and where there had been naked horror, there was suddenly nothing but swirling dust, sparkling with a magical light which was silver again, without any hint of yellow or green.

Harmis came slowly to his feet.

Averil rose too. She was unhurt and untransformed. Her rugged face was as plain as it had ever been; whatever measure of beauty it contained had not been stolen from it by the invisible hand which had sought to wreck her features.

Nicodemus had not been so lucky. Although he was whole, and not a withered skeleton, his heart had stopped when he despatched the dregs of his power to aid his companions in their fight. He was dead – but he seemed, to judge by the expression in his open eyes, to have died peacefully. It was as though he had not been looking upon horrors at all, but only shedding a compassionate tear for all that had been done but now was finished.

Averil picked up her crystal rod, and sat down upon the empty throne – not because she saw herself as a queen, but because she was very tired and needed to rest.

Harmis took from his pocket the single gold coin Asmunda had given him, intending to seal a bargain which, in the end, he had refused to make. He dropped it on to Faramond's body; it was the last tribute which the dead prince would ever have from any of his people. Then he took Lavarock's mirror from his pouch, and looked at his own face reflected there.

He still bore the faded scars left there by the pox which he had contracted as a child. He always would. But his face was otherwise unspoiled, and the stare which met his own was not terrible in any way at all, but only haggard and human.

Averil had taken a bottle from her cloak, and she offered it to him without speaking.

'No,' he said, quietly. 'I do not need it. The thirst has left me. My soul is once again my own.'

LATER, HE WENT out again into the open air, to taste the rain which was gently falling from the night sky. One by one he went to the six gates of the palace, drawing the bolts which secured them and opening them wide. Then he went back to the audience-chamber, to rejoin Averil.

They were waiting together when the first few people began to arrive.

The first of all was a man in ragged, dusty clothing. His beard was caked with dirt, and his hair was matted and grey. His eyes were like pools of blood with unnaturally-small pupils. His face was blanched and scarred with ancient pock-marks, and was as white as a winding-sheet.

But he was a living man: a human being.

'Is it over?' he said, his voice eerily like the croak of a carrion bird.

'Aye,' said Harmis, gently. 'It is over, for now.'

Others came in, one by one: men, women and children with hollow eyes. Harmis looked at them all, steadily and without distress. After a while, he turned to Averil, and pointed to the glowing light cradled in her two hands.

'The power of magic,' he said, ironically. 'It draws them like moths.'

'It is not power which draws them,' she told him. 'It is hope.'

And when Harmis Detz turned again to the gathering crowd, he was astonished to see a face which he recognized.

It was a boy some twelve or thirteen years old, and though Harmis had not seen him for two years and more he knew him instantly. It was Medard, the son of his brother Lavarock, spared with what remained of the nation's people from the destruction of war, and the plague, and the rats, and the worms of the earth.

'Not power,' repeated the hero, wonderingly – as though he had discovered a truth which he had always known, but had never quite succeeded in making articulate. 'Not power, but hope.'

EPILOGUE

WHEN ORFEO FINISHED his tale dawn was once again breaking over the desert. His head was buzzing, for in telling the tale he had put himself into it – into the mind of Harmis Detz, who had gone to war against a daemonic champion of the god of plague and pestilence. That experience had left a bleak legacy of fear and feeling in Detz's soul, which had possessed the man again when he told his story to Orfeo; the player had become a further inheritor of that fear and feeling, which echoed now within the hidden places of his own being.

Orfeo studied the tired-eyed Caliph of Mahabbah and Lord of the Twin Seas, who might now become an inheritor in his turn, if only he had sufficient imagination and conscience to let him place himself in another man's shoes. Perhaps he had, Orfeo thought – for Alkadi Nasreen surely had more in common with a dour man-at-arms like Harmis Detz than with a languid player like himself.

'You had this tale from the lips of the man himself?' asked the Caliph.

'I did,' replied Orfeo.

'You must have known him very well, to be privy to so many of his secret thoughts. Did you share a prison with him, perchance?' There was a hint of a sneer in the man's voice, but Orfeo knew it was only a defensive reaction.

'I was his guest, for a while,' said Orfeo, evenly. 'I told him stories of my own, and through them he learned to like me and to trust me. He entrusted me with his own tale, because he had become convinced that it needed to be told, to give warning to the world of what kind of things are in it, and what evil work they do.'

'You are more generous, it seems,' said Alkadi Nasreen, bitterly, 'in accepting the hospitality of some men than of others. You are very eager to be gone from here, yet by your own account you have lingered long in other places, freely exchanging your precious wisdom of lore and legend.'

'The vital word, my lord, is *freely*,' countered Orfeo. 'I was brought here as a prisoner, not a guest – and when I became a guest, still I seemed to be a prisoner. If you are a man who insists on making bargains over tales to be told and heard, then I must make the best of your bargains, must I not?'

'Can you not see that I would be your friend, if you would let me?' asked the Caliph, sharply.

'Until you behave as a friend should,' replied the player, 'you must give me leave to doubt it.'

'And this common soldier with whom you exchanged such confidences?' said Nasreen, coldly. 'Did he behave as a friend should?'

'He did,' said Orfeo. 'But he was not a common soldier when I knew him. He was the prince of Khypris, and a great hero to his people. His reputation as a saviour and a liberator was wearing thin, as all such reputations do with the passage of time, but his hold on the nation was quite secure, for he had a clever witch-wife who had become very learned and powerful with the passage of time.'

Alkadi Nasreen had the grace to smile a little at the thought of it. 'You should have said so in the story,' he said.

'You of all men must know that the hearers of a tale love a happy ending, in which the hero marries his sweetheart and becomes a prince.'

'You are quite right,' said Orfeo, lightly. 'And when it is my pleasure to shape a fanciful tale for the amusement of a crowd, I will always contrive its ending thus. But you asked for a tale which was true, and I told you one, and gave it the shape it really had and which properly belongs to it.'

'But that is what I am saying!' objected the pirate king. 'If it is true that the hero married the witch-girl, and became a prince, then you should say so. You are doubly wrong to leave it out – first because it happened, and second because it is the proper end of the tale.'

'Perhaps,' agreed Orfeo, with a politeness so careful that it was all too obvious he did not care to concede the point. 'If my lord was a storyteller, no doubt he would do things differently, and would be a better man than I in consequence.

'In justifying my own ending, I can only say this: that a happy end for two people, in the power they acquire and the joy which they find in one another, is by no means to be despised; but a happier end by far for a story is that the sufferings of one man or a few should be transmuted by effort into the salvation of a nation. That Harmis Detz became prince of Khypris is good, and that he mended his initial lack of affection for the wizard's apprentice is also good – but had neither of those things happened, the significance of my ending would be much the same. On the other hand, had Harmis and Averil decided only to save themselves, fleeing from the gates of Faramond's citadel without facing the thing which was within, that would not have made a proper ending, even if they had gone on to win a better kingdom in a less-troubled land.

'We need not agree on this, my lord, but in my view of things, it is the greater happiness of the greater number which matters more than the selfish hoarding of personal advantage. That a hero is successful certainly matters – but that he fights for the side of right and is successful in his *cause* must matter more. That is why my story ends as it does, with the finest affirmation that I know: *not power, but hope*. That is my notion of what is truly precious, and I will not be moved from it.'

Alkadi Nasreen sighed, and stroked his beard with the hardened fingers of his right hand. 'You are a perverse fellow,' he said. 'I insist that you tell me a story which is true, to illuminate the fate which overtook my brother, and you take the trouble to deliver an extended sermon on the subject of vengeance – in which dead brothers feature with suspicious frequency. *Then* you beg leave to lecture me on the morality of its ending, as if it were a fable which you had concocted for a purpose. Do you insist on making me suspect that you have invented every word of it?'

'Not at all,' said Orfeo. 'It is true that a fable is shaped to display a moral, but that certainly does not mean that a true story has no moral. If we were not in real life faced by moral dilemmas day by day and hour by hour, we would not need to preserve the histories of good and enviable men any more than we would need to invent fables. Whether we are storytellers or pirate kings, we are all engaged in constructing the narratives of our own lives, and we are surely better equipped to bring our own accounts to a righteous end if we study very carefully how other men have fared in the same quest.'

'And by that, I suppose,' said Alkadi Nasreen, 'you mean to insist in your cunning fashion that I must now honour my obligation to you, and give you your horse and your saddle, and thirty crowns from my treasure-chest. If I do not, you will presumably reckon me a villain and not a hero, and will cast me thus in all your future stories!'

'I know that you will honour your promise, my lord,' said Orfeo, quietly. 'As to the story of your life – it will be you, not I, who determines the nature and quality of your role.'

'And yet,' said the Caliph, after a brief pause, 'your story does not quite meet the qualification which I asked of it. I asked to know more about the forces which destroyed my brother, but the Power he worshipped was, by your own account, a god of luxury. I have heard naught of that god in this tale, which is concerned instead with a god of plague and pestilence. In Mahabbah, of course, we acknowledge only One True God, but *that* God frowns on luxury and sends his pestilences sparingly, to punish the faithless.'

'My lord,' said Orfeo, making it clear by his tone that his show of patience was merely a show, 'your brother was destroyed by daemons, which he had sought to control and use for his own ends. Chaos has many faces, of which the god of luxury and the god of disease are but two. All the Great Powers of Chaos may make vile beastmen, and pervert the flesh of their servants in hideous ways – and yet even the most loathsome among them can sometimes contrive to shelter its ugliest minions behind a mask of wonderful beauty. This tale displays all of those truths, and I believe it to be a valuable revelation for those who would learn what baneful threats hang over this vexatious world of ours.

'And with respect, my lord, I must add the observation that if your One God uses plagues only as punishments, then he has a very peculiar notion of who the wicked are, and what degree of guilt they bear. I have seen plague and pestilence in action, and I, like Harmis Detz, can hardly bear to look at the hollow eyes of the little children, who are entirely innocent of the violence and evil which are rife in all the nations of the earth.'

But Alkadi Nasreen, on hearing this, simply gestured dismissively with his hand – and for a moment it was very obvious that he was an Estalian who had taken the turban in order to rule this nest of pirates, and that in giving up the gods of his own folk he had become entirely godless in his most secret thoughts.

'Will you give me my horse?' asked Orfeo, wearily.

'It is done,' said the Caliph. 'You will have your horse, and your saddle, and your coin, which you have earned

with your honesty and patience. The gates of Arjijil are
open to you, and you may go when you please. I will do
more than that, for I will confess to you that when I
offered you this bargain, I spoke very carefully of one
horse and one saddle, thinking that I might keep the boy
you have befriended for a further bargain. I will not do
that now; you may have a second horse and a second saddle, and thirty more coins to see you on your way. I only
ask of you that you should try to think of me as a man who
would and could have been your friend, if circumstance
had only contrived to order it thus.'

Orfeo met his gaze frankly, and said: 'I am glad, my lord,
that you have said this to me. I noticed your omission, I
must confess, but I know that it is sometimes best to come
to an honest bargain by a roundabout way. I am certain
now that we are friends – and that is how I will remember
you, when I am gone.'

The player saw the shadow of a frown cross Alkadi
Nasreen's face, and guessed that the other had hoped he
would promise to stay for a while longer in Arjijil. But the
Caliph said nothing to that effect, and by that silence
Orfeo knew that he was truly free.

What the pirate king did say, eventually, was: 'It is a
pretty thought, that the magic which affects people most
profoundly is not power, but only hope. It is a lie, you
know.'

'If it were stated as simply as that,' agreed Orfeo, 'it
would be a lie. Power, whether magical or political, is certainly an important force in human affairs – but the
exercise of power is mostly ruinous, for the power to do
evil far outstrips the power to do good. What the witch-girl
meant to imply is that the magic which we need, if we are
to live our lives in a better way, is the kind of magic which
increases hope. *That* is true, and because of it all men
should resolve that they will not tolerate any exercise of
power which stifles or decreases hope. Only thus might the
forces of Chaos one day be defeated.'

ABOUT THE AUTHOR

When asked why he dresses entirely in black, Brian Craig claims to be in mourning for H. P. Lovecraft, but the real reason is too dreadful to reveal. The rumour that he joined the British Antarctic Survey in 1993 to 'to get away from it all' is false; he failed the medical and had to join the French Foreign Legion instead. He is not allowed to discuss the reasons for his dishonourable discharge therefrom in 1999, but he is glad that he will now have more time to write and play cricket.

Brian Craig is the author of the three Tales of Orfeo – *Zaragoz, Plague Daemon* and *Storm Warriors* – and *The Wine of Dreams*, as well as the Warhammer 40,000 novel *Pawns of Chaos*. He has contributed short stories to a range of anthologies, including the *Dedalus Book of Femmes Fatales*, edited by Brian Stableford. He is 28 and only looks older because his troubles have aged him.

More Brian Craig from the Black Library

ZARAGOZ
The First Tale of Orfeo

THE SPEAKER WAS standing before the doors which had been opened to admit the dry night air. It was Arcangelo, the priest of law.

'I can tell you a tale,' he said. 'A tale of the citadel of Zaragoz. A tale of betrayal, which happened long ago, but whose tangled threads extend, as the threads of treason always do, across the years and the centuries to the present day.

'I come to warn you all that the choice is soon to be made. If justice cannot come again to Zaragoz, then I promise you that Zaragoz is doomed!'

RIVEN BY POLITICAL *intrigue, the countless petty kingdoms of Estalia are a dangerous land to travel through. When he rescues a mysterious priest from brigands, the minstrel Orfeo is drawn into a deadly power struggle for the citadel of Zaragoz. He is forced to use all the power of his wits and skill at arms to survive enemies fair and foul, human and monstrous.*

More Brian Craig from the Black Library

THE WINE OF DREAMS
A Warhammer novel

THE SWORD FLEW from Reinmar's hand and he just had
time to think, as he was taken off his feet, that when
he landed – flat on his back – he would be wide open
to attack by a plunging dagger or flashing teeth. As
the beastman leapt, Sigurd's arm lashed out in a great
horizontal arc, the palm of his hand held flat. As it
impacted with the beastman's neck Reinmar heard
the snap that broke the creature's spine.

As soon as that, it was over. But it was not a victory.
Now there was no possible room for doubt that there
were monsters abroad in the hills.

DEEP WITHIN THE *shadowy foothills of the Grey
Mountains, a dark and deadly plot is uncovered by an
innocent young merchant. A mysterious stranger leads
young Reinmar Weiland to stumble upon the secrets of a
sinister underworld hidden beneath the very feet of the
unsuspecting Empire – and learn of a legendary elixir,
the mysterious and forbidden Wine of Dreams.*

More Brian Craig from the Black Library

PAWNS OF CHAOS
A Warhammer 40,000 novel

GAVALON HAD ALREADY begun thinking of the bulk of
his forces as 'gunfodder', even though they had never
faced guns before. The guns produced by the
Imperium in their planetary-based factories were by
no means as powerful as those they had brought
from the star-worlds, but they were guns nevertheless
and there was nothing in Gulzacandra that could
compete with them – except, of course, magic. If the
Imperium was to be stopped, magic would be the
force that would do it.

IN THE GRIM *future of Warhammer 40,000,*
mankind is engaged in an eternal conflict with the
armies of Chaos. On the medieval world of Sigmatus,
the hated Imperium is flexing its power with ruthless
efficiency. The rebels have a plan to fight back: summon
a powerful daemon from the warp and unleash it upon
their enemies!

More Warhammer from the Black Library

KONRAD
Book One of the Konrad Trilogy
by David Ferring

KONRAD FIRED AGAIN. Another black arrow found its target, this time in the creature's throat. Blood spurted as the arrow drove itself through the fat furry neck and into the trunk behind, nailing the beastman to the bark.

Both of its arms – the one with spiny claws, the one without – went to its neck, trying to pull the arrow free. Its body twitched spasmodically, there was a liquid gurgle deep in its throat. A final gush of blood pumped from the neck wound, both arms dropped to its sides, and then the thing became absolutely still.

IN THE FIRST volume of this fantasy trilogy, Konrad is forced to leave the village where he has grown up when it is razed to the ground by marauding beastmen. Flung into a life of desperate exile, Konrad must seek the answers to his mysterious past in a land of Chaos and savagery.

More Warhammer from the Black Library

SHADOWBREED
Book Two of the Konrad Trilogy
by David Ferring

THE SECOND CREATURE ran straight onto Konrad's sword, impaling itself. Konrad's earlier vow had been fulfilled: drawing his sword had meant spilling skaven blood.

A moment later, the next skaven's throat was torn out with a single sword sweep. It gurgled, blood bubbling from its mouth and pouring from its neck as it died. He wrenched his blade free, then plunged it into the chest of the next creature. Its hot blood spurted over him, and he laughed in triumph. Four down, a hundred more to come!

IN A TIME *of blood and darkness, the mutated hordes of Chaos rampage across the borders of the civilised world, sowing death and destruction in their wake. Driven by the power of his own mysterious destiny, Konrad continues his fight against the evil forces that seek to destroy the Empire – but at what cost to his own soul?*

More Warhammer from the Black Library

WARBLADE
Book Three of the Konrad Trilogy
by David Ferring

KONRAD LEAPT DOWN at the nearest rider, feet first, knocking him straight out of his saddle. Rolling over as he hit the ground, he was instantly on his feet and diving at the man he had dismounted – except he was not a man...

That was why the riders had seemed so strange. They were not human. They were beastmen. Beastmen wearing the uniforms of the Imperial guard!

THE FORCES OF Chaos tighten their grip on the Empire. Beastmen and skaven run rife in the Old World, slaughtering all who oppose them in the name of their foul gods. As a deadly endgame is played out, Konrad struggles against desperate odds to thwart an evil plot to corrupt the very heart of the Empire. He cannot fail, or the future of humanity is doomed.

More Warhammer from the Black Library

DRACHENFELS
A Genevieve novel
by Kim Newman writing as Jack Yeovil

NOW CONRADIN WAS dead. Sieur Jehan was dead. Heinroth was dead. Ueli was dead. And before the night was over, others – maybe all of the party – would be joining them. Genevieve hadn't thought about dying for a long time. Perhaps tonight Drachenfels would finish Chandagnac's Dark Kiss, and push her at last over the border between life and death.

DETLEF SIERCK, *the self-proclaimed greatest playwright in the world, has declared that his next production will be a recreation of the end of the Great Enchanter Drachenfels – to be staged at the very site of his death, the Fortress of Drachenfels itself. But the castle's dark walls still hide a terrible and deadly secret which may make the first night of Detlef's masterpiece the last of his life.*

More Warhammer from the Black Library

GENEVIEVE UNDEAD
A Genevieve novel
by Kim Newman writing as Jack Yeovil

GENEVIEVE'S MOUTH WAS full of blood. An ancient instinct took over. She fixed her mouth to Schedoni's wound. She sucked, and the old man's blood was pumped into her. Her mind cleared, and she swallowed.

These people were nothing to her. She was a visitor, like Aleksandr and d'Amato and the girl. They had made her play her part, but it wasn't her. She wasn't Genevieve Udolpho, she was Genevieve Dieudonné. She wasn't sixteen, she was six hundred and sixty-nine. She wasn't even human. She was a vampire.

Genevieve drank, and became stronger.

DARK AND TERRIBLE *secrets may be found lurking within the cities of the Old World and the savage wilderness that surrounds them. Genevieve Dieudonné, vampire heroine of Drachenfels, battles to outwit adversaries both magical and mundane, human and beast, in this series of three linked novellas: Stage Blood, The Cold Stark House and Unicorn Ivory.*

More Warhammer from the Black Library

The Gotrek & Felix novels
by William King

THE DWARF TROLLSLAYER *Gotrek Gurnisson and his long-suffering human companion Felix Jaeger are arguably the most infamous heroes of the Warhammer World. Follow their exploits in these novels from the Black Library.*

TROLLSLAYER

TROLLSLAYER IS THE first part of the death saga of Gotrek Gurnisson, as retold by his travelling companion Felix Jaeger. Set in the darkly gothic world of Warhammer, TROLLSLAYER is an episodic novel featuring some of the most extraordinary adventures of this deadly pair of heroes. Monsters, daemons, sorcerers, mutants, orcs, beastmen and worse are to be found as Gotrek strives to achieve a noble death in battle. Felix, of course, only has to survive to tell the tale.

SKAVENSLAYER

THE SECOND GOTREK and Felix adventure – SKAVENSLAYER – is set in the mighty city of Nuln. Seeking to undermine the very fabric of the Empire with their arcane warp-sorcery, the skaven, twisted Chaos rat-men, are at large in the reeking sewers beneath the ancient city. Led by Grey Seer Thanquol, the servants of the Horned Rat are determined to overthrow this bastion of humanity. Against such forces, what possible threat can just two hard-bitten adventurers pose?

DAEMONSLAYER

FOLLOWING THEIR adventures in Nuln, Gotrek and Felix join an expedition northwards in search of the long-lost dwarf hall of Karag Dum. Setting forth for the hideous Realms of Chaos in an experimental dwarf airship, Gotrek and Felix are sworn to succeed or die in the attempt. But greater and more sinister energies are coming into play, as a daemonic power is awoken to fulfil its ancient, deadly promise.

DRAGONSLAYER

IN THE FOURTH instalment in the death-seeking saga of Gotrek and Felix, the fearless duo find themselves pursued by the insidious and ruthless skaven-lord, Grey Seer Thanquol. DRAGONSLAYER sees the fearless Slayer and his sworn companion back aboard an arcane dwarf airship in a search for a golden hoard – and its deadly guardian.

BEASTSLAYER

STORM CLOUDS GATHER around the icy city of Praag as the foul hordes of Chaos lay ruinous siege to northern lands of Kislev. Will the presence of Gotrek and Felix be enough to prevent this ancient city from being overwhelmed by the massed forces of Chaos and their fearsome leader, Arek Daemonclaw?

VAMPIRESLAYER

AS THE FORCES of Chaos gather in the north to threaten the Old World, the Slayer Gotrek and his companion Felix are beset by a new, terrible foe. An evil is forming in darkest Sylvania which threatens to reach out and tear the heart from our band of intrepid heroes. The gripping saga of Gotrek & Felix continues in this epic tale of deadly battle and soul-rending tragedy.

More Warhammer from the Black Library

ZAVANT
By Gordon Rennie

'YOU HAVE EXAMINED the corpse, no doubt?' Graf Otto rasped, looking at Zavant Konniger. 'What are your conclusions?'

Konniger set down his wine glass and composed himself before answering. 'Foul play has been committed, certainly. But it was not a robbery-turned-murder. The victim's killer left a full purse of gold behind him. And Altdorf's footpads and cut-purses may be a bloodthirsty lot, but I have yet to meet one who would make a habit of ripping out his victims' throats with his bare teeth.'

'Surely it is the work of some wild animal, then? Some beast loose within the city walls?'

Konniger paused, sensing that he was being tested. 'Animals kill for food. Whatever killed this poor unfortunate did so only for its own savage pleasure.'

THE OLD WORLD *is a dark and dangerous place, and even the towns and cities offer little shelter, for the evil that stalks their fog-shrouded streets is as deadly as it is elusive. Enter Zavant Konniger, the great sage-detective of Altdorf. Accompanied by his trusty halfling manservant, Vido, this most brilliant scholar must use his incredible powers of deduction to solve the most sinister mysteries of the day.*

More Warhammer from the Black Library

GILEAD'S BLOOD
A Warhammer novel
by Dan Abnett & Nik Vincent

GILEAD GOT TO his feet unsteadily. The dulled blade dropped from his hand with a clatter. 'You dare to speak to me of that?' he hissed. 'Galeth was one with me, my brother, my twin! We were one soul in two bodies! Do you not remember?'

Fithvael bowed his head. 'I do, lord. That is what they said of you...'

'And when he died, I was cut in two! Death entered my soul! Ten years I hunted for the murderer! Hunted for vengeance! And when I found it, even that pleasure did not slake the pain in my heart!'

GILEAD'S BLOOD FOLLOWS the saga of the doom-laden high elf, Gilead Lothain. Along with his faithful retainer Fithvael, Gilead, shadowfast warrior and the last of the line of Tor Anrok, travels the Warhammer world seeking revenge on the servants of Evil.

INFERNO! is the indispensable guide to the worlds of Warhammer and Warhammer 40,000 and the cornerstone of the Black Library. Every issue is crammed full of action packed stories, comic strips and artwork from a growing network of awesome writers and artists including:

- William King
- Brian Craig
- Gav Thorpe

- Dan Abnett
- Barrington J. Bayley
- Gordon Rennie

and many more

Presented every two months, Inferno! magazine brings the Warhammer worlds to life in ways you never thought possible.

For subscription details ring:
US: 1-800-394-GAME   UK: (0115) 91 40000

For more information see our website:
http://www.blacklibrary.co.uk/inferno